GW00361767

The One They Left Behind

THE ONE THEY LEFT BEHIND

Norman Leaney

The Book Guild Ltd.

Sussex, England.

The Book Guild Ltd.
25 High Street,
Lewes, Sussex.

First published 1990
© Norman Leaney 1990
Set in Baskerville

Typesetting by Kudos Graphics
Slinfold, Horsham, West Sussex
Printed in Great Britain by
Antony Rowe Ltd.,
Chippenham, Wiltshire.

British Library Cataloguing in Publication Data
Leaney, Norman
   The one they left behind.
   I. Title
   823'.914 [F]

ISBN 0 86332 480 0

CONTENTS

1

I hurried out of my bedroom into the living room pulling on a jumper. Margaret, our cheerful, pretty auburn-haired eldest sister, was sitting in her usual place of authority at the head of the table. My twin sister, Phyllis, five years younger, the plain one of the three with dark straight hair and a fringe down to her eyebrows, was sitting next to Jean the youngest, a pretty curly black-haired fifteen year old with blue eyes, long black eyelashes, rosy cheeks, and a smile that could even soften Father in one of his moods.

They were arguing excitedly about the games we were going to play, and before taking my usual seat, and joining in, I went to switch on the light.

'We don't need it yet, Ted. Switch it off,' Margaret called out to me.

'Leave it. It is our last night,' Jean pleaded, as I hesitated.

It was Friday evening of September the first, 1939, the last day of our summer holiday, the day when the news bulletins were opening with 'Grave developments,' as hourly the approach of war became a matter of time.

It had been an even better holiday than the previous three years: swimming, tennis and, for me, fishing from the canoe I had built in my bedroom last winter. The four of us got on well together, grateful to be organised and led by Margaret, and though none of us mentioned it, I think we all knew this was the last holiday we Trigsbys would have together as a family.

This was the one time of the year when our parents didn't row. Tonight they had gone to the farewell dance at the Lanca Club, where once a year father played the piano.

As we did every evening, we were preparing to play cards until supper at nine o'clock, not wanting to waste a moment, but too tired to do anything else.

7

A cold wind blowing the grey clouds across the twilight sky had driven us indoors early this evening: into the small bungalow we had stayed in for the past three years, built with a square of railway carriages, the hole in the middle being roofed over to make a good-sized living room.

'Please leave the light on, Margaret. Don't be mean like Daddy,' Phyllis said, with a laugh to take some of the bite out of the remark.

Dad was mean, he had to be; he had never earned enough money to keep a family of four children in the style we thought we were entitled to. His excuse was to blame mother, who worked miracles, providing us with clothes for school, though there were times when our shoes would pinch. We knew there would be rows over the money we had spent, which would be desperately needed as soon as we arrived home; but while on holiday we were too happy to think about that.

'I hope you've got a shilling, when the light goes out that's all,' Margaret replied, smiling and shrugging her shoulders as she shuffled the cards.

We had shared out the counters, and Phyllis and I were bantering about why Jean always had to start first, when somebody thumped loudly on the back door.

'Don't go!' Phyllis said, as I stood up.

I hesitated a moment; an even louder hammering followed, and somebody shouted angrily.

Cautiously creeping through the dark carriage used as a kitchen, I reached the back door, and looking through the glazed half, saw the bulky shape of a man standing at the bottom of the steps.

'You'd better see what he wants,' Margaret whispered from close behind me, as I hesitated to open the door.

'It's Mr Ford,' Phyllis whispered from further back, sounding relieved that it was him. He was the local handyman who did the maintenance of the bungalows for the estate agent responsible for the summer lettings.

'Put those lights out,' he shouted, before the door was half open.

'We won't be able to see! What's it got to do with Mr Ford?' Jean muttered, peeping round the corner at him.

'Haven't you heard the wireless?' he asked, looking very

agitated; standing there in his shirt sleeves, the wind blowing the hair over his face.

'No, Dad says we're to save the battery for him to listen to the news when he comes home at ten o'clock tonight,' I replied, thinking it was none of his business, but it might be wise to humour him. He looked wild, and unfriendly tonight.

'They said on the wireless no lights must be shown along the coast. You've got to put them out at once,' he shouted angrily, wagging his finger at us.

'Sorry, Mr Ford, we didn't know, we'll put it out,' Margaret replied, waving an arm behind her back to Phyllis, or Jean, to go and do it.

'You youngsters don't understand how serious it is, we're almost at war with Germany again,' he shouted, sounding tense and agitated. We'd never seen him like this before.

I watched him hurry away as the light went out, and after closing the door, followed Margaret into the living room.

'Has he gone? Can I put it on again?' Jean whispered.

'No! You must not. Didn't you hear what he said?' Margaret replied, as we laughed.

'I'm not frightened of Germans. I'm frightened of the dark,' Jean muttered with a nervous giggle.

'You would be if they landed,' I said, knowing she couldn't see me laughing in the dark.

'Don't be silly they won't land tonight.'

'They might. They're only waiting for us to leave a light on so they can see where we are.'

'You're horrible, Ted, you always frighten me,' Jean replied, as Phyllis laughed.

'You stay here, Ted, and see they don't put the light on,' Margaret said, before going into the kitchen, leaving us sitting there in the dark.

'I'm frightened,' Jean said, giggling nervously and coming round the table to sit close to me.

'Don't be such a baby. You're only two years younger than me,' Phyllis said, laughing as she grabbed my other arm and cuddled up close to me.

'What's Margaret doing?' Jean asked, after a few minutes of sitting there in the dark.

'I hope she's getting something to drink, but it doesn't sound like it,' I replied, as I heard Margaret bumping her way back.

'Now listen. I've found a candle. I want you to go into all the rooms and pull the curtains; the inner ones as well,' Margaret said, as she sat down.

'We're not going into the bedrooms without a light,' the two girls chorused.

'Ted, you do one side, and I'll do the other. If we pull them carefully and shield the candle it should be all right,' Margaret said, standing up, and going into the nearest room.

'It's stupid. It doesn't need to be as dark as this,' Phyllis grumbled when we'd finished and fumbled our way back into the darkened room.

Margaret lit the half candle, and we watched the little flame grow until we could see each other in the flickering light.

'Ted, go outside and see if it shows,' Margaret said, as it seemed to get brighter as we became used to it.

I walked all round the bungalow. Of course you could see it. The old curtains, after years of washing, had shrunk; there were gaps everywhere.

'It's all right, only a flicker every now and again, when the wind blows the curtain, where that window doesn't shut properly,' I told Margaret, as I sat down.

'Good. Now we've half an hour, and then we'll have hot drinks while we play the last game,' she said, starting to deal the cards.

'Listen!' Jean said, at the sound of someone crunching over the pebbles on the path from the beach.

'It's the Germans invading. We shouldn't have lit the candle,' I whispered, trying not to laugh.

Jean and Phyllis, gave little squeals of fright.

'Shut up, Ted. You should know better than to frighten them like that,' Margaret shouted, as the back door burst open; the girls squealed more loudly, and Mother came in to the room.

'We heard someone coming from the beach,' Jean said excitedly.

'It's your Father. He came back that way to check the blackout from the sea,' Mother said, picking up the matches.

'Mr Ford came over to tell us to put the light out, that's why I lit the candle,' Margaret said, shielding it with her hand as

Father came in the back door.

'I should think the candle will be all right: unless someone mistakes it for the Nab Light House,' Mother replied laughing, and turning to go into the kitchen.

We didn't play any more cards, and after some hot drinks and biscuits went to bed. There was no sense in sitting up in the dark. Father warned us sternly to keep our curtains drawn, and not to put a light on if we had to get up in the night.

'Do you think the Germans will come?' Jean whispered to me.

'Not if you keep the curtains drawn,' I replied, pulling hers open as I went to my room.

2

We arrived home in the early afternoon on Saturday the 2nd of September, feeling as if we had been away for years. All the plans we had made before we left a fortnight ago were dead. Some of the cancellation letters for the Tennis Tournaments we looked forward to for months were on the mat, and the others we knew would soon follow.

Phyllis should be going to a Commercial College to learn shorthand and typing, and Jean back to school to study for Higher School Certificate, but nothing was certain anymore; except as far as Father was concerned. I would never get a job. I would be called up before Christmas.

On Sunday the third of September we made no plans for playing tennis, even though the weather was dry. The Wireless News bulletins had warned us to stand by for an announcement by Mr Chamberlain the Prime Minister, at ten forty-five.

By ten o'clock we had finished breakfast and, as usual, were helping with the tidying up. After helping to carry out the dirty dishes, I put things like the butter and marmalade in the sideboard cupboard. Mother, and Margaret had done the washing up, and the other two girls dried and put things away in the kitchen.

Before half past ten the job was done and we were all in our places listening to the wireless playing solemn music, and talking about our friends in the Territorial Army who would be the first to be called up. The volume of the loudspeaker extension I had wired up to the set in the lounge was just enough if nobody spoke.

'Ted, see if you can make it any louder,' Dad said, looking up from reading the Sunday paper.

To save coal, we only used the lounge in the afternoon and

evenings, the fire never being lit until just before we sat down to lunch at one o'clock. Dad was the only one who used it in the afternoon. The rest of us preferred the dining room with its good coke fire, which was lit by the first one down each morning, usually Mother or myself.

'It won't go any louder,' I said, after checking the control on the extension was at maximum volume.

'You girls will have to be quiet or we won't be able to hear anything,' Dad said, folding up the paper as the music began to fade.

We sat in a strange silence. Margaret, and Jean were sitting next to each other where they usually sat at meals, and Phyllis and I sat opposite to them. Dad and Mum were in the armchairs in front of the fire. Dad had stopped puffing his pipe.

'The Right Honourable Neville Chamberlain, The Prime Minister.'

When his sombre words had been spoken in the same monotonous tone of a year ago, when he had promised us 'peace in our time', mother sobbed, and Jean, and Margaret fell into each other's arms and cried.

'This is a fine way to start a war,' Dad said, lighting his pipe, and sucking furiously to make it burn.

'I don't see any sense in crying,' Phyllis whispered to me.

'I'm frightened of the air raids. The Zeppelins were terrifying in the last war. God knows what it will be like this time,' Mother said, sniffing, and sobbing miserably.

'There might not be any. At least wait until we have a warning before you start crying,' Dad said scornfully.

'You don't know what it was like, you were in France where there weren't any Zeppelin raids,' Mother replied, as Margaret went over to comfort her.

'Fine family I have, crying before it's even started,' he said with a derisive laugh.

'There's the siren! What are we going to do?' Mother asked, getting up out of her armchair.

'Rubbish! I can't hear anything. Can you Ted?' Father asked me, obviously fearing that Mother might have heard something.

We all listened. Jean thought she could hear something, and then the local siren started up.

'What are we going to do?' Mother asked again, looking at me.

'They said we should take our gas masks and sit under the stairs,' I replied, knowing that was unlikely to meet with enthusiasm.

'That's stupid! We'd have to go outside. We can't sit in the coal cellar. It's full of spiders,' Jean said, looking horrified at the very thought of it.

'Well that's what you've got to do if you want to be safe from the bombs,' I replied, as the siren died away.

'We can't do that, Ted!' Mother said, pleading with me to think of something better.

'It will be all right if we go into the hall, and sit on the stairs,' I replied. I had to say something, and I found it difficult not to laugh, even though the sound of the siren made me shiver.

Dad, looking pale, lead the way grabbing the gas masks off their peg on the hallstand as he passed, and then sat on the bottom step, looking at the boxes to find the one with his name on it.

'Shall we put these things on?' Jean asked me, when we'd sorted them out.

'Yes, we'd better. There won't be any time once they get here,' I said, looking at Dad who was already trying his on.

'I don't want to put mine on. When I tried it before I nearly suffocated,' Mother said, struggling to get hers out of the box. 'Put it on for practice,' I said, and Jean put hers on, and started to giggle in it.

'I'm not putting mine on. It doesn't fit, and I can't breathe in it anyway,' Phyllis said, hanging her box on the end of the bannister.

A few minutes later the continuous note of the all-clear sounded, and Jean took her gas mask off.

'Put it on again!' Phyllis said urgently.

'That's the all-clear!' Jean said, looking worried.

'I know, but it was such an improvement you should wear it all the time,' Phyllis replied, and we all laughed, relieved to have survived our first air raid.

*   *   *

'Whatever your Father says, you must try to find a job,' Mother said to me, when Father had gone into the lounge after tea that evening.

'Oh Ted, you don't want to get called up. You'll only get killed,' Jean said, putting her arm round my shoulder.

'Don't be silly. Everyone has to go, but they don't all get killed,' I replied, laughing.

'Of course you will get called up, but if you don't get a job before you go, you will have nowhere to go back to when the war's over,' Mother said, stacking the plates to take to the kitchen.

'It's not worth bothering. I won't have a chance anyway with only five passes,' I replied. It seemed to me that with so much uncertainty it would be simpler to wait until I was called up. I didn't know what I wanted to do, and I had no idea how to go about getting a job.

A few weeks after the declaration of war by Mr Chamberlain, the rumour was it would be all over by Christmas, and I changed my mind. It wasn't worth going to war for a couple of months.

Mother was determined that I should get a job, and persuaded me to write to the Schoolboys Employment Bureau. They replied immediately, requesting me to attend for an interview, and to my horror, Mother insisted on coming with me.

She was very good. She said nothing at the interview as she sat beside me, her frail little figure dwarfed by the large hat she was wearing, reminding me of a toadstool. Sitting very upright with a note book on her lap, she took a shorthand record of everything that was said, much to the embarrassment of the interviewer.

'What sort of post are you looking for, insurance, or banking?' the gentleman in a dark suit, white shirt, and pasty complexion asked, sounding as if he found it all rather boring.

'I want to work in a laboratory. I don't want to work in an office,' I replied, realising as I spoke that I had not the faintest idea what I would do in a laboratory.

'I've been working in an office for twenty years. There's nothing wrong in working in an office, son,' he replied testily, scribbling something on the form in front of him.

'I'm sorry. I didn't mean it that way, I'm sure it suits some people, but I want to work in a laboratory,' I said, noticing a

look from mother, indicating that I was not covering myself
with glory.

'And what do you expect to do in a laboratory?' he asked,
leaning back in his chair, and looking me straight in the eye
for an answer.

'I don't mind. Something to do with chemistry or
electricity,' I replied, feeling a little vague. I had expected
him to be telling me about the exciting jobs that he was
looking for someone to fill.

Those of us who were leaving school in my last term, were
called into the Headmaster's office. He asked us what we
wanted to do. Four out of the six in my group said insurance
or banking, and were warmly approved of. One said he
wanted to be an engineer and was told he should think again,
and I said I didn't know, which he said was slightly better
than wanting to be an engineer. I thought those who wanted
banking or insurance were a dull lot, and I certainly didn't
want to find myself in their company for the rest of my life.

'We don't have many jobs like that. What did you say?
Chemistry, or electricity?' he asked, writing it down very
slowly on the form, and then looking at it as if he wasn't sure
of the spelling.

'Yes, I dont't care what I do as long as I'm doing
experimental work of some sort,' I replied more confidently.
I thought there must be something else besides banking and
insurance.

'Well, I suppose something like that might come along, but
I doubt it. You're quite sure you wouldn't like me to send you
vacancies in insurance companies? We get those all the time,'
he said, pen poised to write, should I change my mind.

I shook my head, and that was that.

'I expect that's the last we'll hear from him,' I said to
Mother on the train going home.

'You must keep trying, and something will turn up. I
understand you not wanting to work in an office, but you
were a bit tactless,' she said thoughtfully, thumbing through
her shorthand notes.

'It will have to be soon. I'm eighteen in a few months, then
nobody will want me,' I reminded her, feeling that it was
hopeless to expect to be taken on when there must be many
better qualified than me.

'If you can get anything, it will help you when the war is over,' Mother said, and I laughed. It hadn't even begun, and it was supposed to be over by Christmas.

For the whole of September and October I felt completely useless. Several of my friends had been taken on by insurance firms or banks where a brother or a father worked, earning money until they were called up. I knew that it would be a disaster for me to work in an office anywhere near my father.

Other friends, to earn a few shillings while waiting to be called up, became ARP messenger boys. I didn't want to do that either. They appeared to ride around on their bicycles all day wearing a steel helmet, and a sash, delighted to be playing even a small part. I didn't feel I could do that. I wanted to do something useful.

Three weeks after my interview in London I was surprised to receive a letter from the gentleman at the Schoolboys' Bureau of Employment. instructing me to go for an interview at a Chemical factory in Rainham, Kent.

Father was not pleased. I had no money, and he considered it to be an extravagant waste of the shilling and six pence fare which he would have to provide. Then, generously, he gave me two shillings the night before, telling me he expected six pence change, but if I wanted to buy a two penny bun, I could take it as an advance of my Saturday pocket money.

*   *   *

'A cheap day return to Rainham, please,' I requested the tired-looking booking clerk, after the last full-fare train had departed.

'Rainham in Kent?' he asked, looking at me with raised eyebrows for an answer.

I nodded. I had no idea where it was, but he ought to know: his trains went there every day. He wandered off to the other end of the office, and wrote on a blank ticket, which he brought back and placed on the counter his side of the grill.

'Two shillings and two pence, please,' he said, looking past me into space.

'This is all I have,' I replied, pushing two shillings under the grill.

'Two shillings and two pence,' he repeated loudly.

'This is all I have with me. I'll let you have the other two pence tonight,' I replied hopefully.

'That is not the way we run our railway,' he said, pushing the money back, and putting the ticket to one side, and shouting, 'next please.'

I knew there was a queue behind me, and I stood my ground.

'Please let me have the ticket, I've an interview for a job, and I haven't time to go home for more money,' I pleaded, hoping, from his weary expression, that he would be pleased to be rid of me for two pence.

'That's not the way to run a railway. Next please,' he called out impatiently.

The lady two back in the queue, who had been fumbling in her purse, reached forward and plonked two pence on the counter.

I pushed it through with the two shillings, grabbed the ticket, thanked her and ran for the train.

After five minutes of the interview I wasn't sure I should have thanked her. She'd certainly wasted two pence. It was a one-to-one event, and my opponent was a thick-set heartless business man. He attacked me for not having Matriculation, and for daring to apply without it. I hadn't the nerve to tell him that I'd been directed by a nit in the employment bureau who had no idea what qualifications he was asking for.

He informed me that I would be paid fifteen shillings a week, until I obtained Matriculation, and then I would receive half-a-crown a year increase, until I obtained a degree in chemistry; failure in any year would result in my employment immediately being terminated.

When he paused I pondered if I should ask him if he would like to cough up the extra two pence for my ticket, and confirm that he hadn't said failure in any year would result in my being exterminated.

In no way could I see myself being successful, and I was ready to withdraw the offer of my services then and there, but he insisted on showing me round the laboratory.

There were about ten boys of between sixteen and twenty, paired with the same number of men between twenty-five and forty, standing at five rows of benches. The atmosphere resembled at best a church, at worst a morgue. They were speaking in whispers, and I couldn't imagine there was ever anything to laugh about.

My guide and tormentor lead me to a pair and asked the senior partner to show me their laboratory book, which he informed me was filled in each day, and signed by him or his deputy each night before they went home. I looked as intelligently as I could at the contents, and managed to suppress a shudder.

We returned to his office and, looking at the clock, I was surprised to see that only half an hour had passed. It had seemed like half a day to me.

'You will have to rent lodgings in Rainham, at thirty shillings a week. The village is two miles away, and there is no transport, so you will require a bicycle,' he said, in no way encouraging me to take the post.

'I'm not sure if my father would be able to pay the extra money for lodgings,' I said, knowing he wouldn't, and in no way would I try to persuade him.

'Let me know as soon as possible. We are anxious to fill the vacancy,' he replied, bringing the ordeal abruptly to a halt.

I thanked him, and I was pleased to escape from the factory, even though I had half an hour to wait at the station for the train back to London.

Father was astonished to learn how rail fares had risen recently, and when he heard a rather shaded version of the interview, showing me in a better light, and the price of digs in line with the inflated railway fares, he confirmed that in no way could he afford to subsidise me while I was studying for a degree.

Before I could write and tell the company of their good fortune, I received a letter from them the next morning; they were not taking the risk of me accepting the post.

The next interview was arranged for me by Father. I travelled to London with him on a half-price ticket, which he bought at the ticket office, explaining to me that he could plead ignorance of the age for half fare if challenged, and stump up the extra, but they would guess I had been doing it since I was fourteen years old.

After a long walk up the back streets near Cannon Street station, we arrived at a dingy building which father seemed to want to pass without being seen. He hurriedly told me to ask for Mr Reisepusine and left before I could confirm the name, and nearly failed to gain entry when I asked the rough-looking character armed with a bucket and mop, for Mr Rice Pudding.

The most impressive thing about Mr Reisepusine was his name. He was a scruffy fat man, and I felt he found me contemptuously small, conducting the interview as if he would like me to be aware of his feelings.

'What makes you think we can employ you?' he asked, taking a noisy sip of coffee.

'I don't, I'm not sure what you do. I suppose you would teach me something that would be useful to you,' I replied, wondering how one became an interviewer.

'Yes, we could teach you to lick stamps for a couple of years,' he replied, laughing too much at his own wit to be able to sip his coffee.

'What would I do after that?' I asked, liking him little more than the previous interviewer.

'If you stuck it for two years, we might find you something, but by then you should have found a better job somewhere else,' he replied, laughing so much he started to cough, and after a few minutes, when he was just able to speak, told me he had no vacancy at the moment, but as he owed Mr Trigsby a favour, he had agreed to interview me for the vacancy of office boy when it occurred.

I told Father the interview had gone well, but there was no vacancy at the moment. I thought I was quite safe, I couldn't imagine Mr Rice Pudding would have me if he could avoid it. I was wrong. A vacancy did occur about six months later, and Father asked me if I wished to consider it. That of course was the war. By then employers were so desparate for staff that they would take anybody they could get.

By the end of October I was beginning to despair. The only money I had was three pence a week pocket money from Father, and a shilling a week from Margaret, who had always been generous with the little money she had left after fares to London, and something to eat for lunch. Without her shilling, I would have been in dire straits, and I was beginning to have second thoughts about being an ARP messenger boy.

It was a Friday morning; mother sorted through the mail, and with a white face, and trembling hand passed to me a letter in a buff—coloured envelope.

3

'I didn't think we'd hear from them again,' I said passing the letter to mother, who was anxiously waiting to learn its contents.

'That's good, I was worried it might be your calling up papers,' she said, smiling with relief as she handed it back to me.

'I'd prefer it was. I haven't recovered yet from the last interview: if this one is as bad, I think I'll volunteer,' I replied. I was beginning to feel I didn't want to work in a laboratory or an office.

The letter instructed me to present myself at ten thirty on the 3rd November at the Telephone Manufacturing Company, St. Mary Cray for an interview as a laboratory assistant.

I was pleased, but worried, that this interview might not be any different from the first two. I went to the library and brought home some books on short wave radio. An hour later I decided I was wasting my time. I knew vaguely what a valve, a condenser, a resistor and an inductor were, and I had built a short wave radio set for listening to Biggin Hill Aerodrome, but I had no idea what questions I would be asked, or what sort of answers would be expected.

Carefully putting my cycle clips on to safeguard my best trousers, the only ones I had, and wearing my only sports jacket, I cycled off with the only hope of a successful mission, being mother's best wishes, ringing in my ears.

It was easy to find the factory from the directions in the letter; on the right, first past the traffic lights, after going under the railway bridge, opposite the large gasometers.

It was a fine morning, and the new two-storey office building looked cheerful in the bright sunshine. The entrance hall was in a large square sixty foot high tower made of glass bricks, with a forty foot radio mast on the top: the last place to be anywhere near in an air raid.

I hated being late, and I arrived over half an hour early for my appointment. The secretary confirmed my name three times. She seemed to think it impossible that I could arrive before the person whose appointment was half an hour before me.

Eventually she accepted me as being whom I said I was, and went away to discuss the next move. She was back almost immediately.

'As you are Mr Trigsby whose interview is at half past ten, and the person due at ten o'clock has not yet arrived, would you mind having your interview now?' she asked anxiously, as if she thought I might say no! Which of course I didn't.

I followed her up the marble staircase to the second floor balcony which ran along the back of the hall, to a laboratory with glass windows on to the corridor. After passing this we came to a large office with eight desks in it, four of which were occupied.

We entered, and she halted at the first desk to introduce me to Mr Thompson, a cheerful man in his mid-twenties with neatly combed red wavy hair. His smart brown tweed suit with a matching tie made me glad I had, as mother had continually reminded me I should, remembered to remove my bicycle clips.

Mr Thompson motioned me to the chair strategically placed so that I could be observed by the other three gentlemen. Two of them looked younger than Mr Thompson. The other was in his forties wearing a dark blue suit, and I thought he looked out of place.

Mr Thompson was pleasant, and easy to talk to about my desire to work in a laboratory, and not an office. He went to great pains to explain that my confession that I had no idea what I would be doing met with his approval, as he didn't know either. He hoped I would be willing to accept whatever jobs turned up, as useful experience towards qualifying me as an engineer in telecommunications. I had only a faint idea of what he was talking about.

He carefully checked my qualifications were five G.S.C. passes, which he seemed to think was good, and assumed I would be prepared to study for a degree in Engineering. I so liked the atmosphere, I would have agreed to have taken

Holy Orders if they were required for the job.

After a pleasant half hour he dismissed me, telling me there were others to interview, including the one who hadn't turned up, so he could not say if I would be accepted, giving me the impression that if nobody better turned up it could be me.

I was feeling optimistic as I was collecting my bicycle, until I was nearly flattened by a maniac who just missed me, stopping inches short with a scream of bicycle brakes. It was Alan Leare. We had been paired at school in all the laboratory subjects for the last five years. He was tall, spoke confidently, and he knew where he was going, and how to get there. He had one fault in my favour, but at that moment I couldn't remember what it was.

'What are you doing here?' I asked, when I'd recovered sufficiently to speak.

'I've come for an interview for a job,' he replied, panting as if he'd been in the milk race.

'I thought you were going to Battersea Polytechnic to take a degree,' I said, having remembered why I was surprised to see him.

'I was. I started there a few weeks ago, but my father was killed in the blackout, and I have to earn some money.'

'Sorry, Alan, that's rotten luck,' I replied, sad that he'd lost a father, and that it had probably cost me the job.

'I'm not sorry to have to work. I didn't really fancy studying full time. It was all right at school. We had a lot of fun didn't we?' he said, smiling, and shrugging his shoulders.

'We've probably come for the same job. I've just finished my interview. What time's yours?' I asked, doubting if I would get the job in preference to him.

'Ten o'clock,' he replied, glancing at his watch as he spoke.

'I should have guessed it. My interview was half past ten.'

'I thought you said you had yours,' he replied, looking puzzled.

'I have. The twit before me hadn't turned up, so they asked me to take his place.'

'I suppose I'd better hurry,' he replied, laughing as he threw his bicycle into the rack.

'Good luck, Alan,' I said, holding out my hand. I liked him. We'd had five exciting years at school, when we'd led each other in and out of more trouble than I had ever believed existed. We could both have done a lot better without each other.

'I hope the best man wins. He needs the job, more than you do,' he said, laughing and shaking my hand, before hurrying towards the front entrance.

'How did it go?' Mother asked eagerly as soon as I was through the back door.

'All right. They are going to let me know,' I replied, hating to tell her I hadn't a chance.

'I'll say a prayer for you on Sunday,' she said, smiling hopefully.

'I shouldn't waste it,' I advised her, laughing. I didn't believe in such things anyway.

'You never know,' she said, handing me a cup of tea.

'Yes I do, I bumped into Alan Leare. He's bound to get it,' I replied, feeling it was silly to raise false hopes.

'I thought he was going somewhere to take a degree,' she replied, looking disappointed.

I wasn't all that bothered, believing that if it was going to happen it would, and there was nothing I could do about it.

'That's right, but his father was killed cycling in the blackout, and he has to find a job,' I said, knowing that she would be sorry. She liked Alan, amd his father.

'Poor boy, it must have been a terrible shock for him. What a pity; you might have got the job if it hadn't happened,' she said, nearly in tears.

'Oh mother, don't worry so,' I said, putting my arm round her shoulders.

I wanted a job, but it was no use crying about it. I was bored, and beginning to think of being an ARP messenger again. I decided to exchange the text books at the library for some good murder mysteries.

I cycled out of the gate holding the books in one hand, and rode smack into Alan as he was parking his bicycle against the kerb outside.

'Who's a maniac?' he asked, laughing as he caught me with one arm, and his bike from falling over with the other.

'What a stupid place to park a bicycle,' I replied, when I had my breath back.

'We've got the job,' he said, still laughing as he propped up his bike.

'How do you know? Mr Thompson said there were others.'

'I was the last one, the others were interviewed on Friday. They were no good they were too well-qualified.'

'They couldn't have been less qualified,' I replied trying to laugh, despite my disappointment. If Alan's father hadn't cycled in the blackout without a rear lamp, it could have been me.

'Can you start next Monday?'

'What do you mean?'

'I mean can you start on Monday?'

'But you said you'd got the job.'

'I did. They want two, and when I told them we'd worked together for years in the labs at school, they thought we were ideal,' Alan said, laughing as if he could well understand my amazement.

'Crikey it's hard to believe. Remember what Joe the chemistry master said? Each of us was bad enough but only the Devil would have brought us together,' I replied, and we went in laughing like a couple of schoolboys to tell Mother the news.

4

'What are you going to wear?" Mother asked, when Alan had gone.

'I suppose I'll wear my blazer, or I could wear my sports jacket,' I replied, feeling flustered. Trust Mother to bring me down to earth with something I would never have thought about until Monday morning.

'You see your father buys you a suit,' she said, fiercely cleaning some egg off a plate she was washing up.

'He'll never do that. He told me last week he had no money, and it will be two years before he recovers from our holiday,' I replied, I didn't want to ask him. He always made me feel as if I were a parasite screwing the last penny out of him. I'd rather turn up in my pyjamas. Anyway, what was wrong with my school blazer? I'd worn one for the last five years.

'When you received compensation for that accident, and he took all the money, he promised to buy you a suit for your first job. You remind him of it now.'

'Mother, that was three years ago, he'll have forgotten,' I replied wearily, knowing it was a waste of time for me to argue.

'No he has not. I reminded him on holiday when we were talking about you getting a job. He was sure you would be called up for the forces, and agreed he'd made the promise, and would keep it,' she said, swishing the water around furiously.

Before Father came down to breakfast on the Saturday morning, Mother called me into the kitchen.

'I had a word with your father last night. I told him you were expecting him to buy you a suit today. Ask him at breakfast when you will be going,' she said, pushing the bacon around in the frying pan.

'How can he buy it for me if he hasn't any money?' I asked. I hated asking him for anything. He always made me feel so sorry for him, I ended up wishing I had some money to give him, or offering to take a cut in my three pence a week pocket money.

'He had at least twelve pounds of your money. See you get a decent suit out of him, not the cheapest one in the shop. It's the last chance you'll have. You understand?' she hissed, at last handing me my tiny breakfast of half a piece of fried bread, half a rasher of bacon, and half a fried egg. I was starving.

A few minutes later, Father came down to breakfast breathing through his second cigarette which he always lit at the top of the stairs; and as usual, he put it to smoke away in the ash tray on the sideboard just behind me.

Normally I would get up and stub it out after he had started his breakfast, and I decided to use this as the opportunity to open the conversation., as I sat down.

'Dad, are you going to buy me a suit today?' I asked feeling it must sound as if I had been rehearsing all night.

Jean giggled, Phyllis pulled a face which made her laugh; Father feigned deafness, and behaved as if I had never spoken.

'If he had to pay for it, you'd never have had a birthday suit,' Phyllis said, in a stage whisper.

I waited until Jean had shut up giggling, and tried again.

'Dad, are you going to buy me a suit today?'

'You don't need a suit to work in a laboratory. They wear overalls,' he said, staring at me with his large blue watery eyes over the rim of the cup he was holding to his lips.

'I've still got to wear something underneath,' I replied, feeling utterly miserable, I agreed with him. I didn't really need one.

'I can't afford to buy you a suit. I need a new one myself,' he said, blinking piteously, and of course I felt sorry for him.

Mother came in with extra rashers on a plate. She had obviously been listening outside the door.

'Do you want me to delay the dinner so that you can buy Ted's suit this morning?' she asked, holding the plate with the bacon on it in front of her.

'No thank you, I've had enough; let the children have it,' he said, generously motioning with his knife to indicate where she should be distributing the bacon.

'Godfrey! Do you wish me to delay the dinner?'

'No, why should I?'

'Well, when are you going to buy a suit for Ted?'

'I might have time this afternoon.'

'Would you like me to take him this morning?' Mother asked, as she shot a piece of bacon on to my plate.

'No, I'll buy it for him,' he replied, sulkily.

Four o'clock that afternoon Father came in from the garden, and had a bath. At five o'clock he came downstairs, and sat in his armchair in the lounge. Mother, having been listening for him, came into the room before his bottom hit the cushions.

'Godfrey, it's gone five o'clock. Are you going to buy Ted a suit or aren't you?' she shouted furiously, and Father cracked.

'It's not, is it? My watch must have stopped. Come on, son. If you want a suit you'd better get a move on,' he said struggling out of his chair.

We hurried down the road with me running to keep up with him to the nearest 'Gents' and Boys'' outfitters in the High Street, only a few minutes away from where we lived.

The shop was called 'Pipes', after the owner, a dapper little man who always wore a black coat with pinstripe trousers. He had short neatly trimmed white hair, and little pince-nez glasses. He was standing in the doorway, rubbing his hands, and probably praying for one last customer even at this late hour. I always smiled when I passed the shop, thinking how well the name fitted his slender figure, including the little bump at the top.

'Good afternoon, Mr Trigsby. Can I be of service to you, sir?' he asked, rubbing his hands harder than ever, and tilting his head to look up to Father, nearly a foot taller.

'I want a suit for my lad here. He's starting work next week. Nothing too expensive mind you,' Father replied, leaving plenty of scope for Mr Pipe to offer anything he had left to sell at five thirty on a Saturday afternoon.

'That won't be a problem. I'm sure we can fit him up with something,' Mr Pipe replied, stroking his chin, and turning his head first one way, and then the other as if he wasn't sure which heap to lead us to first.

We followed him into the far end of the shop, which was almost in darkness. He ran his hand along a row of suits whose colour it was impossible to tell in the dim light.

'Were you thinking of something like this, sir?' he asked, pulling one out, and holding it up.

It was black! That's why there was no colour; it would have served me well if I was going to be a pall-bearer.

'No he doesn't want anything like that. I was thinking of something cheaper, a lot cheaper,' Father said, shaking his head, and turning pale.

'I don't know if I have anything cheaper. These only come out at two pounds fifteen shillings,' Mr Pipe replied, looking very thoughtful.

'Haven't you something in a sale?'

'We did have some special offers this morning, but I think they're all gone. They were very good suits, real bargains they were,' he replied, leading us back towards the entrance.

'No, they're all gone,' he said, staring sadly at the empty window.

'What about the one I saw in the entrance as I came in?' Father asked, walking in that direction.

'I thought that one was sold. Is it still there?' Mr Pipe asked, coming over to have a look. 'Oh, I forgot about that one,' he said, reaching up, and lifting it down.

It was a black and white birds eye pattern, I looked at it in horror. I never liked the idea of a suit. I thought a plain shade of grey might not be too bad; not this colour.

Mr Pipe held it against me.

'How much is it?' Father asked, not sounding too sure about it.

'You can have that one for two pounds,' Mr Pipe replied, after studying the label.

'That's just what we were looking for. That will do you perfectly,' Father said, eagerly trying to tear my blazer off my back, before I could undo the buttons.

'It's a nice generous fit,' Mr Pipe announced, gripping the jacket at the bottom, and jerking it violently down on my shoulders, nearly having me on my knees.

'You happy with it, son?' Dad asked, standing back, and unable to hide the smirk on his face.

'It doesn't fit!' I protested miserably.

'You'll grow into it,' he said, soothingly.

'What about the trousers?' I asked, looking at the waist. I could imagine Phyllis laughing, and saying, 'Hang on a minute, I'll come in there with you.'

'It will be all right with braces, and your Mother can turn up an inch or two at the bottom. She's got until Monday to do it,' he said, full of enthusiasm. It was obvious that he was thrilled to bits at getting away with two pounds.

'You'll take it then, Mr Trigsby?' Mr Pipe asked, delightedly. The only one not over the moon was me.

'There you are, young sir. I expect you'd like to carry it,' Mr Pipe said smiling, as he handed me the bulky parcel, and my father gave him the two pounds.

The row started as soon as Mother met us at the front door.

'You didn't take long. Did you get what you wanted?' she asked me.

'You'll have to do something with the trousers. They will need shortening , an inch or two,' Father remarked casually.

'I can't cut bits off the trousers. The turn-ups never look the same after you've cut bits off. You should have had it done before you paid for it.'

'He couldn't have done it before Monday. You should be able to do a simple thing like that,' Father replied, shrugging his shoulders, indicating he'd done his part now it was up to her.

'If you had gone in the morning there would have been plenty of time to have it altered,' Mother said, her hair falling over her face, as always when she was upset.

I stood there holding the large parcel, as Phyllis and Jean came in.

'Put it on, Ted. Let's see the new office boy,' Jean said, excitedly grabbing the parcel from me, and starting to tear it open, with Phyllis's help.

The suit fell out onto the floor. Phyllis grabbed the coat, and held it up.

'That will never fit you, Ted!' she cried, her eyes wide with astonishment.

There was a moment's silence, as Dad hurriedly left the room, and Mother took over.

'Stop it you girls! Ted, go and put it on. I'll have to see what

I can do,' she said, resigning herself to having lost again, and sounding sorry for me.

I came back into the room, holding the trousers up with one hand, a pair of braces in the other. Jean screamed with laughter, Phyllis smiled, but there was pity in her eyes. Mother cried quietly. She already had a mouth full of pins.

5

Working hard over the weekend, with scissors, needle, thread, and plenty of tucks, Mother succeeded in making the suit fit in several places. Jean and Phyllis enjoyed themselves, with me playing the part of a clown.

With faith in Mother's skill with the needle, and the numerous fittings, I became used to the feel, and more comfortable. But I wished she wouldn't keep muttering through mouthfuls of pins.

'Jesus with all his miracles could never have made a suit out of this.'

On Monday morning, after a last tug at the back, and smoothing of the lapels, I left for my first day at work in plenty of time to arrive at eight thirty for nine o'clock.

Sitting in the entrance hall at a quarter past nine, I was wishing Alan would turn up and listening to a tapping noise growing louder as the seconds past. I looked up and saw a tall thin smartly–dressed lady of some thirty years with high-heeled shoes, clippity clopping noisily along the marble corridor, and watched fascinated as, retaining her balance down the two flights of stairs, she came to a halt in front of me.

'There should be two of you,' she said, sounding as if she did't think it worth the trouble of hobbling all that way just for me.

'He'll be here in a minute,' I replied, knowing Alan well enough to be confident that it was only a matter of when.

'I'm not climbing these stairs twice in one morning. When he arrives ask the girl in the kiosk to ring Miss Shrub, and I'll meet you at the top,' she replied, turning skilfully with a twirl of her many–pleated bottle–green skirt, and clippity clop-piting back the way she had come.

She was almost at the top of the stairs, when the swing door flew open and Alan came through, smiling as he saw me sitting there. I leapt to my feet and shouted up to her.

'Hold on, he's arrived!'

She glanced over the balcony; then with her nose high, continued until she disappeared into the dark corridor at the end, the clippity clops slowly fading away.

'What was all that about?' Alan asked, pulling off his cycle clips.

'She came to collect us; you weren't here, so she's gone away again,' I replied, not expecting him to apologise for being only fifteen minutes late. For him that was early.

'I'm not surprised. You look as if you've come from a magpie's funeral,' he said, laughing as he stood back, eyeing me up and down.

'If you hadn't been late, it would have been all right,' I replied, ignoring his comment.

'Come on then, let's go, and find the lady,' he said, striding across the hall.

We raced up the marble stairs, Alan taking them two at a time, and skipped along the corridor. We could have been back at school, except there were no prefects to send flying as we bumped into them. We passed the offices with glass windows on all sides, and soon spotted the lady in the green skirt pouring out tea in an office with Miss Shrub on the door label.

I banged on the door, as Alan opened it, and we burst in.

She looked coldly at us, and I felt like a naughty schoolboy.

'I told you to ask the telephone operator to ring, and I would come down for you when I was ready,' she said haughtily.

'I thought we could save you a journey,' I replied, hoping such consideration might be worth a cup of tea, but of course I was not allowing for Alan, who watched as she dropped two sugars in the tea cups.

'I don't take sugar, thank you,' he said, with the charm of an elephant.

'You're not taking any tea either,' she replied coldly, walking to the desks and putting the cups down.

'I'll take you to see Mr Rae after you've signed the time book,' she said, coming back to the filing cabinet and taking out a thick foolscap book. She dropped it heavily on to the table beside the cabinet, and began to flick through the pages.

'Sign this book, every morning, when you come in, and before you leave at night, or you won't be paid on Friday,' she said, pointing a long thin finger where we were to sign.

Alan grabbed the pen, and signed his name alongside mine. I took the pen quickly from him and signed alongside his. She looked at the signatures for a moment, sighed, closed the book and dropped it into the filing cabinet.

Mr Rae, whom we judged to be in his early twenties, was a corpulent young man with a scanty supply of red hair, and many freckles. He had the air of a prefect, and his friendly manner contained a large element of superiority. He led us into the laboratory, and showed us where things like transformers, resistors, and capacitors were kept. Even I was aware of the age of some of the components.

He showed us the different power supplies available, and then took us to a battery room at the far end of the corridor, containing a large number of high, and low voltage units.

'Your first job will be to clean this place up, and see the batteries are kept in good order,' he said, as we sniffed at the smell of decay which occurs when batteries are allowed to look after themselves.

He told us to answer the telephone in the laboratory, and to take it in turns to collect the drinks and food for the rest of them at ten thirty and three o'clock each day. Glancing at his watch, he then gave us his order, and told us to hurry up and get the others or we would miss the trolley which waited only a few minutes at the bottom of the back stairs.

'That's a blow, I'm not keen on fagging teas,' I muttered to Alan after we had collected the orders, and the money.

'That's why we got the job. The others were too well-qualified to fag teas. We'd better make the most of their bad luck,' he replied laughing as we hurried down the back stairs to where Mrs Tickle the tea lady was waiting for us.

During tea we chatted with the two others who had been observers at our interviews, and when we wandered down the corridor to the Gents, I compared the atmosphere here, with the laboratory at Rainham.

'They seem a pleasant light−hearted little group,' I said, as we closed the door.

'It would have been different without you, Ted,' Alan replied, clapping me on the back, and roaring with laughter.

'What are you talking about?' I asked, knowing him too well to think he was complimenting me in any way.

'Ted, nobody could be serious with you in that suit,' he replied, laughing so much I could only laugh with him.

'It can't be as bad as all that,' I pleaded hopefully.

'It's not bad, it's excellent. Remember what Joe said, we'd get by as long as nobody took us seriously.'

'It's a tailor-made suit. Dad bought the material for two pounds on Saturday afternoon. Mother spent all Sunday morning undoing it, and Sunday evening sewing it up again.' I said, thinking he might as well know the truth.

'After all that I would have thought it would have fitted somewhere,' he replied laughing, and flicking some water at me.

'It does. It's just mother's so skilful with the needle it doesn't show,' I replied, trying to sound cheerful, and wishing I had worn my blazer as he had.

We rejoined the others, and although I knew now why they were laughing, the remainder of a pleasant morning passed quickly, and I soon found myself pedalling hungrily home to dinner, which I knew would be cold meat and a baked potato, as always on a Monday.

'How did it go?' Mother asked, eyeing me up and down when I came in.

'Very well thank you. I think it should be all right,' I replied, not wishing to tell her it looked as if we were going to fag teas, and clean battery rooms.'

'What did they think of the suit?' she asked anxiously.

'They thought it was marvellous. They asked me if you took orders, they realise you won't need any measurements,' I replied, laughing, and putting my arm round her shoulders. Poor Mother, she tried hard to help.

'Ted, I'm sorry, I'll have another go at it tonight,' she replied, and it was difficult to see if she was crying, or laughing like the rest of them.

'Forget about it, Mother dear, they never said a word, they couldn't stop laughing,' I said, and was pleased Mother was laughing too, as she went to the kitchen to bring in our dinner.

'What was the row about last night?' I asked, when Mother paused with her questioning.

'You.'

'Me! What have I done?'

'Father wants you to give him your pay-packet each week, he says. He'll deduct eight shillings for your lodgings, and give you an allowance for expenses, putting the rest in his bank for you when you want it.'

'That sounds like Dad. What was the row about?' I asked, watching Mother viciously cutting the meat on her plate.

'I told him I needed some extra money, and he should give me four shillings a week, as you were coming home to lunch every day.'

'That sounds reasonable . Did he agree?'

'No he did not. He said that up 'till now, I'd managed to feed you since you left school without extra money, and therefore I didn't need any more.'

'He doesn't sound as if he's improving any,' I replied, as I helped myself to some HP sauce to give some flavour to the cold mutton.

'Ted, you must not give him your money each week,' Mother said, looking at me anxiously, as if I might not be going to agree with her.

'He hasn't said anything to me about it, and I have no intention of doing so if he does,' I replied. I didn't like to tell her I hadn't even thought about it. It was another four days before I got paid, and I still couldn't believe it would actually happen.

'He told me to persuade you today to hand over all your money each week to him, and he'll tell you his big plan tonight. Then he may consider giving me a few shillings more,' Mother said, as she gathered up our plates before going for our sweet.

'Thanks for the warning. I've thought about it. I'll tell him I'm going to handle my own money, and then discuss what he wants from me. You tell him you couldn't persuade me,' I said when she returned with our sweet, apple pie left over from Sunday. I wanted to keep things simple, I knew Dad was more than a match for all of us put together.

The cycle ride for me to the factory was just over or under

ten minutes depending on the wind. There was quite a good bus service which would have cost eight pence a day, and took about half an hour minimum, so I wouldn't be able to come home to dinner.

I spent the afternoon working out a maximum figure for my expenses, including bus fares, lunches, teas, and buns from the trolley; all fully detailed for the meeting with Father.

That evening, after I heard Dad go into the dining-room, I went to the lounge, and sat with a book open on my lap, memorising the figures, while I waited for him to finish his meal and come to sit in his armchair.

At half past six he came in, and sat down with hardly a glance in my direction: opened *The Financial Times*, and began to read. I knew better than to interrupt, and waited. After five minutes he folded the paper noisily. I kept my eyes on my book.

'It was today you started work, wasn't it?' he asked, feeling in his pocket for his matches.

'Yes.' I replied, wishing he'd use the matches on the mantlepiece. It annoyed me the way he was always searching through his pockets for them.

'I thought it was today. How did you get on?'

'All right, thank you; just meeting people, and being shown around,' I replied, noticing he'd found the matches, and would soon disappear in a cloud of smoke as he lit his pipe packed with bonfire mixture.

'Do you realise you've had free board and lodging for seventeen years?' he said, laughing as if it was a huge joke.

'I've never really looked on it like that,' I replied, not at all surprised at his opening question.

'You realise now you're a wage-earner you will have to contribute to the family budget?' he asked, staring at me through the smoke from his pipe, as he sucked and puffed it.

'Certainly. I was talking to Mother about it at dinner time. She suggested that I should hand all my money to you each week, and let you give me something back,' I said, having realised I could save a row if he thought she'd done as she was told.

'That sounds a good idea. You've no experience of handling money. Your mother's a very sensible woman you know,' he said, looking pleased to have Mother take the credit for his plan to handle the huge pay-packet of twenty-two shillings I would receive in a few days.

'Yes, I agree with you, but this time I think Mother's wrong. It's not fair to burden you with looking after my money, even though it is only twenty-two shillings a week.'

'That's a lot of money for somebody with no experience of handling money. When I started work I only received two shillings a week, and I gave it to my father to manage for me,' he said, not looking at all pleased with me.

'It would be better for me to learn to handle money at that level at the start, then a larger sum later on,' I continued, determined that I was going to make a stand with him over everything from now on.

'You are heavily indebted to your mother and I, and now it would help us if you were to show some gratitude to your mother and do as she suggests,' he said, sucking furiously at his pipe, to keep the bonfire mixture alight.

'I know Mother is usually right, but this time I'm sure she's wrong. I will keep my money, and pay a contribution towards the home. If after . . .'

'I agree with your mother. We both think it would be right for you to let me look after your money,' he said, and I could see he was becoming anxious.

'That's good if you both agree. I was going to say that if after two or three months I can't manage, I'll hand it over to you, or Mother. I have worked out my expenses, and I can afford to pay you eight shillings a week.'

'If I were handling your money, I would have been prepared to lend you some over the initial difficult period. You can't expect to pay less than twelve shillings a week towards the home, and don't forget I bought you a suit. You should pay that back,' he said, staring at me angrily.

'I'll pay you back for the suit, and give you and Mother four shillings each,' I said, knowing that he would jump at being paid for the suit.

'How long are you going to take to pay for the suit?' he asked eagerly.

'I'll pay you back in a month,' I replied. He agreed, and I'd got him. Any nonsense in the future, and I would hint at telling Mother he'd had the money back for the suit.

For the first month I had only four shillings a week, but I had never had such a large income before. Compared with the past I was a millionaire.

6

'What are we supposed to be doing?' Alan asked John Picard on the second Monday morning.

John was older than Tony Rae, and much easier to talk to. He had no airs or graces, and was pleased that Tony accepted the heavy responsibilities for managing two young laboratory assistants.

'Helping us in the lab,' he replied, rather vaguely.

'When do we start?' Alan asked, looking at me as I moved closer to hear the reply.

'When we have some work to do,' John replied laughing, probably at the bewildered expressions on our faces.

'Why haven't you any work?' I asked. It seemed strange to me, taking us on to help somebody with nothing to do.

'The company have set up these labs for development contracts. When they come in about six months there will be plenty of work for all of us. Until then you'd better make the most of it. Learn all you can about the use of the lab equipment, and use the rest of the time for study.'

The laboratory was well–equipped by 1939 standards, and for a few weeks we spent our time looking at it, and finding out how it worked, and what it was for.

We visited the battery room, which was well-stocked with high and low voltage cells, and the necessary charging equipment to maintain them. It had been neglected since it was installed, and we put it on our list for attention.

Coil-winding machines were available in the laboratory, for us to teach ourselves to produce wire-wound components, and there were precision electrical bridges to measure them accurately.

Most of this was new to me except from text books, and the poorly-stocked school labs. But Alan, who shunned all sports, giving his spare time to his hobby of building short-wave radios, was a member of the Society of Shortwave Radio Amateurs of Great Britain, and enthusiastically helped me to reduce my ignorance.

By the new year we had a programme where we were studying for Matriculation for two hours in the morning, and two hours in the afternoon, and the remainder of the time we were learning to design, and produced sample components, and building a short-wave radio to give us early warning when the fighters were scrambled at Biggin Hill, the local fighter station.

Those first five months were more fun than school, and every Friday Eric Fisher, Uncle's right-hand man according to him, and the odd job boy according to the others, came and gave us our pay packet.

Mr Thompson, as head of the laboratory, was our boss but we didn't see much of him. He was very busy with the design and manufacture of telephone exchange equipment being produced for India in the main factory in Dulwich.

Mr Handselle — the boss known to all of us as 'Uncle' was a Dutchman with little sense of humour, and had been a fighter pilot in the First World War. He took an interest in Alan when he learned he was a fellow member of the SSAGB I was never even sure if he saw me on the occasions he passed me in the corridor, walking with a measured tread, his head stiff, and trilby hat held close at his side. My first impression proved correct: he was an unfriendly man.

Mr Parsons, the works manager, was a pleasant character, understanding that having nothing to do was not our fault, but ruing the day he accepted an office under our lab, where everything seemed to land on the floor above his head.

The general manager was Mr Murphy, a tall dark Irishman in his fifties, very conscious of his important position in the firm, and believing that as general manager, everybody, including juniors like Alan and me on the research staff, came under him as far as discipline was concerned. Worse still, he seemed to think Alan and I lacked discipline, had no respect for higher authority, and were a bad example to his staff. He was probably correct and eager to have the pleasure of putting it right. Mr Hansdelle, director of research, considered that we were his staff, belonged to him, and what we did was nothing to do with anybody else.

When Mr Murphy complained to him that Alan came in late from lunch, and we had been seen playing on the roof, Mr Hansdelle told him to mind his own business, he needed no assistance in handling staff.

We didn't intentionally annoy anybody, but when we wanted to do something we did it. We didn't think it was necessary to ask permission when we wanted to rig an aerial for our short-wave radio. We found where the key of the door to the roof was and got on with it.

In January, 1940 we moved into two of the empty desks in the office to make it easier for our studying. This was quite a concession for such juniors, and Tony opposed it, but the desks were there and it seemed a waste not to use them.

We had minor skirmishes with Mr Murphy but we managed, due to Uncle's belief that criticism of us reflected on his staff management, to escape unharmed, but John warned us that Mr Murphy was not one to give up easily, and we should be careful not to give him any opportunity to embarrass Uncle.

It was a Monday morning. I was in early as usual, drinking coffee and talking and laughing with John Picard who travelled each day from North London, and had no choice but to be early, or an hour late. The door opened and somebody came into the office. I looked round wondering who it could be. Nobody else was due for another twenty minutes. It was Mr Murphy the general manager.

'Good morning,' I said, conscious that he would disapprove of us laughing and drinking coffee, even if it was before starting time.

'Who is responsible for the state of the battery room?' he asked, without a good morning.

'Alan Leare and I look after it,' I replied, wondering what it had to do with him.

'When was the last time you were in there?' he asked abruptly.

'About a week ago,' I replied, as it dawned on me. We had included it in our programme, and then forgotten about it.

'Last week! You couldn't have been in there last year by the look of it. We'll see what Mr Hansdelle has to say about this,' he said, looking pleased with himself.

'Mr Hansdelle's away today. He'll be in tomorrow morning,' John said, laughing cheerfully.

'I'll see him first thing tomorrow morning,' he replied and departed, slamming the door and striding off down the corridor.

'He's right this time. It is in a state, we haven't been near it since we came,' I said, feeling unhappy about it.

At nine o'clock Alan came in the back way, as usual when he was late.

'When I passed the battery room the door was open,' he said,flinging his scarf on to his desk.

'That was Mr Murphy. He inspected it about an hour ago, and he's reporting to Uncle tomorrow morning,' John said, laughing as Alan scowled at the mention of Murphy's name.

'I knew we'd forgotten something,' Alan said, picking up a pad of store's requisitions before sitting down at his desk.

'It sounds as if Uncle will have a job to pull you two out of the fire this time,' John said shaking his head.

'He won't have to,' Alan replied, starting to fill in the store's requisitions.

By tea-time, at ten o'clock, we had collected from stores, and delivered to the battery room everything we could think of to clean the place out; ten pounds of rags, soaps, Vaseline, polish, mops, scrubbing brushes, buckets, even Brasso for the taps.

We had always worked well together, and we fell into an easy routine, Alan standing on the benches and using his height for the ceiling and top of the walls, and I working lower down and keeping him constantly supplied with clean water. By the end of the morning, we were confident that we would complete in the day, and by five o'clock we were finished. The place was perfect, the white tiles on the walls shining as brightly as the freshly washed ceiling. All dud cells had been dumped, the chargers were humming away, and every cell was topped up to the correct level, and bubbling merrily.

I arrived early Tuesday morning, but only just ahead of Alan. He was not going to miss anything. Murphy popped his head in at eight thirty; rubbing his eyes in disbelief when he saw Alan sitting at his desk, and looked stunned when Alan politely informed him that Mr Hansdelle was a member of the senior staff, and would not be arriving before nine o'clock.

Uncle's office was next to ours, and he used the glazed top half of the wall to see who was in our office, before selecting his victim. As soon as he arrived that morning, John Picard who was next in line to Mr Thompson, popped in and told him Mr Murphy was waiting to see him. Uncle didn't ask why, and John didn't enlighten him of Murphy's sudden phobia for inspecting battery rooms in the early hours of the morning.

Uncle picked up the telephone as John left the office, and shortly after he returned, leaving our door open so that we would be able to hear and see. Mr Murphy passed our office.

'Good morning, Mr Hansdelle. Have you visited your battery room lately?' Mr Murphy shouted, across the office.

'I don't think so,' Uncle replied, looking puzzled. He had probably forgotten where it was.

'It's about time you did,' Murphy said, standing in the doorway with his arms folded.

'Why are you so concerned?' Uncle asked, standing with his hands on his hips.

'I think you should come with me and have a look. It's an absolute disgrace. Whoever is responsible should be sacked. They would be if they were on my staff,' Murphy replied stepping out into the corridor.

Uncle walked slowly towards the door, and Murphy shot ahead of him to lead the way, probably unaware, as we were, that Uncle hesitated because he didn't know which way to turn.

Five minutes later Uncle was back, smiling appreciatively at our maintenance of his battery room. Murphy had a face like thunder. He hesitated as he passed our office, then hurried down the corridor followed by hoots of laughter. He rarely came on our floor after that, except for the Directors' meeting held in Uncle's office fortnightly, and when the development contracts grew to be the major part of the work, every Monday.

7

Before we all went to the bungalow for our holiday in August, 1939, Dad had been ill, and spent the previous three weeks convalescing in a guest house in Wittering.

Early in December, 1939, Dad came home from the office, and from the speed at which the girls disappeared I should have guessed that he was ill again.

Mother hurried off to fetch the doctor, a redoubtable lady who lived and practised in the big house across the road. All the family were on her books except myself. Having suffered the attention of Nurse Jane, my mother's sister, I could imagine a woman doctor could be even worse.

Dad moaned horribly when he wasn't well, and we kept clear when we heard the warning sounds. The girls having disappeared without a word to me, I walked right into it, and found myself holding Dad's hand while Mother went for the doctor.

The doctor asked Mother to describe Father's latest malady and, diagnosing it as the same again, sent her to drink tea in the kitchen with her nurse, Erine, while she saw off the last few patients waiting in the surgery.

I held Father's hand for a long time, and he wasn't pleased. The several times before when he'd been dying, it had been for less than ten minutes, and half an hour had passed already.

'Go and see what's keeping the doctor. I could be dead if she doesn't hurry up,' he said, and let out a terrible groan, which meant I had no hope of being saved by one of the girls blundering in, believing the silence indicated the crisis was over.

'You'll have to let go of my hand first,' I replied, struggling to free it.

'I can't let you go, I'm a very sick man,' he said, tightening his grip.

'I won't be a minute. I'll dash over and come straight back,' I pleaded, tugging to free my hand, convinced no dying man would have the grip of a gorilla.

'No! Ted, I can't let you go.' he said, gripping my hand even tighter.

The doctor arrived half an hour later. My hand was dead and I thought it would never recover, as I nodded self—consciously to her, and hurried out of the room.

'Don't!'

I stopped as I was about to shut the door. It was Phyllis at the bottom of the stairs. Her hushed whisper was to stop me closing the door. Jean was with her. They wanted to hear what was going on. I turned to go into the dining—room as the stairs were blocked, and the door opened for me; Mother was listening there.

She put her finger to her lips, and I stood behind her.

After ten minutes, we heard the doctor closing the consultation, and Mother went out to meet her in the hall.

'I have advised Mr Trigsby to go away for a few weeks. He is in a very poor mental state. He seems reluctant to leave you all over Christmas. You must try to persuade him. Complete rest away from everything for a few weeks will be good for all of you.'

'I'll try but if you can't, I doubt if I can,' Mother replied, sounding disappointed at the doctor's lack of success.

'You do your best, Mrs Trigsby, and if you can't persuade him, come and see me again.'

It was three days before Christmas, 1939. We had done our best not to look happy. We were now all under a nervous strain. Would he go, or wouldn't he?

'The taxi is coming in half an hour, Ted. Make sure Father's cases are in the hall, ready,' Mother said, as she nervously fiddled with her apron.

'I'll go up in a minute, and bring them down,' I replied, as I heard Father moving about in the room above.

'Jean, stop giggling, or your Father will change his mind,' Mother said, trying not to smile herself.

'Go now, Ted, better not risk being late,' Phyllis advised, nervously biting her fingernails.

'I'm waiting for him to finish saying his prayers,' I replied. The way they were behaving I was beginning to feel nervous myself.

'Go on!' Phyllis said, as I still hesitated.

I thought, I might as well get it over. Climbing the stairs as quietly as I could, I passed my bedroom door, and looked into my parents' room: Dad was standing facing me doing his hair in the mirror.

'I've come to take your cases downstairs,' I said, wondering why I always felt awkward when I spoke to him.

'Thank you, Ted. Before you go, kneel at the bed with me, and say a prayer, I may not come back,' he said, looking at me with watery blue eyes.

'Don't say that, Dad. The doctor said you need a complete rest. You'll feel fine after a holiday.' I replied, feeling embarrassed. I didn't know whether he was ill or not.

'That's it. None of you realises how ill I am, your mother certainly doesn't. She just wants me out of the way for Christmas,' he said, dropping to his knees beside the bed.

'Dad, that's not true. Mother is very worried about you,' I said, smiling inwardly, knowing Mother's main worry was that he wouldn't go.

'If you believe that, it shows what a clever liar she is,' he answered, motioning to me to kneel down beside him.

I dropped to my knees, glad the girls wouldn't risk coming upstairs, and see me. They were never caught for a pray. It always seemed to be me. We stayed there for a few minutes, then I stood up, and took the cases downstairs, leaving him on his knees mumbling away.

'Is he ready yet?' Mother asked anxiously.

'He wants you all to go upstairs, for a last prayer with him,' I said, trying to look serious, and then having to dodge as Jean rushed at me laughing.

'Shut up you children. Will you never grow up.' Mother cried, desperately trying to quieten us.

'It's Ted's fault. He's a Palestine.' Jean said, struggling to obey Mother and stop laughing.

'Philistine,' Mother said, the tears in her eyes as she tried not to laugh.

'I thought I'd get the blame,' Phyllis said, pulling a face that produced more giggles from Jean.

The door opened, and Dad came in and sat down at the table without saying a word; Mother hurried to the kitchen to bring him his breakfast, and Jean dashed upstairs spluttering and choking with the giggles, her handkerchief over her mouth.

'You children are going to have a party,' Mother said, as we ran indoors together, after waving goodbye to the taxi.

It seemed as if we knew the phoney war could not last for ever, and we must take this last opportunity for a gathering of friends. Margaret and Mother made it our best Christmas, understanding better than we did how different life would be from now on.

Even Dopey the cat purred louder than ever, perhaps because we allowed him to sleep in Father's armchair, which none of us wanted to sit in. Father would have him out when he returned, but even he loved Dopey, refraining from moving him out of the way with his foot, unless he had his slippers on.

Dopey was Mother's cat. She had tried to give him another name, but it stuck, because it did silly things like curling up in Father's trilby hat whenever it fell on the floor, which was most mornings, when we grabbed our coats off the hallstand. This was another chore for Mother, who went into the hall after each of us left to remove Dopey from the hat, and save it rough treatment from Father if he found it there first.

Father arrived home on the fifth of January, and several weeks later Mother became ill. The doctor diagnosed nervous reaction due to his return, and told her to take two aspirins, and try to forget about him.

After another night of agony, Mother was unable to get up on the Sunday morning, and Margaret went across the road to fetch the doctor.

'Ted, you'll have to tell him.' Margaret said when she returned.

'I don't mind telling him, but he won't take any notice of me,' I replied, ignoring Jean's giggles. She seemed to think everything was funny.

I climbed the stairs stepping carefully over Dopey who lay on the bottom step on Sunday mornings until Mother came down.

'Dad, Margaret's been to the doctor, and she's coming to see Mother any minute. Shall I take your clothes into my

room for you to dress?' I asked, as he looked up, and
groaned.

'I can't get up, I'm too ill, I'm always worse on a Sunday,'
he said pathetically, showing no sign of leaping out of bed.

Mother gave a whimper of pain, and the front door bell
rang. I hurried downstairs, meeting Margaret on the way up.

'Is he out of bed?' she asked, as I paused to let her pass.

'No, he says he's too ill. You'd better have a go,' I replied,
running on down the stairs into the hall, where Jean with all
the strength of a slender fifteen year old was trying to open
the front door, which as usual was stuck.

The doctor on the other side, an impatient woman of fair
proportions, must have decided to give some weighty
assistance. The door flew open, and flung Jean against the
hallstand, knocking off Father's hat, which landed at the
bottom of the stairs, and Dopey leapt into it.

The doctor strode into the hall, not noticing Jean draped
on the hallstand like a boxer on the ropes and, gathering
speed as she approached the stairs, kicked the hat, which let
out a feline shriek, as a furry part of it dashed up the stairs
ahead of her. With remarkable composure she continued,
and must have seen Dopey enter the second door on the left,
which she knew from previous visits was where Mother lay.

The room wih the curtains drawn was in semi-darkness,
and seeing Margaret bending over the bed she must have
thought it was Mother. But Margaret was still trying to
persuade Father to get up and go. Pushing Margaret aside,
she grabbed the patient's wrist and found herself looking into
Dad's unshaven face.

'I've got pains in my legs,' he whimpered, as the doctor
dropped his hand.

'I've come to see Mrs Trigsby,' she said, walking round to
the other side of the bed.

She examined Mother, and decided it was urgent.

'I'll ring the hospital immediately. They'll send an ambulance, and if you come with me, Erine my nurse will tell you
what to get ready,' she said to Margaret, before hurrying
down the stairs, and out the front door faster than she'd
come.

'Mother has to go to hospital. I'm going over with the
doctor to find out from the nurse what Mother will need, and

then I'll go in the ambulance. You carry on with the dinner,' Margaret said, before dashing after the doctor.

Father was so shocked at Mother going to hospital that he had to have his dinner in bed. He never thought anyone else could ever be ill.

This was very useful as it gave Margaret the chance to organise the management of our home without his help. By teatime he recovered sufficiently to arrive on the dot with a good appetite, spending most of the meal, telling us how it was all our fault, for not helping Mother enough, and now we would really have to pull together. He himself of course could do no more than he did before, but he would pray hard for her recovery.

Mother had the operation for peritonitis at eight o'clock in the evening, and it was eleven o'clock before we had the news from the hospital that Mother was as well as could be expected, so it was late before we went to bed.

I agreed to do some shopping before going into work, and Phyllis was to take the day off from college, so the other three would be following their normal routine.

I came downstairs just before eight o'clock which was late for me.

'I'm glad you're all right,' Phyllis said, when I went into the kitchen to collect some breakfast.

'Have the others gone?' I asked, expecting that Father might have had another relapse.

'Dad and Margaret have gone, but I'm worried about Jean. She was terribly ill last night,' she replied, making no attempt to dish out some porridge for me.

'Perhaps she's worried about Mother. She's very emotional, that's why she's always giggling,' I replied, impatient to help myself to porridge. It was past my breakfast time.

'No, it's not that. I think you'd better go and fetch the doctor.'

'Me!'

'Please! I don't want to go, she terrifies me,' she said, pulling a face which would have given Jean the giggles.

'I'll go after breakfast,' I said, picking up a plate to help myself.

'No, go right away, Jean's very ill, and if the doctor starts her rounds, it will be hours before she comes.'

'She can't be that ill!' I said, not wanting to wait that long for breakfast.

'She is. You go and have a look at her,' Phyllis replied, making it clear that I was not getting any breakfast until the doctor came.

I dashed up the stairs. I was hungry, but I was also wary of fetching the doctor unless it was really urgent. I didn't believe we were her favourite patients.

Jean shared a room with Phyllis, and slept nearest to the door. To have a look at her, I crossed the room to pull one of the curtains back. As I did so she groaned.

'What's the matter with you?' I asked, as I stood looking at her flushed face. She was certainly nothing like her usual happy self.

'I was sick most of the night, and my head is throbbing. I've never felt so ill,' she moaned feebly, and I could understand Phyllis worrying about her.

'I'll get the doctor,' I said, going over to close the curtain. The light was obviously painful for her.

* * *

I gave the door bell a long ring, and immediately felt apprehensive. The doctor was not the kind of woman you should meet without having a good breakfast.

The door was opened by Erine her resident Scottish nurse. A friendly woman of some thirty-five years, with a mop of curly red hair, a high shrill voice, and a Scottish accent I could hardly understand.

'It's you Ted. I cannae gie you any news about your mother. You have to ring the hospital. You canna worry the doctor, she's a very busy woman,' she said, surprise, and disapproval filtering through her shrill accent.

'It's Jean. She's ill. We would like the doctor to come and see her,' I replied, as quickly as I could. There was a possibility that she might close the door.

Before Erine could reply, the door of the doctor's surgery, opposite the front door, opened, and she came out at a cracking pace with hat on, and black bag at the ready.

'Where have you been? I wanted you to take my bag to the car,' she said crossly, handing it to Erine, and turning round appearing not to have noticed me.

'Doctor!' Erine called loudly.

The doctor hesitated a moment and then turned back, and

walked slowly and deliberately towards us, looking to Erine
for an explanation, and making me wonder if I were
invisible.

'Ted says Jean is ill, and he would like you to see her before
you go on your rounds,' Erine said, and I was grateful not to
have to make such a bold statement.

'What's wrong with her?' the doctor asked, turning so
abruptly towards me, I moved back a pace, and nearly fell off
the step.

'Jean was very sick last night, and has a terrible headache
this morning,' I said, hoping my medical description was
adequate.

'Has she a temperature?' she asked, looking sternly at me
for more positive evidence.

'I think so, she's very flushed,' I replied, sensing it seemed
a very lame remark, unlikely to meet with her approval.

'Did you take her temperature?'

'No.'

'Hm. Has she been drinking?'

'No, of course not,' I replied, feeling annoyed. None of us
drank. We couldn't afford it, and felt it might be better if our
parents didn't either.

I was annoyed, I had not come prepared to give a detailed
medical report. I turned and left them without saying another
word. I was glad she was not my doctor.

'Well is she coming?' Phyllis asked me, as she handed me a
bowl of porridge.

'I don't know. She annoyed me. She asked if Jean had been
drinking,' I said, laughing. It seemed funny now, but not
when it came from the doctor.

'Oh Ted, you didn't have a row with her. You only had to
ask her to come, you didn't have to start an argument,' Phyllis
replied, reproachfully shaking her head.

Before I could deny it was me, who started it; the front
door bell rang.

'I'll go, it must be the doctor,' Phyllis said, hurrying past
me, before I could warn her to watch for the push.

It didn't matter. Phyllis was no slender seventeen year old,
but in a matter of minutes, I'd only made the tea, and it
wasn't even ready to pour, she was back.

'Who was it?' I asked, believing that the doctor even with

her turn of speed would need longer than that to examine a patient.

'The doctor.'

'It wasn't? Why didn't you stay with her?'

'I did, she's gone, I managed to race her up the stairs, but before I had time to pull the curtains, she was on her way down again. She said there's nothing wrong with Jean, she must have been over eating.'

We'd finished breakfast but were still laughing about the doctor's visit, when the back door opened followed by a loud 'Yoo hoo'. It was Mrs Bush, Mother's perfect charlady.

She was very upset to hear about Mother, and after a few minutes Phyllis told her about Jean.

'You must get the doctor to her, dear,' she said, tying up her apron, and looking very serious.

'We did. She's been,' Phyllis replied, as we both laughed.

'Oh dear, I don't like the sound of it,' Mrs Bush said, standing there with her hands on her hips, and frowning thoughtfully.

'She looks ill to me,' Phyllis admitted, as she carried some plates over to the sink.

'Would you mind if I had a look at her, dear?' she asked, her hands moving to untie her apron.

'Of course not, I'd be glad if you did,' Phyllis replied, leading the way.

Mrs Bush was even quicker than the doctor, I was just about to leave to fetch the shopping, when they were back.

'You'll have to ask the doctor to have another look at Jean,' Phyllis said, shaking with laughter.

'It's your turn,' I replied, and that took the smile off her face.

'Oh no, please Ted, you'll have to tell her Mrs Bush says Jean's got scarlet fever.'

'Are you sure,' I asked, looking at Mrs Bush who nodded her head.

'She's got it all right. There are red blotches behind her ears,' she said, starting to tie her apron again.

'What does that mean? Is it serious?' I asked, wanting to be sure before I crossed the road again.

'Yes. She will have to go to an Isolation hospital for six weeks,' Mrs Bush said, looking very professional, standing there in her apron.

'One of us will have to tell her,' Phyllis said, her smile indicating who the one would be.

'I'll telephone,' I said, inspiration arising from my desire to avoid another face to face meeting.

Erine answered the telephone.

'It's you, Ted.' she informed me in her voice which Phyllis could hear without an earpiece.

'May I speak to the doctor, please,' I replied very formally, wishing Phyllis would stop laughing. She wasn't helping at all.

'I think she's gone. What is it this time?'

'We believe Jean has scarlet fever!'

I heard her put the earpiece down, and I glanced at Phyllis, who was looking questioningly at me, her eyes tearful from laughing. Before I could tell her I thought Erine had fainted, the telephone crackled.

'What makes you think Jean has scarlet fever?' the doctor asked sternly.

'Mrs Bush examined her. She said Jean had blotches behind her ears,' I replied, feeling more at ease speaking on the telephone.

'Who is Mrs Bush, and on whose authority was she examining my patient?'

'I asked her to. She's our charlady.'

The telephone went dead, I replaced the receiver.

'Quick open the front door, clear the way to the stairs,' Phyllis said, excitedly.

'I'll open the front door, it's up to you to chase her up the stairs,' I replied putting the lock on the catch as I eased the front door open, and stood back with the others against the dining room door.

Seconds later, the bell rang; the door opened violently, because the doctor expected it to be stuck. She flew past us, rapidly disappearing round the bend of the stairs, as she took them two at a time. After a few moments of silence, we sensed she was returning.

I moved to open the front door for her, Phyllis rose quickly from the chair into which she had collapsed, and Mrs Bush tactfully withdrew to the dining-room.

The doctor slowly descended the stairs with dignity, and

turned to Phyllis when she reached the hall.

'Jean has scarlet fever. Ring this number, giving my name as your authority. They will give you full instructions, and you must be ready when the ambulance arrives in thirty minutes,' she said, handing Phyllis a piece of paper.

I felt sorry for her as she walked past me looking very tired and smiling wearily as I thanked her for coming.

'I wonder who's next? That's two of you, it always goes in threes you know,' Mrs Bush said, cheerfully.

'Bit difficult if there's only two of you,' Phyllis replied, as she hurried upstairs to prepare Jean for her imminent departure.

8

A week later Mother was sitting up in bed, a feeding tube up her nose, demonstrating her powers of recovery by asking questions to enable her to manage us from her sick-bed.

She was upset to learn Jean was also in hospital, but Jean was good, writing long letters to Mother. Of course they were well-baked to kill the germs, and seasoned with humour, which gave Mother plenty to talk about when we visited her.

The problem came when Mother was well enough to go to the convalescent home in Cray Valley. There were no buses, and taxis were things we couldn't afford. Being the only one with a bicycle, I spent most of that week visiting her. The visit in the dinner hour was easy. I didn't like to take more than an extra half hour, spending half an hour with her from one thirty to two o'clock. It was a long day for Mother, so I went straight from work in the evening. Cycling on a dark night in the black-out was not too bad, if you knew where you were going, but in a strange place it was dangerously exciting.

The first evening, leaving early from work, I arrived at the hospital before it was dark. It was a bright night, and I enjoyed cycling home along the narrow country lanes in the moonlight. Mother told me how the days dragged and how she was longing to be home, so the second evening I stayed with her, again until nearly eight o'clock.

When I came out of the blacked-out hospital, it was a dark rainy night, and it was all I could do to find my bicycle. When I did I soon remembered how useless the shaded bicycle lamp was in these conditions. It barely gave enough light to be seen by someone coming towards you.

Somehow I found my way to the main road up through Cray High Street, and was congratulating myself on knowing where I was, when from the sound of it a pub door opened,

56

and somebody yelled, 'I thought you had hold of him.'

Then I hit him, and went over the handlebars. The howling of the black dog grew fainter as it hurried home to nurse its injuries. I wasn't hurt, only shaken, but lost all sense of direction. I found my bicycle in the gutter. It seemed all right, but the top had come off the lamp, and the battery had gone.

I searched without finding it and, believing it must have gone down the drain, continued the three miles home pushing and riding without any lights at all, the rear light being fed from a lead off the front lamp.

The next day I could only visit Mother in the lunch hour, and had to leave the factory early enough to arrive home before dark.

I was passing the post office only half a mile from home, it wasn't yet dark, when a small soft-roofed sports car pulled from behind a bus, and came straight at me. All I could do when it hit me was leap off the bicycle, and sail over the roof. I cleared the car, and landed on all fours, shaken, and slightly bruised.

After dusting myself down, and rubbing my knee, I went round to the front of the car to see how my bicycle had fared.

'There's a young fellow under the car,' said the middle-aged gentleman, whom I took to be the driver, pulling clear my bicycle with a buckled front wheel.

'Is there?' I asked, being still a little dazed, as we both got down on our hands and knees and peered underneath.

'Where the Hell did he go?' the gentleman asked as we both stood up.

'Are you sure he went underneath?' I asked, the penny beginning to drop.

'There must have been somebody riding the bicycle,' he replied, looking at me as if I were simple.

'It was me, I was riding it. That's my bicycle,' I replied, pointing at the badly buckled front wheel.

'But I thought you went under the car.' he said, looking at me as if he was sure I was a lunatic.

'No I didn't. I went over the top. I landed on all fours, that's why I was rubbing my knee,' I replied, giving it another rub to prove it.

'Anybody hurt?'

We both turned round to see a special wartime constable,

with notebook in his hand standing behind us. There was something familiar about him, but I couldn't place him.

'No I'm not hurt, apart from the odd bruise,' I replied, watching him examining my bicycle.

'You must have been very lucky. I thought when I saw the bike lying there, that you must have gone underneath,' he said, looking at me with his pencil poised as if he was about to write an obituary.

He took all the particulars, and the gentleman in the car ran me home with the bike in the back, promising to call in the next morning to take it to be repaired.

About ten minutes after he'd gone there was a knock at the door. I opened it, and recognised the policeman standing there with his hat in his hand.

'It's you, Tom.' I said as I ushered him in before we broke the black−out. I recognised him now without his hat. He was a member of our tennis club.

I thought I'd better call in, Ted. I forgot to ask if you had a lamp on the bicycle.'

'Yes, of course,' I replied, without thinking.

'Was it switched on?' he asked, laughing.

'Yes it was,' I replied, truthfully enough if one didn't go into details about it containing a battery.

'That's all,' he said, closing his note book.

It was Friday, and I had no bicycle to go and see Mother. I hoped I might get it repaired by the afternoon, but it was unlikely, and I needed it to cycle around looking for a battery.

I came home Friday evening, worried at the thought of Mother waiting in vain for a visit to break up the monotony. The house seemed strangely quiet as I came through the kitchen, and found nobody in the dining-room, where the girls preferred to sit by the fire.

I was about to go upstairs to my room, when I changed my mind, and turned and opened the lounge door. They were all there, including Mother in her armchair, looking frail but cheerful.

'Mother, I was pitying you all alone waiting for a visitor,' I said, as I went over to give her a kiss.

'The doctor told me this afternoon I could come home tomorrow. I told her the place was too far away in the wilds for any of you to visit me, and you had nearly been killed by running over a dog in the black-out.'

'Mother! I wasn't nearly killed.'

'It doesn't matter, it did the trick. She said, 'Be dressed in half an hour, and I'll run you home in the car,' and here I am,' she said, sitting there looking contented with Dopey purring away on her lap.

'Now your mother's home, you've got to help her and see she doesn't do too much,' Father said, blowing clouds of smoke from that evil pipe into the air.

'They always help me, and I have Mrs Bush in the day. The only time I may need some help is if they're all out at supper,' Mother replied, as she sat back in her chair gently stroking Dopey.

'I can get the supper, that's nothing to worry about,' Father replied.

That evening Father went to get the supper at quarter to nine. He came in five minutes later, with two plates in one hand, and two saucers in the other. He put them down on the table, and removed a cup from each of his jacket pockets. After tapping the bits of tobacco out of them he put them on the saucers.

He then returned to the kitchen, to come back with six dry biscuits in one hand, a pat of wrapped butter on a plate with some cheese in the other, and after sinking down exhausted, he pulled two knives out of his top pocket.

'I think that's everything,' he said as he dropped two biscuits on to Mother's plate, opened the butter and, after taking some, pushed it across the little table to her.

'That's fine, I won't be a minute,' Mother said, and when she came back ten minutes later with the tea, he was sitting there waiting.

'I thought there was something I'd forgotten,' he said, taking a sip of the tea Mother had poured out for him.

That was the first and last time he ever got the supper.

9

Christmas, 1939 had come and gone, and the War wasn't over. It hadn't even begun. Alan and I felt frustrated, and insecure. We had nothing to do that could remotely contribute to the prosperity of the company or winning the War. We didn't waste any time, and we weren't bored. We were sticking to our study plans at work, and at home in the evenings, taking correspondence courses to sit the external London Matriculation in July, 1940.

Mr Anthony Eden announced on the fourteenth of May the need for a Local Volunteer Defence Force (LDV), armed with American rifles, and five rounds of ammunition, when it arrived, to make up for the dubious victory at Dunkirk.

Several weeks after his announcement we had another air raid practice in the factory, and this time we were to go to the air raid shelters, to which we had been assigned. We'd had many practices and the utter confusion, and the lack of understanding of the urgency, some believed could have been disastrous if the enemy had not allowed us all this time to practice. But of course, with one real air raid, we got the hang of it.

Like many others, despite the urgent pleas of the head air raid warden over the tannoy, Alan and I strolled nonchalantly down the corridor. We came to a small table outside the store cupboard which was to be used as an armoury for the factory, when the promised weapons arrived, and on the table were some LDV arm bands. We had discovered at school the power of a prefects' badge, even if you weren't a prefect, and we both instantly saw the possibilities of these as we helped ourselves to one each.

By the time we arrived at the front door, we had the power

60

of authority upside down half way up our arms.

Mr Thompson and several of the senior staff were standing around chatting in the warm sunshine.

'Come on, we know the drill. Move the little one's first, and the big 'uns will follow,' Alan reminded me, and we went a few yards down the path to the shelter, and began to hurry them along.

In less than five minutes we were in control, and as we moved in to direct Mr Thompson, he asked us where shelter number five was.

When they were all shepherded in, way ahead of many of the others, we saw coming towards us Mr McCloud the corporal whom we had heard was to be promoted to sergeant as soon as the unit was officially established.

'All present and correct, Sergeant,' Alan announced, bringing his two left feet to attention.

Sergeant McCloud could not conceal a smile of amusement, mixed with a puzzled expression, having no idea who we were or what we were doing, and he was the one in charge.

'You on the front door are you?' he asked, having arrived at the only possible conclusion, but of course unable to remember appointing us to this prime position of authority.

'Yes, Sir.' Alan said, as I moved forward to direct a straggler.

'Try and get here sooner next time. It might be the real thing,' he said, and from then on we were members of the factory LDV. We hadn't a lot of confidence in our comrades as a fighting unit, but we thought that going down a shelter would be less fun.

The realities of war began to come to us. We had several real alarms, and one of these occurred at eleven o'clock, a few days after the arrival of our rifles and clips of five rounds of ammunition.

I was hurrying past the armoury wearing my armband, to meet Alan at our chosen spot guarding the front entrance, when Sergeant McCloud stopped me.

'Go to the canteen with Mr Payne, and remain on guard, until the all-clear,' he barked, handing me a rifle and a clip of five rounds.

I recognised Mr Payne. He was the rather cocky young lad

I knew as Humphrey, waiting there holding a rifle awkwardly with one hand and five rounds gingerly in the other.

I wasn't pleased. These raids could last an hour, and I didn't think I could stand Humphrey for that long, but in war, orders is orders, and I hurried off with him to the canteen, which was deserted, with all the chairs stacked on the tables.

'You'd better load,' Humphrey said, in a manner that seemed to imply that he was in charge.

'Why?' I asked, purely to show that I was not recognising his authority to give me orders.

'We're guarding the factory from sabotage by enemy parachutists. That's why,' he said, giving me a disdainful look, for being ignorant after Mr Eden's proclamation explaining why we were needed.

'There aren't any enemy parachutists, so we don't need to load,' I replied. I had a good reason for not loading. I didn't know how to.

'They are not going to send us a postcard. We have to be ready for them at any time. You load and I'll guard the door until you're ready,' he replied moving towards the door.

'Wait a minute. Do you know how to load?' I asked him, wondering if he might be as ignorant as myself.

'Of course. Do you?'

'Yes,' I replied. I wasn't going to admit it to him. He was probably bluffing anyway.

Two years ago, I had been released from the school OTC by mutual consent after only a few weeks as a member. It was obvious that I would destroy any chance of the house winning the platoon cup. The only thing I remembered of the loading drill was: first release safety catch; I did this discreetly, so that Humphrey couldn't see, and managed to pull the bolt back. I was pleased with my progress as I paused, wondering what came next, and watching him trying to pull the bolt back without releasing the safety catch.

'I can't get the bolt back,' he said, looking embarrassed.

'Release the safety catch,' I replied, feeling that I had established my superiority.

He fiddled around and eventually managed to release the catch, and withdrew the bolt. We both struggled for some minutes to cram the five rounds into the magazine, and finished up by nervously pushing home the bolt.

Each pulling a chair off a table, we sat down sweating from fear, and nervous exhaustion. To Hell with parachutists. They would have to come to us. We weren't even going to the door to look for them.

Of course we'd hardly sat down when the all—clear sounded. Humphrey looked at me and I guessed what was coming.

'How do you unload?' he asked me, his pale face showing the strain, with no pretence of any knowledge.

'I have no idea. That's why I didn't want to load in the first place,' I replied, adding to his misery.

'I thought you knew,' he said, putting the blame on me.

'I did once, but only in theory. At school they wouldn't even let me try with dummies in case I ruined the platoon rifle,' I replied, revelling in my ignorance.

'You must have some idea. This is the first time I've ever held a rifle,' he said, excusing himself pathetically.

I understood his feelings. It would be a bit of a let down if McCloud told us we shouldn't have loaded anyway.

I sat there fiddling with the bolt and thinking hard. I knew I must not let my finger go anywhere near the trigger.

After a few minutes, I discovered that pulling the bolt back brought the round with it, but of course I couldn't release it. Impatiently I jerked the bolt back, and the round flew out across the floor. We were both so pleased we repeated the performance until all the rounds were scattered under the tables on the canteen floor.

After laying the rifles on a table, we crawled about the floor collecting them.

I carefully slid my five into the clip, and was ready to go.

'Have you got a spare one?' Humphrey asked, looking at me with pleading brown eyes.

'No, I only picked up five. I expect it's somewhere on the floor,' I replied, as the dirtiest white coat in the factory came through the inner door.

'What are you boys doing in my canteen?' the manager asked, not seeming to appreciate the importance of guarding his canteen against hungry parachutists during an air raid.

'We were on guard,' Humphrey replied, sounding embarrassed.

'Christ! I hope you boys know how to handle those guns. They look a bit big for you,' he said, hooting with laughter as he went to the kitchen.

'Don't go crawling under the tables until he's gone,' I whispered to Humphrey, who was already on his hands and knees.

Five minutes passed. We still hadn't found it, and the canteen manager was opening the shutters on the counter.

'You still here! The all-clear went half an hour ago,' he called out to us.

'We'll have to go,' I whispered to Humphrey, ignoring the manager. We didn't want to be there when the workers rushed in throwing chairs off the tables.

'I can't go back, one short,' Humphrey said, so pitifully, I felt sorry for him.

'Yes, you can. McCloud won't notice. Sergeants can't count up to five. That's why the army only forms fours,' I replied, feeling happy I'd got my five.

Then I had an idea.

'Pull your bolt back,' I said, having seen the manager disappear to the back of the kitchen.

'I tried that. It's empty.'

'Pull it back. Let me have a look,' I said, sure the silly twit had left one up the spout.

He was right. The magazine and the spout were empty.

'You might as well uncock it,' I said, as he returned the bolt.

'How do I do that?' he asked, pleased to learn from me.

'Press the trigger.'

He did that, and I told him to put the safety catch on.

'You're still cocked,' he said, pointing to my rifle.

I had my finger on the trigger, when he shouted at me.

'Wait a minute!'

I hated pulling triggers. I was always frightened of a bang, so I waited.

'What's the matter?' I asked. Something in his manner annoyed me again.

'Have a look and see it's clear first,' he said. He was beginning to assume command now I'd taught him all I knew.

'I've looked, it's clear,' I replied, feeling annoyed at the suggestion that I should have one up the spout.

'It's best to check first,' he replied, nodding his head as if he knew it all.

I jerked the bolt back, and a round flew out across the canteen.

Humphrey dived after it, and came up smiling with it held firmly in his hand. He was pretty decent. He didn't say a word as we hurried off to the armoury.

'Where the bloody Hell have you two been?' Sergeant McCloud bellowed at us.

'We didn't hear the all-clear,' I replied knowing he'd love that.

'Christ! You must be stone deaf. The siren's only a few yards up the road,' he shouted, snatching the rifles and the clips from us, in too much of a hurry to count anything, or check if the rifles were cocked, much less question us any further. He'd lost nearly five minutes of his lunch hour.

I was having a cup of tea with Alan in the afternoon. I thought I wouldn't tell him about my first guard duty without him.

'Did you get a rifle this morning?' I asked him, knowing there had been a limited number, and it was first come first served.

'Yes, I had a clip of five rounds as well,' he replied, proudly.

'Did you load?' I asked, thinking that he would know if anybody did.

'Christ no. I've no idea how, and if I did, I wouldn't be able to unload.'

10

It was some weeks after we'd become members of the LDV that John Picard returned from one of his regular meetings with Uncle, and told us that Mr Hansdelle would like to see both of us in his office, immediately.

We had been behaving well recently, and neither of us could think of any reason why we were apprehensive when we stood on the carpet in front of his desk.

'I am pleased you have both joined my unit,' he said, his lips parting to give the impression of a smile.

Neither of us made a clear response, and I had no idea what he was talking about.

'The situation is very serious, and we must be prepared for the worst,' he continued, looking as if it had already happened.

'I'm sorry, I don't understand,' I said, feeling irritated. His manner seemed to confuse me. If life were as serious as he made it appear, I would have given up long ago.

'I'm welcoming you to my unit,' he said sternly, annoyed that I was so slow in the uptake.

'LDV,' Alan whispered to me and even as he spoke the awful truth struck me: he was telling us that he was our commanding officer.

'I have a plan for running lines of communication, which are very important for the defence of the factory. This is what I want you to do,' he said, passing a scruffy sheet of paper across the desk.

Alan picked it up, and studied it, and then passed it to me. I couldn't make anything of it at all.

'I'm sorry I don't understand this,' I said. I should not have been surprised. I never could understand his sketches, I always had to ask John Picard to translate for me.

'You are not very bright, Trigsby. It is very simple. The 'T' is for tower and the 'S' is for shelter,' he replied, underlining the 'T' which looked liked a Greek lambda, and the 'S's' which looked like pushed−over eights, and made the whole thing still a mystery to me.

'When would you like us to start?' Alan asked, looking at the sketch, as if he wasn't sure he was holding it the right way up.

'Right away. It is urgent, we could be invaded any time. But don't let it interfere with your work,' he replied, standing up with his hands on his hips, and turning round and looking out of the window. We left the office, John having warned us that this was the way Uncle terminated an interview.

'You didn't have to tell him you couldn't understand it,' Alan said when we were back in the office.

'How could we do it for him if we didn't know what he wanted?' I asked. I knew Alan was right, but Uncle brought the worst out in me. I think he reminded me of Father.

'We still don't know what he wants. This is the big job we've been waiting for. He obviously doesn't realise we've nothing to do, and this will keep us going for weeks,' Alan said, laughing and sketching enthusiastically on a clean sheet of foolscap.

'I don't know how I shall survive with him as my commanding officer,' I said. It didn't seem to worry Alan, but it certainly worried me.

'Forget about it, come and help me with Uncle's mark-one communication network,' Alan replied, moving over, and putting a clean sheet of foolscap in front of me.

After three days of filling up sheets of paper we had a good plan of what we were going to do, and several sheets of the items we would need, some of which, like insulators, hooks, and terminals, we could get from stores, the others, like poles, sand, cement, shovels, and pickaxes, we had no idea yet how we would come by, but Alan had no doubt that the problems would all be solved.

The wires would be carried on nine poles about ten feet high. They would have to be cemented into the ground, and would connect the tower to the two outside shelters and the middle one.

Friday morning we were full of enthusiasm, discussing the

things we had managed to get, and ideas for the impossibles, among them four hundred yards of waterproof twin wire, when Mr Thompson banged on the window for us.

'We could do with some help. It will seriously reduce our study time,' Alan said, as we broke off to see what he wanted.

'You've been here six months, and the work we took you on for has not arrived, but it will come. Your approach to solving your main problem of having no work, has at times caused concern with the senior management but nothing serious, and you have taken every opportunity to keep yourselves usefully occupied, including your studying.' he said, smiling as he paused, leaving us wondering where it was leading. It didn't sound as if we were going to be sacked.

'We're not complaining,' Alan said with a grin in my direction. It seemed that Mr Thompson might not know of our latest project.

'No, you haven't complained, but you know each other well. How do you think it would be if there were four of you?' he asked, leaning back on his chair to view the better our reactions.

'Four!' Alan asked, as if it was an impossible thought to conjure up.

'There are two more of about the same age as yourselves starting Monday. I'm sure the first few days will be all right, but if they behave as you two did when you first arrived, Murphy will do his nut,' he said laughing, almost as if he was looking forward to it.

'With nothing for us to do, why do you want two more?' I asked. It had been getting more difficult. We needed something other than studying, and if this present job from Uncle hadn't arrived our morale would have been at rock-bottom.

'When the development contracts are placed we will need all the lab staff we can get, and that won't be the time to recruit them,' he said, picking up a slide—rule to indicate that he had no more time to spare to enlighten us further.

I felt unhappy about this turn of events, realising that we had trained ourselves with little help from anybody else. The invaluable assistance I had received had all come from Alan.

We had learnt by going into offices, and workshops, and asking the most senior-looking man what his people did. This was resented by some, who made it clear that they viewed us as privileged layabouts, others were more helpful.

Some had good reason to resent telling us how the system worked. Learning about stock control, enabled us to find out what was in stores, and then use our ingenuity to have it released to us.

This ranged from chatting up the stock control clerk, or the store's clerk, or accidentally initialling the requisition in the right place. We were, of course, only overcoming obstacles to getting the job done, and in the case of our latest project we saw it as a matter of survival for King and Country.

Monday morning Tony Rae introduced us to Harry Williams and Jimmy Potts. They seemed to us every bit as sensible as we were. Harry was of average height, slim build, and if I'd known about these things, I would have guessed him to be a ladies' man.

Jimmy Potts was a thick−set young fellow, who didn't seem to be all that bright at first, and on occasions no match for Alan or even myself. But we soon found that he was a steady worker, and could be relied on to keep out of trouble. By the end of the first day they had heard about our project and Jimmy was enthusiastic to help. Harry, dressed in a new blue suit, stopped short at anything which might dirty his hands or clothes.

'Our first problem is to obtain the poles to carry the wire,' Alan announced on Tuesday morning.

'I saw them delivering scaffolding, sand, cement − the lot, for building the depot storehouse near the station when I cycled past this morning,' Jimmy Potts said, laughing at the possibilities.

'That sounds hopeful. Do you think they'd miss a few?' Alan asked, eagerly.

'No. They delivered hundreds of them,' Jimmy said, rubbing his hands as if he couldn't wait to get started.

'That's what we want, but it's a bit far away,' Alan muttered, looking thoughtful.

'We've got bikes, we could go and reccy the place,' I suggested, not feeling too keen on a firm decision to hump scaffolding poles a mile and a half, even if it was downhill.

'We might be able to get them to deliver a few. It's for the LDV to defend our factory, against the parachutists,' Jimmy said, pulling out his cycle clips.

The three of us decided we would sneak out after tea, leaving Harry to look after the lab. He didn't have a bicycle. He came in on the bus.

'I don't like it. I can't give you permission, and for God's sake don't get arrested,' John Picard, said when we told him where we were going.

It was about a mile from the factory, mostly up hill, which was good for transporting heavy loads in the other direction. When we arrived, like most stations through the day, the place was deserted.

The poles had been dumped just off the road. They were about twenty feet long, and so heavy that the three of us were needed to lift one of them.

'There's nobody to ask. Let's see if we can move one,' Alan suggested, motioning me to bring my bike over.

I held my bike steady, and the two of them lifted the end on to the handlebars, then Jimmy moved his bike behind mine, and we slid his along, as we raised the pole. After a few yards my bike fell over and the pole crashed to the ground, fortunately doing no damage to us or the bicycles.

'That was daft. We will use only two bicycles, but put the pole on about six feet from each end, and the third man can steady the pole in the middle as we go along,' Alan said, as we anxiously examined our bicycles for damage from the previous try.

This time it worked; Alan put his bicycle inside the station entrance for safety in case there were any thieves about, and then we set off down the road. It was not too difficult, but we certainly needed Alan's strength in the middle when we went round corners. The worst was yet to come, being the 'T' junction onto the main road, about a thousand yards from the right turn into the factory.

Alan went on ahead to the main road, to ensure that we could negotiate the turn without knocking over the traffic lights.

'I think we may have a problem,' he said when he returned.

'We can do it, if you bend it in the middle,' Jimmy said laughing, and making me think he was likely to be the kind of asset Mr Thompson had been afraid of.

'There's a policeman on a bicycle coming up the road,' Alan replied, looking more amused than worried.

'We must get him to help us round the corner,' Jimmy said, laughing as he rested on the pole.

We waited, and after a few minutes, the policeman came to the traffic lights which obliging went to red. As he waited there, Alan waved him over.

'I had to leave my bicycle at the station, could you help these two chaps as far as the electronics factory?' Alan asked him.

'I wondered where you were taking it to,' he said, as he straightened up after resting his bicycle against the lights, and removing his cycle clips.

'It just needs steadying in the middle, I'll help you round the corner,' Alan said as the lights changed, and we began to move slowly forward.

How like Alan I thought, as he thanked the policeman, and hurried away up the hill to the station. In a few minutes we were at the entrance to the factory and Harry, who had been watching for us, came running out to help.

We thanked the policeman, and after watching us, being watched by nearly everybody on the second floor, he turned and strode at the steady pace of the law to collect his bicycle, and proceed to the police station round the corner.

'It's going to take a long time to collect a dozen, you've been nearly two hours already. Another five minutes, and you'd have been knocked over by the workers rushing out for dinner,' Harry said, as we stopped on the waste ground between the tower and the shelters.

'It will take about a week, but we could get away with only six if we cut them in half,' I replied. I didn't fancy another eight journeys. It was very slow, and quite dangerous coming down the hill.

'Where's Alan?' Harry asked.

'He went back for his bike. That's why we had the policeman to help. I expect he's gone off home to lunch now.' I replied, getting ready to do the same.

11

'Here comes Alan,' Harry said, as a cyclist swept across the road, and round the back of the building.

'I don't think we should go back for another pole this afternoon. That copper is bound to get suspicious if he sees us again,' Jimmy said, yawning, and looking not so much worried as not built for working in the afternoon.

'Of course we can. Having done it once, the copper will accept that we normally wheel poles around the countryside,' I replied, as Alan came in, grabbed a stool, and joined us at the bench looking out of the window.

'We can't get any more poles from the station. We were lucky to get that one,' he said, still panting from the eight mile cycle ride, he did every lunch time.

'I hope they don't want it back,' I replied, fearing the worst.

'If they do they'll have to fetch it. We'll never get it up the hill.' Jimmy said, looking as if he wasn't going to try anyway.

'They would if they knew we'd got it. There were eight of them. It seems they went into that little hut for tea, just as we arrived. I told them we were working on local defence, and needed some poles, and something to stick them in the ground, and they said that if I didn't buzz off they'd show me where I could stick em,' Alan said, smiling, as we all laughed.

'Unpatriotic bastards. We ought to shoot them,' Jimmy said, pointing an imaginary rifle at the gasworks opposite.

'I think we might get a barrow load of aggregate. They had masses of that, and the cement is stored just inside that little hut,' Alan said thoughtfully.

'We don't need aggregate. There's plenty on that waste ground, left over from building the shelters,' I replied. I didn't fancy wheeling a barrow load of aggregate, even if it was downhill.

'I went to see Uncle when you were taking that pole for a bicycle ride,' Harry said, laughing as he leaned back balancing on the stool.

'You went to see Uncle?' Alan asked him looking as surprised as I was. We were here over a month before we went into his office, and it wasn't a friendly visit.

'He sent for me,' Harry said, looking very superior.

'Sent for you! Did he want another jam bun?' I asked. I'd thought he was the smooth well—dressed type who would impress Uncle.

'That's what comes of wearing a smart blue suit,' Jimmy said, pointing his imaginary rifle at Harry.

'He told me that he was so exhausted trying to explain his simple diagram to you, he forgot to tell you, there were plenty of poles for carrying the wire, behind shelter number five,' Harry said, grinning and getting ready to duck.

'You liar. Why didn't you tell us before?' Alan said, laughing with the rest of us.

'I'm not. I didn't tell you before because I didn't want to spoil your fun. I thought you enjoyed wheeling poles on bicycles,' Harry replied, laughing, as Jimmy scowled at him.

Alan leapt to his feet, 'Come on, we'd better go and have a look, and see what's there.'

'If there's nothing there, we'll use him as a pole. We'll fix his feet in the ground without any cement,' Jimmy said as the three of us raced to see who could get through the door first. Of course we stuck, and while we were making a little noise, Mr Thompson came walking up the corridor.

'Please try to remember that Mr Murphy has big ears, not that he needs them to hear you. Mr Leare and Mr Trigsby, you at least should know better,' he said, leaving us feeling like naughty school boys.

There were at least a dozen scaffolding poles stacked behind the shelter, left over from building the office block. We had wasted a lot of war effort, but it had been an interesting exercise.

We found some spades, and Jimmy brought in a pickaxe, which we needed despite our careful selection of soft spots to dig, and we spent the whole of Wednesday marking out and digging the holes.

We had plenty of sand and aggregate, but no cement.

'I vote we send Harry to ask Uncle for the money for a bag of cement,' Jimmy said, when we'd discussed the problem for the third time that day without finding a solution.

'I can't see Uncle doing that, he expects us to use our initiative, and get everything for nothing,' Alan said, doodling with his pencil on a piece of paper.

'We've got to do something. We won't win the war sitting here all day in our best suits like Harry,' Jimmy said, looking desperate.

'I've only got one suit, and I'm not mucking it up working as a navvy. It's all right for you three, you're dressed for the part,' Harry replied, sitting back, looking a picture of complacency.

'Ted's suit is nearly new,' Alan said, giving me a nudge.

'Is it? Well that goes to show why navvies don't wear suits,' Harry replied, and whatever he meant the others thought it was funny.

'When we've had tea, Ted and I will go back to the station, and see if we can cadge something off the foreman. I think it will be better with two of us,' Alan said, and Jimmy readily agreed that we should have a try without him, with all his enthusiasm he didn't like cycling up the hill.

We arrived at the station at about half past three, and the men on the building site were starting to pack up for the night.

'He looks kind and helpful,' Alan whispered, as we approached one of the men standing apart from the others.

'This morning somebody offered us a little aggregate, to help with an LDV job we have to do,' Alan said, smiling in that friendly manner of his that fooled most people, including me.

'It wasn't me, mate. It must have been the gaffer over there with the hat. He might give you a bit of aggregate, there's plenty about, but you won't get much out of him I can tell you,' he replied, pointing to a big fellow cleaning a cement mixer by bashing the side with a pick-axe handle.

'Should we wait until he's finished beating hell out of the mixer?' I suggested as we walked towards the foreman.

'We're doing a job for the LDV. Have you a little aggregate we could have?' Alan asked him as he paused for a rest.

'I can't give you anything. If you like to take a little when I'm not looking, there's a barrow over there. But mind you bring the barrow back,' he said, resting on the pickaxe handle.

'Thanks, we'll bring the barrow straight back. We have to come back for our bikes anyway,' Alan replied, turning to walk towards it.

'Hold on. You can't take it now. There's a shovel over there, load up the barrow and push it round the side of the hut. Come back in half an hour, and we'll all be gone. Put the barrow back where it is now,' he said, turning, and thumping with increased vigour at the barrel of the mixer.

We went over to the heavy steel barrow leaning up against the side of the shed. The door was open and stacked up just inside were sacks of cement.

'Look round, and see if anyone's watching us,' Alan said urgently.

'Can't see anyone'

Alan shot into the hut, lifted down a bag of cement, and dropped it quickly into the barrow, where it couldn't be seen. Almost before it disappeared I was pushing it over to the aggregate, which we shovelled on top until the bag was hidden. We didn't want too much. The barrow was heavy enough for me with only the cement in it. After leaving it round the side, we rode off down the hill to the factory.

'That's the easy part,' Alan said as we put our bicycles back in the rack.

An hour later, Alan and I arrived back for the barrow, and the foreman was still there.

We told him what we were doing, and he was very relaxed and friendly now that the men had gone.

'Don't you want a bag of cement as well?' he asked, moving towards the hut where it was stored.

'No thank you. We managed to get one,' Alan replied, starting to push the barrow down the hill.

12

Uncle was pleased with the communication system we produced from his sketch, and though Alan got the credit that he deserved, Uncle thought we must have all worked well together on it.

Mr Thompson thought his fears might have been unnecessary, but I could see the mix of personalities was likely to prove him right first time, and would yet produce situations to meet with his and Uncle's disapproval.

Jimmy was keen to join anything to have a gun in his hand should we be invaded, and having been a member of his school OTC was able to show Alan and me how to load and unload, a simple enough task when you know, but as I had found, not that simple when you didn't. Harry was never interested in being anywhere near either end of a gun, and all he ever did was resign from the LDV he never joined.

As 1940 wore on, and air raids increased after Dunkirk, we became more worried about the invasion, believing we needed not only a rifle and ammunition, but to be in a unit that would be competently led, and a force to be reckoned with.

Jimmy and I joined our local unit, and received a rifle and five rounds of ammunition to take home. Alan did the same in his area. We didn't tell Uncle because we still believed that it might be useful to have access to a rifle and ammunition at work.

Unfortunately our relations with Sergeant McCloud were not good, we being in his eyes, not ours, junior to him. We were the only ones to whom he could issue orders like, 'Clean the rifles' and 'Tidy up', and of course when we wore denims, we were the ones he could tell to smarten up, this being impossible as the fitting made it difficult to tell if you were standing at ease or attention.

After the rifles and ammunition had been distributed, it was discovered that the minority had not fired a rifle for over twenty years, the majority had never handled a gun at all, and didn't even know how to load. Those who had any experience were convinced that five rounds was useless, it would take at least twenty rounds to hit a double—decker bus. To remedy this, despite the shortage of ammunition, LDV units were sent off each weekend to firing ranges, of which there were a few, to allow each individual to fire five rounds. Factory units like ours were included.

When Uncle received the call most of the workers were on overtime, and would not allow themselves to be spared. They needed the money. Uncle had to scrape the barrel to find five. He could never raise ten men.

Mr Thompson was working at the main factory at weekends. Alan claimed that he was too busy looking after his widowed mother, and it finally boiled down to Uncle, Sergeant McCloud, Jimmy Potts, myself, and Wendy.

With such quality five would obviously suffice. If Wendy hadn't been going we couldn't have gone. There was no transport here. It was still at Dunkirk. In such an emergency we were expected to provide our own.

Uncle was taking his sergeant, and wasn't going to ruin the upholstery in the back of his car with our hobnailed army boots, war or no war. But Wendy had a Ruby saloon, one of the small eight horsepower cars produced before the War, and for many of us the only car we could ever imagine owning, a good chariot in which to go to war.

Wendene was called Wendy because of his name, and because he was a little elf-like man in his late thirties who looked like Peter Pan. He certainly wasn't five feet tall, was an Oxford BA, which meant nothing to us, but we knew that he was a genius. We had taken part in some of his demonstrations of memory, when he had beaten three of us at chess without once looking at the boards, and at the same time playing solo with three others.

I was six inches taller than him, and had been issued with small denim overalls: so big, they never touched me anywhere, and even Mother, who had proved herself able to work miracles with a needle, claimed that nothing could be done about it, but they fitted me a lot better than Wendy's did.

We met at the factory at seven o'clock Sunday morning in denim overalls, the only uniform we had, carrying as much food and drink as we were able to find for a long day, with no idea when we would be returning, or if we would ever get there.

There was no air raid warning when we left St Mary Cray heading for Croydon, on a typical warm July day with plenty of breaks in the cloud, hoping to make Bisley in Surrey in about four hours.

Jimmy and I had no idea where Bisley was, but we were confident that Wendy would remember the way, until we discovered that he'd never been there.

'I found an old ordnance map, could you look out a route?' he asked, handing me a large bundle of folded squares of paper which it would be impossible to open in the front of the Ruby without obscuring his view.

'I can't read a map in a car. I'll be sick,' I protested, passing it over the back to Jimmy, who was comfortably filling all of the back seat.

'Can you give me some idea where to look?' Jimmy asked, as he unfolded the tatty sheets.

'It's near Woking, or Guildford. I'll start by heading for Croydon,' Wendy replied, giving us the impression that he knew where he was going.

It was comfortable in the little car. We hardly knew we were moving. At no time did Wendy exceed twenty-five miles an hour. He could never be accused of taking corners on two wheels, he reduced the speed by half at every sign of a bend. After ten miles, Jimmy and I were in new territory; one didn't know places more than that radius with only a bicycle for transport.

'We could do with some signposts,' Jimmy announced, struggling to find our position on the map.

'That's why I bought the map. I wouldn't have needed it if there were signposts,' Wendy replied, which surprised me; I thought both were necessary.

'Do you know where we are now?' Jimmy asked, giving me a wink as I looked back at him.

'Yes, I'm all right as far as Leatherhead.'

'I'm glad about that because I'm lost,' Jimmy replied, and then whispered to me, 'I didn't know we went to Leatherhead.'

'Let me have the map,' Wendy said, holding up his left hand to receive it.

'You can't drive and look at the map, even at this speed,' Jimmy gasped, looking at me with his mouth open in horror.

We pulled into the side, a fire engine raced past, and a little Air Raid Warden sheltering under the usual large white helmet crossed the road, and knocked on Wendy's window.

'You know there's an air raid on?' he asked officiously, in a loud voice shrill with the tension of the moment.

'No, you can't hear anything in a car,' Wendy replied, holding in his left hand the fistful of map that Jimmy had passed to him.

'What are you doing with that map in an air raid?' the Warden asked suspiciously.

'Tell him we're looking for somewhere to land,' Jimmy whispered.

'We're lost without the signposts. Is this the main road for Leatherhead?' Wendy asked, grinning at Jimmy's remark.

'It might be.'

'What do you mean it might be?' Wendy asked, with his best Peter Pan smile.

'I mean that we don't tell strangers the way round these parts. That's careless talk, especially when we've just had a stick across the main road. Where are you going?' he asked, looking very formidable under that big helmet.

'Bisley.'

'Bisley! What you going there for?'

'Rifle practice.'

'Don't you start being funny with me, mate.'

This was too much for Jimmy, and me. We both laughed, and poor Wendy smiled, despite all his efforts to look serious. We had thought it funny to be going forty miles to fire five rounds, but this character made it seem hilarious.

'Here comes the law,' Jimmy said, as a large policeman crossed the road to see what was going on.

'Are you having trouble, Charlie?' he asked the Warden, smiling at us as he spoke.

'They say they're going to Bisley for rifle practice,' he

replied, as if it sounded highly suspicious to him.

'May I see your identity cards, please gentlemen?' the policeman requested politely, knowing of course that no spy would have such a document.

We handed ours to Wendy who passed them on with his. The policeman glanced at them and handed them back.

'Where are you from?' he asked sternly, looking at each of us in turn.

'St. Mary Cray,' Wendy replied,

'Is that near Brighton?' the policeman asked, looking intently at Wendy.

'No. It's near Orpington,' Wendy replied, and we all laughed, knowing that it was the trick question for spies.

'What time were you hoping to get to Bisley?' the policeman asked, smiling now that we had passed the tests, and elbowing the warden to one side as he spoke.

'About twelve o'clock. If somebody will tell us which way to go,' Wendy replied, hopefully smiling at the policeman.

'You might do it, that's the all-clear going now. Take the first on the right and then turn left, go as far as you can, and then turn left again, that should take you clear of that last stick. Good luck,' the policeman said, making us jump with fright, as he finished his farewell with a thump on the flimsy roof with his fist.

We were grateful to the British constable for directing us. Without him we would never have learned how to fire a gun.

Stopping many times to find the way from Wendy's tatty map, by diversions caused by bombs falling on our route, and avoiding asking the way from the numerous wardens looking suspiciously at us every time we studied the map. We eventually arrived at one o'clock, having had half an hour to eat some of our food, in case those in command had not allowed for it in their itinerary.

We hardly recognised Uncle. It was the first time any of us had worn our uniforms. We thought it amusing, but his face fell when he recognised us.

'What happened to you, Peter? I've been here over an hour. We've had to go down the list. We won't be firing until three o'clock,' Uncle said, trying to avoid looking at us.

'We had a job finding our way, and several times we were delayed by enemy action,' Wendy replied smiling, obviously amused at the sight of Uncle balancing his little titfer on his large round hairless head.

'There're three of you to navigate, you've no excuse for losing your way,' Uncle said angrily, not realising how lucky we were to have arrived at all.

'It's not easy to read a map without any signposts, when you're making deviations to avoid bomb holes,' Wendy replied, quite impervious to Uncle's criticism.

'I had the same problems. I was here at eleven o'clock. You must expect delays from enemy action,' Uncle replied, sounding to me as if the pips on his shoulder had gone to his head.

'I did but when we started we forgot that the Wardens were on the other side,' Wendy replied, looking pleased as we backed him up with our loud laughter.

'I left at eight o'clock. You should have left earlier.'

'We left at seven,' Wendy replied, smiling at us, and obviously enjoying treating Uncle as the straight man in the comedy.

'At that rate, I'll be lucky if I see you until tomorrow afternoon,' Uncle said testily, as he waved to Sergeant McCloud who had suddenly appeared with his two stripes.

'Form up!' McCloud shouted at us.

We had no idea how to form up in threes, so we formed a diagonal line with Wendy in the middle.

Even Uncle had to smile.

'Single file,' McCloud shouted, and Jimmy and I fell in behind Wendy. With McCloud one side, and Uncle on the other we marched all five out of step to collect our rifles and five rounds each. Poor Jimmy with his OCTU training was in a helpless state laughing, and when McCloud called a halt, Wendy's feet continued marching. His mind was high in the clouds.

We had to wait an hour until we marched to the firing point and five minutes later we put our rifles in a buggy, and waited another half hour to be marched back to the car park. We didn't even know if we'd hit the target, but then Wendy told us that he'd heard they didn't tell you if you hadn't, because of the effect on morale. He didn't say whose morale, but we thought Uncle looked depressed.

13

We had received our Anderson shelter in May, 1940, but as there hadn't been any air raids, only warnings, we had been in no hurry to erect it. Now air raids on the fighter bases, including Biggin Hill only five miles away, had become frequent, and on several occasions I cycled home from the tennis club, with Phyllis and Jean running beside me, while planes were fighting overhead. The need for the shelter could no longer be ignored.

I took the responsibility for erecting it with my friend John Manning. We had known each other for years, and I had spent a lot of time with him and his sister Julie. We enjoyed doing things together, and he considered himself an expert having been accepted to start studying for a degree in Civil Engineering at Imperial College in the coming September. We were both eighteen years old and bursting with enthusiasm to undertake such a responsible job devoid of any supervision, Father being happy for us to get on with it providing there were no labour costs.

It took two weekends to dig the chalk from the eight foot square by five feet deep hole, and to build the concrete base with sides and a back to form three foot high ledges on which to rest the shelter, and some steps to get back up to ground level.

The third Saturday, soon after breakfast, we sweated our way down the garden path with the heavy steel structure, and successfully manoeuvred it to the edge of the hole.

'I'll fetch the rope,' John said, and turned and trotted back to the house to collect the tow rope that we had borrowed to use as a cradle, to lower the shell on to the concrete ledges.

We knew our neighbours at the end of the garden, where Father had generously allocated the plot of ground, were keen to help. They were big strong fellows, both father and son having worked for years in the London docks humping huge loads of every shape and size. Digging, cement mixing, and humping shelters was a happy bit of light relief for them. But John and I had managed to refuse their offers.

I stood resting waiting for John to return, when I heard a noise behind me. Turning round I saw to my annoyance Bob the father and Sid the son from next door, peering over the fence.

'Are you ready to drop it in the hole, Ted?' Bob called out, as the two of them stood resting their great forearms on the top of the fence.

'Yes, John's just gone to get some rope,' I replied gruffly. We'd got this far, and now we didn't want any help with the part we'd been looking forward to, the real engineering task of lowering the shell skilfully onto the walls.

'You don't need any rope,' Bob said, turning and giving a nod to Sid.

They leapt over the fence, and in less than two minutes lifted the heavy load of steel onto the ledges, checked that it was central, and jumped back again.

I didn't thank them. I had nothing to be grateful for, and I nearly threw a brick over the fence when I heard them chortling with laughter.

'How did it get there?' John asked when he arrived with the rope, and saw me shovelling earth over it.

'Those two buggers from next door jumped over the fence and dropped it in,' I said, handing him a spade.

The shelter had three bunks down each side, and barely two feet clearance in the middle. Being below ground, it was safe from blast and gave one some confidence, if one did not dwell on the effect of a near miss.

We all felt that cold fear when the sirens wailed, often after gunfire had flapped the letter box up and down. I never admitted to being afraid to the girls, and didn't believe that I would ever go in the shelter.

They had no inhibitions. The sirens went at about seven o'clock most evenings, and they dropped everything and fled. In our house of six persons and one toilet you could be sure of a seat from half past six onwards. They didn't hang about.

Some evenings, when I came home late after the siren had gone, I would find things scattered everywhere, including all the ornaments off the sideboard and mantelpiece.

By July, Margaret's company had moved from London to a large old house in the country near Crocken Hill, making a shorter and safer journey each day, with less chance of air raids. Phyllis, having completed her shorthand and typing course, was also working there. We were pleased with our jobs, but Jean was not happy at school.

'Ted, you've got to help me. I shall end up a spinster like the old aunts,' she said to me the evening I found her sitting in Mother's chair in the drawing-room, waiting for Father to come in after his dinner.

We had often joked about her studying to go to University and one day becoming a teacher. But that was so far away, it didn't seem important.

'I thought you were going to marry John when you grew up,' I replied, not seeing how I could help her avoid being a spinster.

'Don't be funny. He's too mean anyway, but I might have to if I go to University,' she said, looking sad and forlorn, as if she was already an old maid.

'But you're brainy, you got Matric when you were fourteen. You will have a wonderful time sailing through a degree. I haven't even got Matric yet, and I'm eighteen,' I replied, feeling that I was the one who needed help.

'I'm not brainy. If I'd had any sense I would have failed. You designed and built boats and wirelesses, and made things out of wood. You worked on things you liked doing, you were always happy; except after exams. I did nothing else but study, that's all I ever did, and that's the only reason I did it, I couldn't think of anything else to do, and look where I am now. If it wasn't for you and Margaret, I'd have no money, and never go anywhere,' she said, looking pretty as always when she worked herself up, until her curls fell over her dark blue eyes.

'You've only been doing 'Highers' for a year, you ought to give it a bit longer', I said, surprised that she would give up so soon.

'I never wanted to start, and the longer I go on the more difficult it will be to stop. I'm telling Dad tonight I'm not going back after the holidays,' she said, looking very determined.

'What are you going to do instead?' I asked. I never thought of her as being just another shorthand typist.

'I'm going to learn shorthand and typing, like the others. You've got to help me.'

Before I could ask her how I could help, Dad came in and as usual plonked down like a sack of potatoes into his armchair.

'Dad, I want to leave school, and take a course in shorthand and typing,' Jean said, looking straight at the top of his head.

He was leaning right over with his head parallel to the carpet, slapping his pockets in turn, and listening to hear which one he put the matches in. Jean should have known better. She was wasting time talking to him until he'd lit the bonfire in that filthy old pipe he was holding between his teeth.

She waited, pulling a face at me, and watching him sucking and blowing clouds of smoke, with showers of sparks flying in all directions, until he was ready to reply.

'What did you say, Baby?' He asked, blowing another cloud of pungent smoke into the room.

Jean winced. Being called Baby at sixteen years of age was something else she hated.

'I want to leave school, and do a course of shorthand and typing,' she repeated, waving some of the smoke away from her head.

'No baby, you have brains, you don't want to do that. The others did that because they were no use for anything else, like your mother,' he replied, laughing and then coughing as he sucked in when he should have puffed out.

'I don't want to go back to school, I want to get a job and earn some money,' Jean said, looking hard at me to say something to help her.

'You want to get a degree, and then get a real job, not as a shorthand typist,' he replied, sucking furiously at the pipe to try and keep it going.

'That will take me four years. I can't wait that long for money and clothes,' she replied, looking at Father disappearing again as the bonfire responded to his noisy efforts.

'It will be worth waiting for. I'm prepared to make sacrifices for you. You don't need clothes now. You'll get plenty when you have a good job,' he said, looking at her over his glasses, which had slipped down his long nose.

'*You* don't make any sacrifices, I just have to do without. Ever since I started school I never even had a new pair of knickers. Everything I've had was handed down. I want to leave school, learn shorthand and typing, and earn some money to clothe myself now, not when I'm an old woman of twenty–two,' she said, giving me a desperate look to join in.

'I can understand Jean's feelings. I've been at work for over six months, and I'm only just able to think about a luxury like a pair of white socks for tennis, or having a decent suit which I feel comfortable in,'I said, hoping that in some way I might be helping her.

'You were all right! You had a suit when you started work. I hope you're not forgetting, now you think you're independent. I can tell you, you couldn't get digs for the price you pay to live here,' he said, wagging that filthy pipe at me.

'Dad, I'm not going back to school. I hate it. If I do I shall only fail and waste your money,' Jean said, looking annoyed at me for giving him the chance to change the subject.

'What are you going to do? I'm not paying for you to go to commercial College to learn to be an office skivvy. You go back to school, Baby, and get a degree, there's a good girl,' he said, leaning forward and looking at her, while he thumped his pockets again to find the matches.

'I'm not a Baby! And I'm not going back to school, and I don't want you to pay for me to go to college,' Jean replied, near to tears as she jumped up and ran out of the room.

'I can guess who's put her up to this,' Father said, puffing at his pipe and staring at me through the smoke.

'Nobody has put her up to anything. When she was studying for Matric, she did nothing else but study. She hated it, and couldn't wait for it to end. Then you . . .'

'It was your Mother! I can see her hand in it, and probably Margaret, and it wouldn't surprise me if her sister Alice had something to do with it,' he said, fiddling furiously to get a match out of the box.

'Nobody put her up to it. She's only trying to tell you that she doesn't want to be dependent on you for another four years. She wants to earn some money now,' I replied, hating the way he could never believe that we had minds of our own.

'I've educated four of you, given you holidays, and done my best for you, and you have all turned against me. Why? I'll tell you why; it's because of your mother, she's set you all against me,' he said, leaning back in the chair, staring straight at me and daring me to deny it.

I couldn't tell him why, but he was right. I was the only one who ever said a good word for him, but I found it increasingly difficult. I waited as he picked up his *Financial Times* and buried his head in it, then I quietly left him on his own.

'Ted, Mum wants to talk to you about Jean,' Phyllis whispered, as I was about to climb the stairs to my room.

I turned and followed her into the dining-room. Mother was sitting in her chair near the fire.

'Ted, tell Jean that she's got to stay at school, she won't listen to me,' Mother said angrily.

'There's no sense in making her stay at school if she doesn't want to,' I replied. I couldn't think why Mother was worried. She was quite happy for Margaret and Phyllis to leave school and earn some money as soon as possible.

'You're working for a degree, and she's brainier than you are. Tell her that she's got to go on with it,' Mother said, picking at her thumbnail as she spoke.

'I wouldn't have wanted to study full time, with no money for four years, even if I had the chance. I had nothing when I started work. Surely you remember the suit Dad bought me. It didn't last six months,' I replied, understanding very well how Jean must feel.

'Ted is working to become an engineer. Even if he doesn't get a degree, the time won't have been wasted, and he's earning money while he's doing it. All I will get is a job as a teacher, and end up as an old maid like the aunts,' Jean said, sitting down and turning her back on Mother.

'It's nothing to do with it. Aunty Alice is a shorthand typist, and Jane is a nurse,' Mother said, looking confused.

'There's something wrong there, Jean. Mother was a shorthand typist, and look what happened to her,' Phyllis said, pulling a face, and they both laughed, breaking the tension.

'I'm not going back to school. I've told Dad, and when he's worked out how much he will save he won't argue any more,' Jean said, shrugging her shoulders as if she had made up her mind and that was the end of it.

'He won't pay for you to go to the commercial college, and we can't afford to help. What are you going to do?' Mother asked, looking even more worried as Jean turned round to face her.

'I have the text books Margaret and Phyllis used: I'm going to teach myself. Aunty Alice says that she'll give me the same tests she gives her evening pupils every fortnight, and correct them for me, and give me a written statement of my standard for a reference when I've finished.'

'You can't do that. Father will be furious when he finds out that you've been to Aunty Alice. He'll blame me too,' Mother said, sitting up like a startled hen.

'Don't be silly, Mother. He'll never know. Who's going to tell him?' Phyllis said, as we all laughed at the look of horror on Mother's face.

'He's bound to find out, and I know he'll blame me,' Mother moaned, picking furiously at her thumbnail.

'No he won't. He hasn't found out that you've visited them every Thursday for the last ten years,' Jean said, laughing as Mother opened her mouth in dismay.

'Stop it, Jean, he'll hear you; I've told you never to mention that when he's in the house,' she said, shaking wih emotion.

'If you don't tell him that I go on a Monday, I won't tell him that you go every Thursday,' Jean replied, laughing at Mother waving her hand at her to shut up.

'You've already arranged it then,' Mother said sulkily.

'Of course I have. I told you last week I was not going back to school. You said that Dad would never pay for me to go to college, so I rang Aunty Alice when you were out.'

'You never told me. I think you're very deceitful,' Mother replied, pouting and looking near to tears.

'I didn't want to worry you in case Dad agreed to pay for me. Now he won't, it doesn't matter,' Jean said, coming over, and putting her arm round Mother's shoulders to comfort her.

Father never told Jean that he had written to the school,

but Mother spotted the reply in the post, accepting his notice of her leaving.

Jean obtained a well-paid post as a shorthand typist, in an oil company. They were very pleased with her proficiency, but not surprised, as she had the benefit of a private tutor. Father never asked how she had done it, but in his view any fool could be a shorthand typist.

14

'You ought to come and see our bomb,' Jimmy Potts said that morning as we sat in the lab drinking our tea.

'I don't want to see anybody's bomb,' I replied. I knew that looking at bomb damage was bad for the nerves.

'I didn't think there were any round here last night,' Alan said, taking a bite into one of those huge cheese rolls that require jacking your mouth open to get it in.

'It missed by about half a mile, but we heard it. I'm surprised you didn't hear it, Ted,' he said, looking thoughtfully over the top of his tea cup at me.

'I was in bed asleep last night, though come to think of it, something did wake me about three o'clock. But I didn't hear any planes, so I went to sleep again.'

'It was about that time. You must have heard it. Come back with me tonight, and I'll show you what a real bomb will do,' he said, with that funny little laugh of his.

'I've seen plenty of real bombs,' I replied, I didn't mind cycling back with him to Petts Wood. It wasn't far out of my way, but I didn't think I'd bother.

'Are you coming back with me tonight?' he asked, at tea time in the afternoon.

'I don't think so, thank you,' I replied, thinking that it was a bit of a fag cycling up the hill.

'I wish I hadn't,' Alan said, staring mournfully out of the window.

'When did you see it?' I asked. He hadn't told me that he was going.

'I went back with Jimmy on the way home to dinner.'

'Is it that bad?'

'It's terrible. I think we ought to surrender,' he replied, smiling ruefully.

'I'll come with you and have a look,' I said. I couldn't imagine anything bad enough to worry Alan.

We were two hundred yards away from Acorn Avenue when I noticed the tiles off the roofs, and most of the windows boarded up.

'I thought you told me it was in Acorn Avenue,' I said, looking at the damaged houses which were still standing. What scared me was seeing a pile of bricks, and realising that I could be lying underneath.

'I did. This is only the blast,' he replied as we turned into the Avenue and stopped.

There were six houses each side flattened, if you could call piles of bricks flat, and dozens more damaged by blast.

'Christ! It must have been more than one bomb,' I said, understanding why Alan had wished he hadn't come.

'It's called a land-mine,' Jimmy explained as we stood astride our bikes, resting our arms on the handlebars, and staring at the mess.

'I'd better get on home,' I said, feeling sick, I would never have slept in the house if I'd known they were dropping things like this.

I stayed later at the club that evening. I was in no hurry to tell the girls I was too frightened to sleep in the house. It was a bright night, with the moon showing quite frequently through the fast-moving clouds, and several raiders buzzing about.

They were all in the shelter, and I went round to the back door which was never locked, and trod carefully through the kitchen to the stairs in case one of them had rushed out at the last minute, leaving the usual cushions and chairs on the floor. I hesitated before taking my pillow off the bed. It was tempting to lie down, and forget about bloody land-mines.

I listened, and thought I heard a plane, grabbed the pillow, and dashed down the stairs, and out the back door, distinctly hearing a whistle as I closed it behind me.

I leapt down the four steps from the back door, and ran as fast as I could along the concrete path towards the shelter fifty yards away. The whistle was becoming louder, and I knew that I would never reach the shelter before the bomb landed. Suddenly, there was a loud crack from the concrete road on the other side of the fence. I stopped as quickly as I could and, still gasping for breath went to the fence, and looked over at a single little incendiary bomb burning brightly in the middle of the road.

'Was that you running down the path?' Phyllis asked me as I stood panting at the entrance to the shelter.

'Yes, who did you think it was?' I replied, as casually as I could.

'It didn't sound like you. Were you frightened?' she asked, sounding as if she couldn't believe it.

'No of course not. I thought it was going to rain,' I replied, and we both laughed.

After that all I could do was wish her good night, and go back to the house. On the way I picked up my pillow, which I had dropped when I had leapt in terror down the steps from the back door.

I lay awake listening to every plane, until the all-clear went at half past five. Then I fell into a deep sleep until Phyllis woke me up at half past seven with a cup of tea.

'I don't know how you can sleep so soundly. I'm so frightened that I lie awake all night in the shelter,' she said, putting the tea on the chair beside me.

I had a hurried shave before bolting my breakfast, and dashing off to work.

'You look as if you had a bad night,' Alan said when we met on the way in; unusual for me to be that late.

'I didn't sleep last night, but I don't think I would have been any better off if I'd gone in our shelter,' I replied, wondering what I was going to do tonight.

'Why don't you come back here? Wendy and several others use the shelter every night,' Jimmy suggested, sounding a bit guilty, but of course I didn't blame him. I expected to crack up sometime.

'Thanks for the idea. I'll wander up and have a chat with him,' I replied, feeling more cheerful at the possibility.

'You need to wear plenty of clothes and bring a top and bottom blanket. It can be quite cold,' Wendy said when I told him I was thinking of joining them in the shelter.

I didn't tell the family what I was doing. I should have done. If the house, and the shelter at the factory had been hit on the same night, they might have spent hours looking for my pieces at home, and puzzling over the identity of them at work. I just didn't think.

I arrived at the shelter at half past ten. The alert had been on since seven o'clock. The evenings were drawing in now. September was running out fast.

Elsie, the only lady among the four of us, I knew well. She was an assistant draughtswoman and we'd had many chats at her board when she did detailing for me. It was always about the injustice that prevented her from rising above assistant, while a man automatically became a draughtsman when he was twenty-one, whatever sort of idiot he was.

Appy, a small dark-haired, white-faced fellow, probably under thirty, was also there with Ivan Gurre, his exiled Russian friend. I had spoken to them occasionally, and been warned by Tony Rae, to avoid them. They were Communists.

'Much going on outside?' Wendy asked, as we listened to a faint rumbling of guns.

'Not much, very scattered, probably sent to keep us awake,' I replied. It had been quite an easy ride. If guns fired at anything near, I usually sheltered somewhere for a few minutes. That hadn't been necessary.

'You didn't see any blonde six foot nuns marching with steel helmets under their wimples?' Appy asked, cheerfully.

'I did but they were praying outside "The Coach and Horses" for the sinners to bring them out a pint,' I replied, having expected some nonsense from them.

It was all very cheerful, and in less than half an hour I settled down and fell into a deep sleep, knowing no more until I heard Wendy talking.

'I'll go out and have a look,' I heard him say, and I was just able to make out the shape of a small figure wrapped in a blanket, and wearing a pixie bonnet.

'You're right, Elsie, they're having an early morning. It's the all-clear,' he said, when he came back.

'What's the time?' I asked, feeling wonderfully refreshed after the first good sleep I'd had for ages.

'The all-clear's gone, and it's only five past five according to Elsie's watch, he said, climbing back on to the bench and pulling the blanket up to his chin.

'I think I'll go home,' I said, getting up and folding my blankets and pillow into a bundle to strap on my shoulders.

'You don't need to go home for breakfast for another two hours. Why don't you stay here?' Wendy asked, his head just visible on his pillow.

'I can get two hours in my own bed, if I hurry,' I replied, moving towards the exit.

It was a stange dawn. The clouds had thinned, and the moon was still bright. I made good progress with the wind behind me, and in five minutes I was half way home, about a hundred yards from the village hall, whose striking clock had given me the hour, and half hour on many a night when I lay awake unable to sleep. Suddenly it struck. Instantly I knew that it was the half hour, half past five. It couldn't be, the pace I'd been going I should have been here by quarter past at the latest. Then I was looking up at the hands, clearly indicating that it was one thirty. Elsie's watch must have been a few minutes fast, and had read one twenty-five. She had read it as five past five.

I hesitated, wondering whether to return, and then the sirens started wailing in the distance. I cursed them all, and went home to bed.

A few mornings later, Alan called in early. He often did this when he'd been on allnight duty with the Home Guard, and we cycled into work together.

We were less than a hundred yards from the factory when we found scaffold poles on trestles barring our way. Alan was leading and, spotting a small opening, he negotiated it skilfully, with a sharp right, sharp left hand wiggle, with hardly a noticeable reduction of speed. I followed and as no traffic could pass the barrier, we shot into the factory on the wrong side of the road. We didn't think to question why there was no man on duty at the gate, and were pleasantly surprised to find the cycle racks empty.

We would normally have gone in the main entrance, but the large side doors into the factory were open. It being a shorter distance going through the inspection department, Alan dashed ahead in that direction, and I followed.

'Christ, what on earth happened last night?' Alan said, as we stopped short looking at the equipment we would have to scramble over to reach the connecting door to the offices.

'We'd better go the other way,' I suggested. It was such a shambles that it would be quicker walking further to the front entrance.

'We could clear a path lifting the racks. It will have to be done by someone, we might as well make a start,' Alan suggested, beginning to lift the one nearest him.

We lifted upright a dozen heavy racks to clear a path to the door and, feeling exhausted, I decided that a rest and a pot of tea would help.

I had a job persuading Alan. He enjoyed such feats of strength, and wanted to continue, not hoping as I was that when we came back somebody else would have finished the job.

The door opened onto the main hall, and we reached our office without seeing anybody, only to find that the windows were wide open, with the cold morning air making it distinctly uncomfortable.

'Who's the bloody fresh-air fiend who's been opening these windows, and all the lab windows too?' Alan said, helping me to shut them as soon as he'd put the kettle on.

We'd hardly sat down after closing the office windows, waiting for the kettle to boil, when I heard heavy footsteps coming up the corridor. We both turned round as the door opened, and Mr Parsons, the work's manager, filled the doorway with his large frame, stooping slightly to avoid bumping his head.

'I should have known it would be you two,' he said, coming into the room.

'Cup of tea?' Alan asked cheerfully.

'I suppose that you didn't notice a barrier across the road when you came in this morning?' he said, going to the window, opening it, and looking up the road in that direction.

'We saw it. We went through the gap left for cyclists,' Alan replied, grinning at me as he went over to pour the tea.

'The barrier was there to stop anybody coming into the factory. Everybody else turned back, but not you two,' Parsons said, looking sadly at us, as if we had somehow disappointed him.

'Sorry, have we done something wrong?' I asked, watching Alan looking at the cups to find the clean one for Mr Parsons.

'There's a land-mine in the gas works, and if it goes off, there won't be much of this place left. I came in and opened

hall the windows you've just closed, and lay down all the racks
you just stood up. Why the Hell can't you behave like everybody else?' he said smiling, and gratefully accepting the tea Alan handed to him.

'Sorry, we'll open all the windows, and lay the racks down again, after we've finished our tea,' Alan said, opening a window as he spoke.

A telephone started to ring, and Parons hurriedly put his tea down, spilling most of it, and shot out of the door.

'He was very brave to come in on his own knowing that there was a land-mine in the gas works,' Alan said, draining his cup, and then starting to open the other windows.

'We wouldn't have done if we'd known, would we?' I said, getting up and moving towards the door.

'No bloody fear. Let's forget about the windows and to hell with the racks,' Alan said, hurrying out of the door in front of me as the telephone rang.

I hesitated. We weren't interested in customers at the moment. Then I changed my mind.

'Hello, Trans Lab here.'

'You can relax, the phone call was to say that the mine has been defused,' Parson's voice bellowed out.

Next time we were speaking to him, he told us that we showed great courage in agreeing to open the windows and lay down the racks after he'd told us there was a land-mine in the gas works. We both smiled modestly.

15

I was convincing myself as I shaved that I was meant to sleep in my own bed, and that I would make no more attempts to find a safe haven, when the telephone rang. The girls were back from the shelter, and were having a cup of tea before coming up to use the bathroom, and I heard Margaret answer the call.

I glanced at my watch as I went downstairs to breakfast. It was half past seven, the girls had not come up, and they were going to be late for their transport to Crocken Hill if they didn't hurry up.

I picked the paper off the mat and walked into the dining-room still reading the headlines as I sat down and Phyllis put a cup of tea beside me.

'Thank you. You'll be late if you're going to wash this morning,' I said, without looking up.

'We're not going in. Mr Price telephoned. He didn't say why. He's going to ring back later,' Phyllis said as Margaret came in with my breakfast.

'The service is improving round here,' I remarked as she put it down with a flourish.

'We've got the morning off,' she said, sticking her nose in the air to make me envious.

'Lucky for some. I can't be spared,' I replied, as they both went off upstairs.

I came into lunch at the usual time, and Mother had it waiting for me.

'The girls are being evacuated to Denton,' she said, looking sad about it.

'Are they? Where's that?' I asked. The Company had only recently evacuated from London to Crocken Hill.

'It's only a small village, North of London. They will be

living and working in the old manor house the company took
over some time ago. They are coming home at weekends, but
I shall miss them,' she said, and I thought she looked as if
she'd been crying.

'It will be a lot safer than Crocken Hill,' I replied, to cheer
her up.

'Of course you haven't heard. You were at work when Mr
Price phoned the second time. The old manor at Crocken
Hill was hit by a land-mine last night. It's completely
destroyed. Some of those living there were killed. Bob and
Flicker are in hospital, and the girls have gone to help recover
things from the wreckage.'

'Oh dear, how terrible!' I replied, feeling that awful
coldness again that I experienced when I went to Acorn
Avenue.

'Ted! Are you all right? You look very pale,' Mother said,
looking hard at me..

'I'm not surprised. We were out there only a few nights ago
playing a table-tennis match with them,' I replied, knowing
I'd be sleeping in the factory shelter again tonight.

I arrived at the factory shelter at about nine o'clock with
my two blankets, a pillow, and my old alarm clock. I wasn't
taking any more chances with Elsie's watch.

I was welcomed by Ivan, whom I liked and found good
company. I first met him in the canteen when he surprised
me by asking for a game of table-tennis after we'd both
beaten a big show-off at the game.

'Do you play snooker?' he asked, when we were folding
the table to stow it away.

'I don't have much chance, not belonging to a club, and
there are no halls around this way,' I replied, wondering
where he would play.

'I'll take you to my club, if you like,' he said, pulling a diary
out of his pocket.

We arranged to meet outside the 'White Hart' on Monday
night the next week, and when I arrived at seven o'clock he
was there waiting for me.

'I'm glad you're punctual. We want to make sure of a table
before the other bastards arrive,' he said as he led the way
towards some shops further down the road. It was too dark in
the black out for me to have any idea where we were going.

We went through a blackout curtain into a dimly-lit hall, climbed a flight of stairs to the first floor, and entered a large comfortably furnished room, with a bar, and a full-size snooker table.

'Is the other table free?' he asked the steward, as I signed the visitors' book, and he paid for a couple of drinks.

The steward nodded, and Ivan led me into a back room, well furnished with green leather seats along the walls, and a well-kept snooker table.

We played three frames and he thrashed me. He was a very good player, but I was puzzled by the well-dressed gentlemen who kept coming to the door to see if the table was occupied.

'What club is this?' I asked Ivan when we were having another drink in the bar afterwards.

'My visitor wants to know the name of this club,' Ivan said to the steward who seemed to be on very good terms with him.

'This is the Conservative Club, sir,' he replied, and I wondered how well he knew Ivan, remembering Johnny Rae's warning to me to be careful of Ivan the Communist.

Now we were in the shelter with only one small light at each end, there was no heating, and only candles for extra lighting.

'We review the week on Wednesday nights,' Wendy said, as I squeezed past him, causing the candle stuck in the beer bottle to flicker violently.

'Carry on, I'll listen for a while and then, I'm going to have an early night,' I replied, meaning just that, as I spread my blankets on a clear space.

'I put some extra tea in the flask. Would you like some?' Elsie said, holding a cup out to me as I sat down.

'Well, Ted, when are they going to invade us?' Ivan asked, as he made room for me to sit beside him.

'How should I know?' I replied, sipping the hot tea.

'I would have thought that they would have let Sergeant McCloud know by now, so that he and Uncle can deploy their troops to the best advantage,' Ivan said, with a grin on his rugged face.

'They won't invade. They'll be having second thoughts now Sergeant McCloud and Ted have five rounds each,'

Appy said, his thin pointed nose making him look sinister in the candlelight when he smiled.

'There won't be any invasion. The bullets are for the workers when they revolt after the Governement makes peace with Hitler, and joins Germany in a war against Russia,' Elsie replied, as a burst of ack-ack sounded horribly close.

'You're blinded by your hatred of the enemies of the left. There is only one enemy at the moment, and it's Russia that doesn't recognise this,' Wendy said, taking an apple offered to him by Appy from a large brown paper bag.

'I can't believe the Germans are using all this effort against the fighter bases, and softening us up for nothing,' I said, as several loud thumps seemed to be bombs and not ack-ack. They were too far away for us to hear any whistles, but close enough to be uncomfortable.

'We don't need enemies with allies like that, do we?' Wendy replied, winking at me.

We talked for hours with the candle growing shorter and dimmer, and munching apples that Elsie had brought from her garden. I didn't realise until my fourth that they were windfalls, which explained the meaty taste.

'You have to forget your bourgeois fastidiousness when you're living like a rat in a hole.' Ivan said, laughing at my disgust when I discovered I'd been munching maggots for hours.

'I would have thought that one of you left-wingers would have had the decency to warn me,' I said, when we trooped the fifty yards to the toilet in the front hall before turning in at one o'clock.

I didn't sleep. I could feel those perishing maggots turning over every time I did, and I couldn't stop arguing with Ivan and Appy. When my alarm did bring me to full consciousness, I found that I hadn't set it correctly. They'd all gone, and I was late.

I couldn't go to work without shaving or having some breakfast, and when I hurried in half an hour late, Alan and Jimmy were talking to our Sergeant with only two stripes.

I walked over to them, wondering what he wanted. Relationships had been strained lately. We refused to go to lectures in the canteen, preferring to attend those given for our local units.

Jimmy saw me and, moving out of McCloud's view, began pointing to his arm, where he now had three stripes.

'Captain McCloud,' I said, springing to attention.

'There's a lecture you have to attend tonight in the canteen,' he said, ignoring my attempt to flatter him.

'What's it about?' I asked, determined that I was not going to come all the way back to the factory canteen for a lecture I'd already had.

'It doesn't matter what it's about. I expect you to be there at seven thirty.'

'I can't go tonight.' I replied, trying to think of a good reason.

'There is no excuse for missing these lectures. There is a war on,' he said, stretching himself to his full five foot six inches.

'At least you could tell us what it's about,' I replied, noticing Harry Williams, who wasn't in the Home Guard, coming over to hear what was going on.

'It's on the Mills Bomb.'

'We went to that one on Friday with the Petts Wood Unit, didn't we?' I replied, turning to Jimmy for confirmation.

'I went on Thursday night at Keston. It was good, wasn't it? I liked the bit about pulling the pin out, and waiting before throwing it at the nearest sergeant,' Alan said, chattily.

'I don't care whether you've been or not. It's an order. You are coming tonight,' McCloud said, sternly like a Sergeant.

'I haven't been and I'm not coming tonight,' Harry said laughing, as if he didn't care if he got us three shot.

McCloud looked like a very cross Sergeant as he turned smartly on his heel, and marched out to Harry's 'Left, right, left, right.'

'You're a bastard, Harry. You could get us all shot,' Alan said, as the sound of McCloud's boots faded away in the distance.

'They couldn't spare the bullets,' Harry replied, still laughing, having thoroughly enjoyed himself.

We knew why McCloud was so mad. We were the only ones he had any chance of getting to attend. The others came under Parsons or Murphy, and they would never agree to release their men from overtime to play soldiers with Uncle and McCloud.

It was half past two that afternoon when Tony Rae came into the lab.

'Cotton, Leare, Trigsby, and Williams. Uncle wants you in his office, right away,' he announced holding a piece of paper in his hand.

'What's he want me for?' Williams asked, obviously concluding, as we did, that it concerned our talk with McCloud in the morning.

'He said all of you, and gave me this piece of paper, and your name's on it,' Tony said, pointing to it.

'That's McCloud's writing,' Alan said, as he examined the names.

'It's nothing to do with me then. I'm not in the LDV,' Harry said, standing back for us to go.

'Oh yes it is. You cheeked the Sergeant, and you're coming with us, whether you're in the LDV or not. Come on,' Alan said, and with him one side and Jimmy the other, and me encouraging from behind, Harry had no choice.

I slipped in front when we reached Uncle's office, and opened the door. We burst in. Uncle jumped up, looking as if he thought that we were going to attack him. Then he turned round, looking out of the window with his hands on his hips, as he did when he wanted you to go.

I glanced through the glass partition to see John Picard and Tony Rae laughing as they stood where they could see us without Uncle seeing them.

'I have a complaint, about insubordination,' Uncle said, when he faced us lined up on the mat in front of his desk.

I noticed Alan putting on his best expression of innocence, which had never worked before, and I couldn't see working now. But our combined expressions and unusual silence must have done something, because Uncle waited for us to protest.

'Well?' he asked, looking at me, and I thought as usual, that I had better do the explaining.

'The only thing I can think of is that Sergeant McCloud asked us if we were going to the lecture tonight, and we told him that we went to the lecture on the Mills bomb last Friday. But I don't think we were insubordinate,' I replied, turning to Alan and the others for support.

'No! We certainly weren't insubordinate,' Alan said,

looking very hurt that it should even be suggested.

'You belong to my unit, and when my Sergeant organises training lectures, I expect you to turn up,' he said, turning half towards the window, and then turning back suddenly, and staring angrily at me.

'We take the first opportunity we can to go to the training lectures. An invasion is supposed to be imminent, and we want to be prepared as soon as possible,' I replied, noticing the others including Harry, nodding their approval.

'I want you to attend the lectures here. You should not have joined your local units,' he said as if he thought it was a rotten thing for us to have done.

'I joined my local unit because if invasion comes, I want to be sure of what I'm going to do. The factory closes down every night and at weekends, and it seems to me that we are relying on the Germans playing the game and not attacking us then,' I replied, feeling angry at being told what I could join, and what I couldn't. I didn't start the bloody war.

'Do you think I haven't a plan?' he asked, looking indignantly at me.

'I'm sure you have, but in an invasion we don't want to defend the factory, we want to defend our homes,' I replied, warming to the argument, and noticing a nod from Jimmy, and a look of doubt on Alan's face.

'Do you think you can choose where you will fight? What a stupid boy you are. I'm not sure I want you in my unit,' he said, hands on hips and staring fiercely at me.

'I am happy with my local unit, and they are pleased to have me. If you don't want me, I would like to resign,' I said, seeing this as the way out.

'You may resign if you wish to. I would prefer to be without you,' he said, staring angrily at me.

'Thank you, I will resign,' I replied quickly, in case he changed his mind.

'What about the rest of you?' he asked, turning to the others.

'I will resign,' Alan and Jimmy said, as he looked at each in turn.

'And you, Mr Williams?' he asked as Harry hesitated, as well he might, not being a member.

'Yes, please,' he said cheerfully.

'Right, your resignations are accepted,' Uncle said, standing up and turning his back on us, his hands on his hips as he stared out of the window.

16

I felt a great relief when I went home the evening after resigning from Uncle's Home Guard Unit. We didn't like each other, and the little I saw of him at work was more than enough for me.

I had enjoyed the trip to Bisley, and the occasion when I was posted to the tower with Mr Thompson and Uncle, and a crippled German fighter was circling to find somewhere to land. Mr Thompson wanted to have a shot at it, and Uncle, as his commanding officer, kept telling him to be careful, the gun was loaded.

The next morning the warning went about nine o'clock, and a few minutes later the factory Air Raid Warden gave his usual announcement over the tannoy.

'This is your Air Raid Warden, Bill Rogers, speaking. An alert has been sounded. Please go quickly and quietly to your shelters. Do not run. Thank you. This is Air Raid Warden Rogers speaking.'

'That means us,' Alan said, as we went round the laboratory switching off soldering irons in particular, and anything else we found on.

There were no main switches in those days. We had been taking this precaution since we returned from the shelter one day to find our black—out curtains on fire, having been blown on to an iron by the wind through the windows which were always opened to reduce the effects of blast.

'I suppose we'd better,' I replied, as we walked reluctantly along the corridor.

'We could have a pee first, to make sure we're the last there,' Alan said, and we went on past the stairs, and the radio lab to the toilets, which served our top corridor. It had two cubicles, two wash basins, standing room for two, and a two-door coat cupboard.

We took our time washing our hands, hoping the all-clear might go at any minute.

'I reckon we could stay here, nobody will know,' Alan said, as he waited for me to finish with the towel.

'I shouldn't think anybody would come,' I replied, feeling that it was a come down having to go to the shelter.

'If they do, we could hide in the coat cupboards, there's plenty of room for one each side,' Alan said, opening the door to make sure.

I wasn't too happy with the idea. We would have to go to the shelter sometime so we might as well start now. We stood leaning our backs against the wall. There were only the usual seats, and we didn't fancy using them. Suddenly Alan turned and our eyes met as we listened to loud footsteps hurrying down the corridor. They should have gone down the stairs, but they didn't. They came on, passing the radio lab next door. We leapt into the cupboards and closed the doors.

The door banged open, and somebody in a hurry came in. I kept still, hardly daring to breathe. Then my cupboard door opened, and Mr Thompson tried to hang his coat on my nose.

'What the Hell are you doing in there?' he asked, as if he'd never found anybody in a coat cupboard before.

I jumped out, took his coat which he was still holding up, and hung it on the peg for him.

'It's part of the service,' I said, smiling, hoping he would think it funny, and shutting the door quickly, hardly daring to look at Alan plainly visible to me.

'Why aren't you in the shelter? You boys don't seem to have any sense at all. It's dangerous being in a building in an air raid. The shelters are provided for your protection.'

'These early morning raids only last ten minutes, and I was in the toilet when the warning went. So it was hardly worth going to the shelter,' I said, giving the first excuse that came into my head.

'You know perfectly well. You . . .'

'There goes the all-clear,' I said, relieved to have proved my case.

'That is not the point. You must go to the shelter as soon as you can. I didn't expect to have to tell you,' he said, as we walked out of the toilet, and up the corridor, and then he changed the subject, and said no more about it until half past ten, when we were having tea in the office.

'When I went into the toilet this morning, I found Ted in the coat cupboard, during the air raid. That's a very stupid thing to do. You boys must obey the air raid instructions, the same as everybody else. It's for your own safety,' he said, pausing and looking to see how we were responding.

We stood in silence, Alan looking particularly composed and angelic. I couldn't even look at him without wanting to laugh, and find myself even lower down the merit list. Mr Thompson continued; 'I will be going to India shortly to install equipment, some of which you have been testing, and then dribbling along the corridor to the packers. I am aware of your high spirits, but you have to have a more responsible attitude. The only one of you likely to survive, in my judgement, is Alan. Can't you speak to them, Alan, and get them to grow up?' he said, turning to Alan, who was smiling modestly.

'Don't worry about them, Mr Thompson. They have improved since they came, and I can promise you that I will see Ted goes to the shelter in future,' Alan replied, smiling and winking at me.

I knew we were high-spirited, and of the incident Mr Thompson was alluding to concerning dribbling all the way to the packers. It was when Jimmy and Harry tried to see who could carry the most units. Half way down the corridor Jimmy dropped one and Harry, hurrying beside him, caught it with his foot. It shot down the corridor ending up at Mr Thompson's feet as he came out of the radio lab. I felt as if we ought to say something in our defence.

'The real problem is work. We need something to do, the testing could be done by any one of us, but it is shared out to be fair to us all,' I said, feeling glad he didn't know half of what went on.

'I understand that, but you must try to be patient. The work will come. Uncle has no sense of humour, and there are some of you he doesn't like. Be careful,' he said, looking at me, and then picking up his pen and continuing with his work.

Things did not improve, but we did survive. The door lever handles to the lab to allow easy opening with arms full of equipment were still bent through one hundred and eighty degrees, so they opened up instead of down, and eventually broke off.

At regular discreet intervals, Alan and Jimmy would watch for me to go to the toilet. One of them would wait to see me come out at the end of the corridor, and signal to the other to drop several times a heavy copper crucible on to the floor above Parson's head, and then retire to the office and watch through the lab window.

'What the Hell have you been doing?' Parsons, the works manager, would yell at me innocently working at the bench above where he had been sitting.

'I've only just come back into the lab,' I would reply, knowing very well what it was all about.

'That's what you told me the last time. You'd better see that it doesn't happen again,' he would say, and he was a big fellow in his late thirties, played rugby, and I was never sure he wouldn't thump me. And of course it did happen again in a few weeks.

Tony Rae was in charge of us and all lab equipment, and he was very conscious of this heavy responsibility to the extent that he suffered from *folie de grandeur*. He was the next in age to us, about three years older, and worried that he might be mistaken for one of us.

There were twenty cupboards in the corridor for storing expensive precision measuring equipment, and other items like special cable and connectors. The Yale keys were held in the office, excepting number one cupboard, that was held by Tony Rae, and nobody else. It held delicate precision meters that we had to use for measurements, and he insisted on handing them out personally and checking them back. That meant that on Monday when he was away all day on a degree course, we had to do without: in no way would he leave the key with anybody else.

One Monday, Jimmy and Alan, with nothing better to do, were exploring the contents of the cupboards, and Alan opened one of them with the wrong key.

We of course tried each key in turn, and we discovered one that opened number one cupboard. We agreed to use this information sensibly, so that there would be no reason why Tony should ever find out that we had access to his Aladdin's cave.

Many of us had milk in the morning, and there were always arguments about who should take the empty bottles downstairs, and to save a row about something so stupid, I took them down to be collected once a week for several months.

'Will you see you clear those bottles each day, Ted? I don't like them left for a week,' Tony Rae, said to me very officiously.

'I've been clearing them for weeks, it's somebody else's turn now,' I replied, so irritated at his manner of asking that I was determined I would never again clear them at the end of the week.

'You will do as you're told,' he said in such a manner that I couldn't possibly move them, especially as Alan and Jimmy were standing there laughing, and Tony would not have dared to ask them.

After three weeks the bottles were beginning to appear everywhere, in drawers, on shelves, in overcoat pockets, behind black-out curtains, anywhere they might be hidden for a few hours, and those finding them would line them up on the window sill.

Friday afternoon Tony gave me a final warning.

'If those milk bottles are still here on Tuesday when I come in, I'll speak to Mr Hansdelle about your insubordination,' he said, knowing I wouldn't like that.

'Don't worry, Ted. We'll move 'em for you,' Alan said on Monday morning, and by Monday night they'd gone, and I was grateful to them. There are certain times when you learn who your real friends are.

'I see you've done as you were told, see you move them each day now,' Tony said, very pleased with the outcome of his threat.

I ignored his remark and asked him if I could have a meter from number one cupboard.

'I'll get it for you after tea,' he replied. He often made us wait.

About half an hour later I followed him out of the office and stood by his side in the corridor as he fiddled about finding the key on his crowded keyring.

At last he put it in the lock, turned the key sharply, and

ceremoniously opened the door.

I heard him gasp, and looked past him into the cupboard. I saw on the shelf, at eye—level, rows of milk bottles.

He let out a howl of rage and I ran. I shot through the lab door as bottles came flying past. If I hadn't been quick he could have killed me. My kind colleagues had filled them with water.

It was shortly after this that the army department expressed concern that we were working in the laboratory on classified defence contracts, and going home every night without locking up.

Tony was thrilled. He had several keys cut, and a spare was sealed in a little box on the wall beside the door, with a notice saying 'Glass may only be broken in an emergency'. The key lay on a little shelf in the box.

'That won't be any good. Every time the door bangs, the key will fall off the shelf to the bottom of the box,' Alan said, giving me a wink to confirm his verdict.

'Then you'd better see that you don't slam the door,' Tony replied aggressively, as if we weren't trying to be helpful.

'It's not only the door slamming. What about vibration from gunfire, or bombs?' I suggested hopefully.

'I'm telling you, there will be trouble if any of you tamper with those boxes,' Tony said, as he went to see Uncle who had just knocked on the window for him.

'I think that if we tap carefully with a small hammer, we'll be able to get it off the shelf,' Alan said, obviously having taken Tony's warning as a challenge.

'We'll wait for an air raid, and I'll come in early next morning, and do it,' I said, as John came back into the office.

John Picard and I had a go at it the next morning before Tony came in, and found it very easy with good firm taps to move the key about, and we had a noisy raid two nights later.

'The key's fallen off the shelf in the key box outside our lab,' I told Tony when he came in.

'I'm not surprised, there was a lot of gunfire last night. It's a wonder it didn't have the boxes off the wall,' Alan said, convincingly.

'No amount of gunfire would do that,' Tony said angrily, as he left the office to have a look.

'He's not going to be pleased about it,' John Picard said,

laughing, as Tony came back.

'The one outside the radio lab is all right. If it is you, Ted, I warn you that Uncle will hear about it,' he said, scowling at us as he sat down at his desk.

'You wouldn't get so much vibration near the radio lab with the brickwork of the tower being so much nearer,' John suggested helpfully.

'Rubbish! I know you bastards are responsible for it,' Tony replied angrily, getting to his feet.

'You're supposed to be an engineer, you should be looking for the technical reasons, not trying to blame poor old Ted,' Alan said, and as we all laughed, he left the office.

We discovered that he had been removing the screws sealed with wax, to take the front off the box, and put the key back on the shelf. After gunfire had shaken the key off the shelf several times, Tony screwed a large hook in the box, and hung the key on it: there was no way we could dislodge the key without smashing the box.

The Home Guard telephone link we had set up for Uncle used old hand generator sets. To ring one turned the little handle and the generator sent a powerful ringing supply down the line. Tony brought one of them in to the office and put it on my desk.

'What's that for?' I asked, wondering why he should dump it on me.

'It doesn't work. Uncle told me to give it to you to mend,' he said, as he walked to his desk.

'Why me?' I asked, surprised to be chosen for such an honour.

'He said that you might just manage it, if it were something simple. I told him that if it were that simple there would be nothing wrong with it,' Tony replied. He was still annoyed about the key falling off the shelf, even though he'd solved the problem.

I had other work now, but knew that Uncle would expect me to look at the hand set at the same time. He was right in a way becaise there was a lot of waiting for things to warm up in those days.

I took the outer case off, and decided to remove the generator coil. There were no volts, and it might be a broken wire. I removed the permanent magnet by slipping the coil off and put it on the bench. My screwdriver, about a foot away, clanged against it.

John had just handed me the means of removing the key from its hook. We had tried magnets but none had the power of this one.

Uncle came into the lab about eleven o'clock after his morning stroll to the toilet.

'Don't waste time on that, Trigsby. You should be able to mend it in between working on the converter,' he said peering at the coil on the bench.

'When do you want it?' I asked, knowing that there were no spares and one leg of his network was out of action.

'As soon as possible. You should be able to do it in a day.'

'I haven't found the fault yet. It might not be repairable,' I replied. I knew that I could not get the key off the hook until Friday night, so it couldn't be ready before then.

'It's Friday tomorrow. We've got an exercise on Saturday. You'd better work on it as much as you can. We must have it for the weekend,' he said, turning and walking slowly out of the lab.

I found and repaired the fault, tested it and then took it to pieces again, and left it on the bench. Uncle always stayed late on a Friday, and I told him I would have it ready before I left.

As soon as the others had gone, including Tony of course, I took the magnet and removed the key from the hook, making sure that it fell below the shelf. I assembled the hand set, gave one final check and took it into Uncle.

Tony didn't come in until Tuesday. Monday he was on a day course for the final of his part-time degree.

'Ted's getting a proper creep,' John said to Alan on Monday morning.

'I know he stayed late working for Uncle's Home Guard Unit. He must have heard about Uncle's vacancy for a corporal,' Alan said, laughing.

'I'm trying to get in his good books. You're all right,' I replied, wondering if Alan might be suspicious.

It was on the following Friday. Alan came into the office. Only John and I were there. Tony was in the Lab.

'The key's gone!' Alan said, as if he didn't expect us to believe him.

'What key?' I asked, hoping that I sounded innocent.

'The lab key. It's not in the box,' Alan replied, looking amazed.

'It must be. Unless Tony took it out,' I replied, looking at John who was laughing in disbelief.

'Tony will explode! Does he know?' John asked, as the door opened, and Tony came in.

'Do I know what?' Tony said, as he closed the door.

'Alan says there's no key in the box,' I said, laughing, to try and sound relaxed.

'There had bloody well better be,' Tony said, rushing out of the door.

'Was it you, Ted?' John asked, as Alan led the way for us to see the evidence.

'Good Lord, no. I thought it was you.'

'I wouldn't know how to start. I suppose it must have been Alan then,' he said hanging back as we discussed who it could be.

'It was very clever of him to come and announce it, if he did,' I said, following him to join the other two, and have a look.

I had carefully pulled the key, close to the front of the box, so there was no hope of seeing it without taking the front off.

'It has gone then. I thought they were pulling your leg,' John said, as we stood looking at the empty hook.

'Take the front off, it might still be in the box,' I suggested, pleased to tell Tony what to do.

'I'm just going to do that,' Tony said, producing a screwdriver from his top pocket.

'If it isn't there it could mean that there's a spy in the factory, trying to find out what goes on in the lab,' John said, looking at me and winking.

'If there is, and he finds out, perhaps he'll tell us,' Alan replied, and we roared with laughter.

'It's not funny! There's going to be a row about this,' Tony said, cleaning the sealing wax out of the screw heads.

'I think you owe us an apology, Tony. You as good as accused us when we suggested that the vibration from gunfire might have caused the key to fall off the shelf. Now it looks as if we were both wrong. It was somebody else,' I said, as we crowded Tony to make it difficult for him to use the screwdriver.

'If it was somebody else it was only because they beat you to it,' Tony said, fiercely unscrewing the last screw.

'It's not very kind of you to always suspect your colleagues above everybody else,' John said, winking at me, and just then the front came off, and the key fell on the floor.

A notice was circulated along the whole of the top floor reminding us all that the keys were there for an emergency, and after that it never happened again, I never had another hand set to repair.

17

Despite the increasing tempo of the air raids, Jean continued with her crash course of shorthand and typing, with Aunty Alice's help. Father knew that she was working all day at it, but he didn't know she went to see Aunty every Monday, anymore than he knew of Mother's visits every Thursday.

Aunty Alice lived with her sister Jane, a nurse, the oracle for all medical matters in the family, whose cures and preventatives, with her predictions of our demise should we fail to follow them to the letter, had terrified us when we were young, and still had some influence, especially on Jean, for whom she had special concern as her godmother.

'How's it going?' I asked Jean one Monday when she returned from her visit to Aunty Alice looking depressed.

'Fine I'm well ahead of Aunty's class. In a month I should be qualified as much as I can be, without going to a full-time college,' she replied, seeming to cheer up a bit.

'That's good. I thought you looked as if you'd had a bad day.'

'Well, I did really. Aunty Jane was there again today, and she always probes as to how I am, in the most intimate way: I hate it,' she replied, pulling a face to show her disgust.

'Can't you tell her a few symptoms that will keep her guessing?' I replied.

I couldn't understand why Mother and the girls still worried about Aunty Jane's predictions. It was different when we were kids, but now we were grown-ups, Jean was seventeen. But even Mother and Margaret still quoted Aunty Jane as if she were some mythical medical marvel instead of just a nurse. It wasn't as if her predictions had ever come true. According to her, Phyllis and I, as twins had been too small and delicate to survive at birth, and every two or three years we were destined to die of some childish malady. Jean, with her dark hair, and blue eyes, was also considered too fragile to survive.

There were many stories Mother told us over the years that we loved to listen to and laugh about. The one that always left Jean helpless was about the pots. Aunty Jane had come to stay to nurse us through a crisis when we were four, and Jean was two years old. She took us over completely; we were weighed daily, had our height measured weekly, and our bowels were a subject for daily discussion. Every morning after breakfast we would have to sit on our pots in the nursery on a mat in front of the gas fire.

Aunty insisted that I should sit in the middle. Jean didn't like me sitting next to her. She told Mother I pinched her bottom, which was not true. I was not that sort of boy. Mother told Phyllis and me to change places. Knowing no better, we did just that, leaving the pots where they were, and then we changed back when we heard Aunty coming up the stairs.

Phyllis was constipated, and I was not, and I liked syrup of figs, and she didn't. From then on I performed like an express train, which of course went to Phyllis's credit, and I had repeated doses of syrup of figs. It was a week before Mother discovered the reason for our phenomenal changes in performance, and she was too frightened to tell Aunty, who never found out as she had to leave us in a hurry to nurse another patient in a crisis. We had survived all these years and they still worried about her predictions.

'I wouldn't dare do that, she was on about TB again today. She asked how you were as well. She still thinks, with blue eyes and black hair, that unless we wrap ourselves in cotton wool, we'll be dead before we're twenty-one,' Jean said, putting her case on the table and starting to open it.

'Just ignore her, she's a menace. I believe Dad's right when he says she's a witch with no broomstick,' I replied. I believed that she meant well, but couldn't help worrying that she might be right one day.

'You wear trousers: you're all right. She comes over to me, lifts up my frock, and says I told you last week to buy yourself some flannel knickers. Wearing those cotton things will give you kidney trouble if you don't die of TB first,' Jean said, laughing as she sat down.

'Tell her you can't afford them.'

'I dare not do that. She'll give me two pairs, and then want to inspect them every week, to make sure I'm wearing them. You know what she's like.'

'I'm glad she doesn't inspect me anymore. I can concentrate on surviving the war,' I said, smiling smugly.

'It's only because you're nearly twenty, and she thinks that you're as good as dead,' Jean replied, smiling as I winced.

'I should think the safest place in an air raid, would be to sit next to her. If the Russians didn't get her I can't believe the Germans will,' I replied laughing, believing it wouldn't be worth it.

'That's another thing. She says I shouldn't go in the shelter. It's too damp. She doesn't understand. I'm scared of being blown to bits. You'd think I went there for fun,' she said, looking through the papers in her case.

'You'll be all right. If we were as fragile as she says, we wouldn't be able to play tennis and hockey the way we do,' I replied, for my own comfort as much as Jean's.

'They should have shot her when she was in Russia during the Revolution,' Jean said, smiling at the thought of anybody daring to shoot Aunty Jane.

'She wasn't there long enough. You know what Dad says: she only went over there to start it, and then came straight back home again'

'What do you think of this?' Jean asked, handing me a sheet of typing.

'It seems very good,' I said, when I had finished reading it. It was a reference from Aunty Alice, saying that as Jean's private tutor, she would have no hesitation in recommending her for the post.

'You don't think it's too much, do you? She does lay it on a bit, doesn't she?' Jean replied, as I handed it back to her.

'No, that will do fine. You've got to have something if you don't go to a commercial college,' I replied, watching her putting it back in the case.

'Aunty said it's for an oil company to which she recommends her good pupils, and she is going to recommend me next time they have a vacancy,' Jean said, as she closed her case.

'Did Aunty Jane say anthing about Mother?' I asked. We

were worried: Mother was looking very tired, which was not surprising as she didn't sleep at all in the shelter. Being all skin and bone, she needed a soft mattress.

'Yes. She said that she gave her some sleeping tablets, and told me to make sure she took them. I didn't dare tell her that Mother wouldn't take anything she gave her after the last time when we couldn't wake her up, and found Aunty Jane had told her to take two instead of a half,' Jean replied, laughing as Mother came in.

'You're not going down the shelter?' she asked Jean, glancing at the clock, which showed nearly eight o'clock.

'In a minute. The warning hasn't gone, has it?' Jean asked anxiously.

'No, I don't think so. If you will sleep downstairs in the lounge, Ted, I think I'll try sleeping in the armchair tonight,' Mother said, wearily.

'Yes, I'll fetch my eiderdown and a pillow and sleep on the floor. There's plenty of room,' I replied, pleased that Mother might get a few hours sleep in the warm.

When Dad heard that Mother was not going to the shelter, he decided to sleep in his armchair, and Jean went to the shelter at about nine o'clock. She didn't fancy having to rush down there half asleep in the middle of the night if the siren went.

I didn't know how long we'd been asleep. We had put the light out at nine thirty for Mother to have as much rest as possible, if the warning should go.

'Ted! Ted! Wake up! They're dropping things,' Mother was shouting hysterically.

'Stay where you are, I'll put the light on,' I shouted. I was frightened she would blunder into something, might even tread on me.

'What's the matter? I didn't hear anything. Shut up, Mother! You must have been dreaming. Waking us up like that! The first decent sleep I've had for ages,' Father grumbled from under the blanket in his armchair.

'Ted, they were dropping things, I heard them,' Mother called out excitedly, and I was able to find her in the dark from the direction of her voice, and press her gently against the wall, while I felt for the light switch.

'You sit down, I'll get a cup of tea, and then take you down to the shelter,' I said, as I led her to her armchair.

'No, Ted, I want to go to the shelter. I don't want any tea,' she replied, still shaking with fright.

'All right. I'll take you down. What about you, Dad? Are you going to stay here?' I asked, not wishing to make two journeys if it could be avoided.

'Are you coming back?' he asked, the blanket held up to his chin.

'Yes, I shall only be five minutes,' I replied, opening the door, and leading Mother by the hand.

She mumbled on, all the way to the shelter.

'I wasn't dreaming,Ted. I heard the whistle, something hit the roof and crashed into the road,' she kept saying, and I kept telling her that I believed her.

Jean was fast asleep. We didn't wake her, and I tucked the blankets around Mother as best I could.

'Did you hear anything?' Father asked, when I got back.

'No, but something must have frightened Mother. She's very upset,' I replied. I didn't believe it was a bomb, it might have been a shell cap. They made quite a noise, whistling through the air, and smashing tiles when they thudded on to the roof.

'It was probably only a gun that went off. You know what she's like,' he said scornfully.

'I do know what she's like. She goes shopping every day to be sure that we get our rations, even though she's terrified of the raids. She can't help being frightened, we all are,' I replied, feeling annoyed at his constant belittling of Mother.

'She's a coward, always crying before she's hurt. She cries if the girls are late home, she cried when she thought you were being called up,' he said, looking at me as if to dare me to defend her any further.

'Of course she's frightened of something happening to any of us. Mothers are like that,' I replied. I felt that if anybody was a coward it was him.

'What about you? When are you joining up? I'm ashamed. All the other girls and boys are joining up, but not my family.'

'I don't know. I expect I shall be called up soon. If I'm not I'll probably volunteer. I feel left out with all my friends away in the forces.'

'I'm pleased to hear that. I fought in the last war, and I wouldn't like to think that a son of mine was ducking out, 'he said, sitting back as if he was proud to have done his bit.

'You didn't exactly volunteer did you? From what I understand, you only married Mother to avoid being called up. Then they changed the rules. She had to have a baby, and you never forgave Margaret for arriving a week too late, because you had to go just the same,' I said, furious with him, of all people, suggesting that anybody was ducking out.

'I suppose I've to thank your mother for those damned lies. I'll tell . . .' he said. He wasn't angry, he was almost in tears, but his words were drowned by a series of sharp bangs that seemed to come from just outside the front door, rattling the windows, and banging the letter-box up and down.

'Those were bombs, Ted. Mother was right,' he shouted, struggling out of his armchair.

'That was gunfire from a mobile Bofors,' I replied, as another barrage of six rounds were loosed off.

My nerves won't stand this. You'll have to help me down to the shelter,' he whined. When he thought they were bombs, they were bombs.

It was two o'clock, a half moon had risen when I came back, and I went to the front of the house to see if there was a gun parked outside. I looked over the gate, and lying in a dent in the road was a huge block of concrete. Poor Mother, she must have heard it glance off the roof, where even in the moonlight, I could see the smashed tiles.

The next morning we found that a small bomb had fallen in the road, about a hundred yards from the shelter. Nobody was hurt, but there was minor blast damage to the houses nearby. The biggest piece of concrete had flown two hundred yards, not quite clearing our house, and breaking a dozen tiles, when it bounced off and made a dent in the road outside. We were lucky again, but they were getting nearer.

Mother, having been proved right, went each night to the shelter with Jean and Dad, until well into November.

18

By the end of November we had only occasional day or night nuisance raids, and though they could be frightening, they were soon over.

Young people coming home on leave from the forces, were keen to go to dances and cinemas, but one could never be sure that there would not be an air raid, and one always felt vulnerable in a large building.

Early in January, despite all Mother's pleas to her not to, Jean decided to go the the cinema alongside the railway at Petts Wood. It was the last evening of her boyfriend's leave, and there had been no raids for a month. The programme started at half past six. At eight o'clock the warning went, and a heavy fire-bomb raid began.

Mother was prepared; the oil lamp, and the matches were still kept in the shelter; the bedding still stored ready to hand was grabbed and a few minutes after the warning had gone, she and Dad were in the shelter.

'I told Jean not to go. She doesn't think about the worry she causes me,' Mother said, sobbing away as if we'd seen the last of her.

'I'll go to the station to meet them, and take a helmet for her,' I replied, keen to see what was going on. Mainly incendiaries seemed to be dropping all over the place, and they weren't as frightening as ordinary bombs.

Unfortunately there were two ways one could come from the station; one slightly quicker than the other. I took the short way, especially as there was more shelter under trees if it became too noisy; not that they gave much protection.

The booking office was empty when I arrived and, going onto the platform, I found the ticket collector watching the incendiaries burning down the line towards Petts Wood.

121

'Has there been a train in from Petts Wood recently?' I asked, just as a loud whistle indicated that something bigger was coming, and we both dashed to lie down near the wall.

'There was one about fifteen minutes ago,' he replied, as we dusted ourselves down.

'You didn't notice an RAF corporal with a dark-haired girl come through the barrier, did you?' I asked, feeling sure that I must have missed them.

'No, they were all blondes tonight with sergeants,' he replied, not very helpfully.

'I'm looking for my sister. She went to Petts Wood to the cinema. She has dark hair and is about my height.'

'I can't remember. They might have gone through. I had other things to think about,' he replied, head on one side listening to the drone of a plane, which appeared to be overhead.

I waited until a reasonable break in the gunfire meant that what had gone up could all have come down, and hurried back home.

I'd been less than half an hour, and I looked in the shelter to see if I'd missed them.

'Haven't you gone yet? I thought it was Jean,' Mother said, sounding very disappointed.

'No, I'm just going,' I replied, dashing off again.

This time the porter told me that a train came in just after I left, and there wouldn't be another for an hour, if at all.

My civil engineering friend, John Manning, lived near the station, and I decided to call on his mother and sister to see if they were all right. His father was abroad, and John was doing well at his civil engineering studies, but he only came home from university at weekends. Julie his sister, the same age as Jean, who was training to become a masseuse at Orpington Hospital, and her mother, were alone during the week.

As I approached their road, I saw the fire wardens in their funny bonnets, carrying small sandbags which they dropped on the incendiaries, to put them out. It wasn't really necessary for those in the road. They could be left to burn, but it was good for morale, until the beastly Germans put an explosive charge in to make things more exciting.

'Hello. What are you doing here?'

It was Julie, standing in the shadow of the large oak tree at the entrance to her house. She had a little sandbag resting on her shoulder, and her tin bonnet made her look like an eighteenth century governess.

'I came to see if you needed any help,' I replied, laughing at her in that bonnet.

'I know why you're laughing,' she said tilting it back at an angle.

'I think they designed these bonnets to raise morale by giving us all a good laugh,' I replied, pleased to see her coping so well. She was a competent girl whom I was fond of, and she had a steady boyfriend in the Navy.

'It seems to have quietened down now, they were dropping everywhere at one time. How about coming in for a cup of tea?' she said, putting her sandbag on the low wall, and then leading the way to the back door.

'What about your leader? Will he mind you knocking off to drink tea?' I asked, knowing fire wardens were on duty until the all-clear sounded.

'I wouldn't think so, I haven't seen him tonight,' she said laughing.

'He should be around. This is the worst fire-raid we've ever had in this area.'

'He doesn't come out, even when nothing happens. We believe he works out his strategy under the dining-room table, until the all-clear goes,' she replied, knocking loudly on the kitchen door for her mother to put out the light, and unlock the door.

They always made me welcome, and I enjoyed the tea, and the chat, having spent a lot of time in the past with her and John, before he went to university.

'Were you serious about Major Waller?' I asked Julie, when we decided that we ought to go out again and see what was going on. I had never liked him but I couldn't believe he could be that bad.

'I am. It's true,' Julie replied laughing, as she put her bonnet on over her curls.

'I wouldn't mind so much if he didn't talk about you and John the way he does,' her mother said, shaking her head to show her disapproval.

'What does he say about me?' I asked, knowing it

was unlikely to be very flattering.

Waller was ex-Indian Army, very pompous, fond of whisky, and thought me a sissy because I didn't drink or smoke. I never stayed long if I found him there when I called in.

'He told Mrs Peel next door we should all be in the forces, people like us received white feathers in the last war,' Julie replied, as she stood by the door waiting for me.

'He's a pompous old ass, I wouldn't worry about him,' I said, putting on my helmet.

'Mother does, don't you?' Julie replied, as we stood waiting for her mother to put the light out before we opened the back door.

'I think it's hurtful to say things like that, especially as he's not much of a hero,' she said, switching off the light.

It was a pleasant night, with only patchy white clouds. The searchlights and guns were operating a long way off now, as Julie walked up the road with me towards the station.

'This is Major Waller's place, isn't it?' I asked, as we paused at the house at the end of the road.

'Yes, we won't see any sign of him,' she said, starting to walk on.

'Let's knock on the door and ask him if he's all right,' I said, knowing that if he was at home he should definitely have been outside, and I welcomed a chance of embarrassing him.

We walked up the open drive to the front door, and I banged hard with the knocker, several times. We waited, but nobody came to the door.

'Are you sure he's in?' I asked. I couldn't believe he wouldn't even answer the door.

'He's in all right. I told you, he never comes out if there's a raid. We don't mind. We'd rather he didn't,' Julie said, as we stood there listening to faint rumbles of gunfire echoing from far away.

'Shall we go round the back?' I asked. There were no gates, just a wide path to the back door.

'Yes, let's. I can show you where he is,' Julie said, with that little infectious laugh of hers, and starting to lead the way.

We climbed up the stairs to the veranda, and looked through the curtains which were partly drawn. A heavy table was against the far wall, and underneath we could just make out the figures of the Major and his wife.

'Now do you believe me,' Julie said, as we went down the steps of the veranda.

'I do but it's almost unbelievable,' I replied as we both laughed.

'It's better for all of us if he stays there isn't it?' Julie said, and I left her patrolling her little patch, as the all-clear began to sound in the distance. It was the end of the raid, and we had been lucky again.

19

By September, 1940, we still had only minor jobs to do. Mr Thompson had left for India, and after some hairy horse play in the lab, when Uncle looked in one day and found us dancing round a pot of flaming wax, we were deployed. Harry Williams and I remained in the main Laboratory, and jimmy Potts and Alan went to the radio lab, first on the left at the top of the stairs next to the toilets.

Alan and Jimmy worked for Doctor Bagner, a clever German Jew, who was arrested for a time under the Detainee B regulations, and Captain Vayne who obtained his commission in the 1914−18 War, where his hearing had been impaired.

After a few weeks of working for the Captain in the radio lab, I visited Alan's mother. She was worried about Alan. He shouted at her when he came home. She was relieved when I told her that poor Alan spent all day shouting at the Captain, and as a consequence shouted at the rest of us because he couldn't switch off.

Vayne liked to be known as the Captain, and he didn't like Uncle telling him what to do. Just over twenty years ago, in the First World War, Uncle had been a member of the Flying Corps, of which Captain Vayne had a very poor opinion. Having been up to his eyes in mud and bullets, he thought Uncle should have been doing the same, instead of swanning about the sky.

Most days Uncle would visit the toilet at eleven o'clock, that was how he caught us dancing round the flaming pot, and call in to the radio lab on the way back. When the Captain became wise to it, he would go for a walk as soon as Uncle passed the radio lab. No fool, Uncle, he called in before visiting the gents, and the Captain tried to delay him until he was hopping from one leg to the other.

Uncle used the toilet downstairs, and then came into the lab, and the poor Captain was convinced that Uncle had acquired a spare bladder.

Not to be beaten, Captain Vayne changed his strategy completely. When Uncle left the radio laboratory, he would allow two minutes, then open the door and shout up the corridor.

'Uncle is a bloody fool.'

He explained that Uncle should stay in his office. That's why he was given an office, to prevent him from annoying people like us who wanted to work, so if he hadn't got back in two minutes then he deserved to hear that he was a bloody fool.

This went on for weeks before Vayne became bored with it, and we wondered if Uncle ever heard him, until one morning John Picard was about to leave Uncle's office.

'Just a minute, Mr Picard. Who's Uncle?' Uncle asked, standing up as always when somebody was leaving his office.

'I don't know,' John replied, after a thoughtful few moments.

'I thought you might know,' Uncle replied, looking disappointed.

'Why do you ask?' John said, his hand on the door handle.

'I heard Captain Vayne shouting about him twice last week, and I wondered who he was.' Uncle said, frowning and looking very puzzled.

'What did he say about him?' John asked, unable to resist the temptation to learn more.

'It was something about him being a bloody fool,' Uncle said, folding his arms in his Buddah mode.

'It could have been anybody. There's a lot of those about.' John said, and they both laughed as he left the office.

Alan's main job was to operate a small transceiver from Uncle's house for the Captain to make measurements of signal strength. Alan would get into a groove and not break off his transmitting for instructions, or appear to doze off and not answer the calls when he was supposed to be listening.

I heard the Captain shouting about this to Alan on several occasions. Alan would just shrug his shoulders and laugh. But one day it got beyond a joke.

'Trigsby speaking,' I said, when I picked up the phone, and then winced as a bellow from the other end deafened me.

I held the phone at arm's length, and interpreted the message from the Captain to be that he wanted me to go over to Uncle's house and wake Alan up.

'I'll go right away' I shouted into the mouthpiece, welcoming the opportunity to get out of the lab into the sunshine.

'Will you go right away?' Vayne bellowed back, before I replaced the receiver.

I wasn't sure if I'd come to the right house, but I rang the bell, knowing that I'd soon find out: Mrs Hansdelle was a very attractive young woman. She certainly hadn't been around in the last war.

The door was opened by a delightful blonde girl of some eighteen years, about my height and wearing a pleated knee-length, light blue skirt.

'Sorry, I think I've come to the wrong house,' I said reluctantly, when I got my breath back.

'Who did you wish?' she asked in a foreign accent, smiling sweetly.

I could have replied none other than herself, Harry would have done.

'I'm looking for Mr Hansdelle's house,' I said, wondering if her English was good enough to understand me.

'Yes, you come,' she said, standing aside for me to enter.

I hesitated, she couldn't have understood, and it wasn't my birthday.

'Come in, please. You find Mr Alan,' she said, nodding her head up and down.

I shot through the door. Alan had not been sleeping, and it would be worth something for me to keep my mouth shut. She tripped up the stairs, with me not too close behind, past a bedroom, and up another flight of stairs to the attic, where Alan was gabbling away into a microphone.

'You rotten bastard, Alan, hogging all this to yourself. I remember when we used to share things,' I said, as he raised a hand in greeting.

'Mrs Hansdelle only left yesterday. This is the first time I've met her,' he replied, laughing with his finger on the transmitter switch.

'The way she welcomed me, it wouldn't take long to get to know her,' I replied, turning and smiling at her leaning against the doorpost.

'What brought you here?' Alan asked, standing up and stretching his legs.

'Vayne couldn't raise you, and sent me over to wake you up.'

'I wasn't asleep,' Alan replied, laughing.

'I bet you weren't,' I said, giving the girl a sideways glance.

'Mr Alan, your friend like tea?' she asked, smiling and looking from one to the other of us.

'You bet he does,' I replied, eagerly.

'I no understand. You say Yes?' she asked, looking at me with those big blue eyes.

'Yes, yes please,' I said, and raced after her down the stairs.

We sat on the settee in the lounge drinking tea, and trying to communicate. She was Dutch, and could speak a little English. I managed to learn that her name was Fokki, her family were in Holland, and she could not go back. She was very unhappy, we were the first young people she had met since she came some months ago. Uncle's wife and three year old son had gone somewhere safe, and she was leaving to go to another family in a few days.

'Come on, we'd better be going, if you don't want to meet Uncle coming home for lunch,' Alan said, standing in the doorway with his coat over his shoulder.

'Goodbye, Fokki,' I said, as I stood up.

'Goodbye, I never see you again,' she said sadly, and gave me a peck on the cheek.

'I'll see you after lunch,' Alan said pushing me out, and hurrying down the steps.

Alan really does have all the luck, I thought the next morning as I sat at my bench. The most excitement I had was twiddling the dials of an oscillator.

'Has that mate of yours arrived yet?'

I recognised the voice without having to turn round. It was Uncle's odd–job boy, Eric Fisher, a forty year old whom we considered non-technical. He claimed to have had a dock-yard apprenticeship qualifying him as a marine engineer, which he assured us made him superior to the rest of us.

'He's just behind you,' I replied as I looked round and saw

Alan coming in the door to get the key to the radio lab.

'The boss rang through, and gave me a job for you two lads,' he said, rubbing his hands together, pleased at the chance to give us orders.

'What sort of job?' I asked, not relishing doing anything under instructions, not that he was a bad chap. Alan and I didn't like people like him telling us what to do.

'It's about time you did some real work, instead of fiddling with those bloody knobs,' he replied, as I turned down the power control on the oscillator.

'I suppose it can wait until I've opened up the radio lab?' Alan asked, holding the key in his hand.

'It's a long job, you'll need to get quite a bit out of the stores. Uncle caught a packet last night, and his windows need patching up.' he replied, pushing a store's requisition pad already filled up in front of me.

'Poor old Uncle. Was he hurt?' I asked, more concerned as to how Fokki had fared, as I glanced at the pad.

'No, he sleeps in the shelter, with McCloud and a few others. If you need anything else add it on over my signature, that will be all right,' he replied, with an air of importance.

It was gone ten o'clock when we had amassed all the bits and pieces to take over to Uncle's, but we didn't wait for tea, we were too anxious to get on with the job.

'Please to come in,' Fokki greeted the two eager handy boys, standing on the doorstep, and we needed no second invitation.

We made a programme while we were having tea and biscuits in the breakfast-room with Fokki. Starting with Uncle's bedroom, then Fokki's, and the various other rooms. There was not a lot to do really. Fokki had done all the clearing up before we arrived.

By eleven o'clock we were back for more tea, and Fokki generously produced some William pears that Uncle had grown in his garden.

'You dance?' Fokki asked Alan, putting a record on the gramophone.

'No, he does,' Alan said, nodding at me.

I stood up, and held my arms out to hold her.

'You teach me,' she said, smiling as I took her in my arms.

'I'd better go and do the work,' Alan said, and left us to it.

What a pal he was.

After such a lovely morning, we arranged to come back, and finish off after two o'clock, when Uncle would have returned to work.

By half past three Alan had finished, and was tidying upstairs; the dirty cups were still on the table. I was going through the whisk in the quickstep, when Fokki stumbled. I helped her up, and saw her face change from happy mischievous laughter, to something akin to pain, and I tried to pull her close to me to comfort her, but she struggled fiercely to break away. What on earth had gone wrong? She had enjoyed dancing cheek to cheek, and holding me tight. Something must have happened.

Hearing a noise behind me, I turned to see Uncle standing in the doorway.

'I suppose Mr Leare will be doing all the work,' he said, looking at me with those cold blue eyes.

'We had just finished – Alan is tidying up,' I replied, breathlessly.

'You can go back. I'll find Mr Leare,' he said, standing aside for me to make my exit, which I did feeling as high as a tortoise, and without a word to Fokki. I'm sure that she would have let me kiss her goodbye, but I couldn't try with him standing there.

20

The first week in January, 1941, Alan and I considered the war-time hazards of going to London for evening classes at Battersea Polytechnic were at a reasonable level, and we descended on them to enrol on the appropriate evening.

'You can't start in January. You have to start in September,' each Tutor told us in turn.

'We couldn't start in September with air raids in progress on most nights even before we left the factory,' we explained, wondering how many classes were actually held.

'Come back next September. You can enrol then.' they repeated patiently.

'We're not waiting all that time,' we insisted, and shaking their heads sadly, they took our money and enrolled us.

The journey was from St Mary Cray station to Battersea Park, taking an hour and a half, and requiring a change at Victoria for the Battersea Park train.

At five thirty, the factory management allowed the race to start for the five thirty-seven train from the far platform over the footbridge. It was all up hill with the last part about one in ten. If you were young and fit without a head wind, you could do it uncomfortably in six minutes.

Mr Murphy, for the sake of discipline, insisted that Uncle should not allow us to leave any earlier than the rest. We managed a small advantage by waiting at the fire-door below the battery room, which became a big advantage when we realised he couldn't see us, because we didn't have to pass his office, and we left ten minutes earlier, knowing that Uncle wouln't know either.

We needed to be early, because we had to purchase a student ticket, half the price of an ordinary fare.

To begin with, we were lucky. George the ticket clerk an

ex-schoolfriend, stood ready for the hand over like an Olympic relay runner, urging us on as we raced towards the footbridge, and the train roared in. After a few months he became bored with the job. He hardly saw a soul all day, we were the only excitement, and that was very quickly over, so he volunteered for air crew.

His successor was a younger fellow who was pleased to help, and we continued for three years, until he was called up. Then an old hand arrived, skilled in making a job of it by challenging every customer to justify his right to be sold a ticket to travel on his railway.

We heard about the new ticket office terror from friends who travelled each day at reduced rates, for a multiplicity of ingenious reasons which this fellow challenged repeatedly, making their travels more expensive than ever before.

'He can't stop me having a ticket to Orpington after all these years,' I said to Alan when we were discussing the fact that we, as students, should be a privileged class, and be immune from such inconveniences.

'Have you read the small print on the pass?' Alan asked, looking very serious.

'Of course not, I've better things to do,' I replied, turning it over.

It was, I discovered, quite clearly stated that it was required to be renewed each year, and in no circumstances could it be taken that it would be renewed without a new application giving all the details up-dated.

'We're three years out of date. I thought it would be valid as long as we were students,' Alan said, shaking his head as if he couldn't believe it.

We left early that evening, giving us time for argument.

'May I have the ticket made out to Orpington, please,' I asked politely slipping my pass under the grill.

'I shouldn't think so, the pass is only valid for the station at which it is presented.' he said, examining the pass as he spoke.

'I always have had the ticket made out for Orpington,' I replied, dreading that he would notice it was three years out of date.

'You can have it from here, or not at all.'

'All right, I suppose I will have to have it from here,' I said, pushing the money under the grill.

He handed me the ticket, and Alan pushed his underneath. He seemed to examine it for ages, I was half way over the bridge before Alan caught me up.

We wrote off for our student passes to be renewed, only to receive a letter of regret saying that they stopped issuing student passes two years ago. It was a pity. We had to continue for another year with those grubby old passes. We felt anxious every time we used it.

One of the lectures for Physics including practical was only held on a Friday afternoon, with engineering drawing from seven o'clock the same evening.

We went boldly in to ask Uncle for Friday afternoon off to attend.

'What time will you have to leave here?' he asked, when we explained that the only train was from Orpington Station at one thirty.

'About ten to one,' Alan replied, having worked out that we could just do it, leaving at one o'clock if wind and speed of ticket clerks were in our favour. The last mile from the high street was all up hill, and the last two hundred yards, to where we could leave our bicycles, was the steepest of all. Even with that train we would arrive half an hour late for the lecture.

'You can't expect to have time off for study during a war.' he said, arms folded, and looking as unbending as a brass Buddah.

'We'll do overtime when we're not at college, and Saturdays, when we are' Alan said. We'd agreed that he would do all the talking, my star was still below the horizon as far as Uncle was concerned.

'You can go if you don't leave before one o'clock,' he said, getting to his feet, and turning his back on us.

'Thank you very much,' we chorused and left the office.

We did it for two years, and we never missed the train, or had more than two minutes to spare. We would fall into an empty carriage and lie one each side along the seat, panting away until we reached the next station.

The evening lectures used to end at nine forty-five. Our train left at nine fifty. We could catch it if we ran flat out, a dangerous thing to do in the blackout. On really dark nights the local louts would entertain themselves by lining the entrance to the booking hall with bottles of all shapes and sizes: the first to enter would kick violently to clear the lot. If one trod on one one would probably miss the train, and break one's neck.

Failure to catch this train meant crossing to Queen's Road station on the other side of the road. It was important to know the drill. The half dozen would-be passengers sat in the dark in the waiting-room against the wall, staring fixedly at a special indicator high in a corner of the ceiling. When a train was going to stop, the indicator dropped down, and gave for a few seconds the destination and the platform. You then ran at once to the platform, the porters blowing whistles and threatening to leave you behind if you faltered. Regular travellers could be recognised by the pronounced crick in their necks as they sat in the carriage or on the seats in the waiting-room.

At Denmark Hill the porters were waiting for us, with shouts of;

'Everybody out! All change! Over the bridge for the Bromley train. Hurry along the train is about to leave.'

Then the whistles blew, and the shouts continued, as doors slammed the whole length of the dark train. The breathless passengers could never relax; even when arriving at their desired station they peered fearfully out of the train in case they had misread the dimly-lit name of the last station, and found that they had gone too far, and that there was no return train that night.

The worst part of those journeys was being hungry. We could never arrive before the refectory closed, even if we had the money. We used to stand on the platform by the chocolate machines, waiting for the train, wishing there was chocolate in them as there used to be in the good old days. One night the machines were filled with chocolate and toffee. Between us we hadn't the coins to fit, and there was nothing we could do but curse our luck until the train came in.

Alan and I always found something to laugh about on those journeys, but we were working quite long hours with little time for exercise or relaxation. One morning I came home from an all-night guard duty, which I had gone to straight from classes, with the rotten headache that I'd had for several days and been unable to shift with a large number of tablets. I couldn't eat breakfast, which worried Mother, partly because of the entreaties of the Government not to waste food: it was a quarter of a ration of bacon, a quarter of a slice of fried bread, and half a fried egg.

'Go and see Dr Grant. He'll give you something for your headache, and he may even give you a tonic,' Mother said, as I sat there looking miserable.

'It's only a headache, it will go,' I replied. I had little faith in doctors.

Mother insisted and, not feeling strong enough to resist, I ended up in the Doctor's surgery. He was a friendly little man whom I had only met on rare occasions, as when I dislocated my collar-bone playing tennis. He thought it a joke when the hospital decided it was best to do nothing, and it would be better if I gave up playing tennis, telling me at nineteen that there were plenty of other pleasures in life. I knew that but I wanted to enjoy them all.

'Well, what have you been up to this time?' he asked, when I sat down in the chair in front of his desk.

'Nothing. I've had a rotten headache for several days, and it won't go,' I replied, feeling embarrassed at such a feeble reason for visiting him.

'Tell me, what you did last week?' he said, scribbling on a pad as he spoke.

'I went to work each day, and I went to evening classes, and did Home Guard duty one night,' I replied, as briefly as I could.

'What time do you start and finish work?' he asked patiently.

'I start at eight o'clock and finish at five thirty.'

'What time do you go to classes?'

At five thirty.'

How can you go to classes at five thirty if you don't leave work until five thirty?' he asked, pencil poised.

'Sorry, I meant I start going to classes as soon as I leave work.'

'Now come on, I want to know what you do. Give me in detail an average day.'

'I leave work at five thirty to catch the five thirty-seven train from Cray station to Victoria. I then catch the train to Battersea at six forty, and arrive at the polytechnic at seven o'clock,' I replied pausing to see if he was satisfied so far.

'Go on,' he said, as he finished writing.

'The class finishes at nine forty-five, and I run flat out to Battersea station to catch the nine fifty to Victoria. I catch the ten fifteen from Victoria to Orpington, and get home about half past eleven.'

'I want to know when you eat. Start with breakfast,' he said, drawing a line across the page.

'I have breakfast at seven thirty, a cheese roll and cup of tea at ten thirty, dinner at home at one fifteen, and tea and a jam bun at three o'clock,' I said wondering what sort of joke he was thinking about this time.

'Go on,' he said as he stopped writing.

'I've finished.'

'All right, how long do you have to eat your lunch, and what do you eat before going to bed?'

'I have half an hour to eat my lunch, and I don't have anything after three o'clock. There isn't any time,' I said, hoping that he had enough to go on with. I was becoming irritated with his questions; they weren't making my headache any better.

'Right, I see,' he said, reaching for a pad, and starting to write.

I wondered what he saw, and waited for him to tell me.

'You didn't say when you did your Home Guard duties.'

'I parade Sunday mornings at eight o'clock, and do one all night every ten days. When it falls on a class night, I go straight there.'

'Good. Now send this in to your place of work, and come back and see me in a fortnight.' he said handing me the form he had just filled in.

I looked at it. My head was bad but I could make out the date. It seemed months away.

'I can't take any time off from work,' I said, imagining Uncle's sarcasm if I took a day off, much less a week.

'You suffer from headaches because you are flogging yourself to death. Have a couple of weeks off, and see how you feel. If your headaches have gone, and you look better than you do now, I'll sign you off,' he said laughing, as if he found it all very funny.

'I can't send this in for a month. We're very busy.' I

replied, feeling shattered. If I sent this in I'd never be able to face Uncle again.

I sent it in, and after a week at home, despite plenty of studying and course work to do, I felt lost and alone. All my friends were in the forces, Margaret and Phyllis were away the whole week, and Jean left at eight, and didn't come home until six o'clock.

I went back to the doctor the next week, and he promised to sign me off in a week's time if I still wished him to. I went back the next week, feeling much better and eager to return to work.

'You young people are stupid. You're killing yourselves as surely as if you were being shot, but if that's what you want you can have it,' he said, handing me the certificate.

Before I had gone sick, I had been working on a breadboard model of an amplifier, which Uncle was hoping to flog to the Major and Captain, from the Army Department, who came regularly to progress equipment we were developing for them.

'Mr Trigsby will have it ready to demonstrate next time you're here,' Uncle promised them, and he knew, as well as I did, that I had no hope of being ready for at least a month and they came every fortnight.

'Where have you been?' Uncle asked me, when he came into the lab the first morning I was back, and found me working on the breadboard.

'I wasn't feeling well, and I sent in a medical certificate,' I replied, wishing I'd never come back.

'I was told that it said you were suffering from nervous debility, whatever that means.' he said, sarcastically.

'I felt ill for several days before I went to the doctor, and I'm glad he gave me time off. I feel better now,' I replied, realising now how foolish I was. It would have made no difference however long I was away. Uncle would always think it was not justified. I should have taken a month.

21

The company were in trouble with staff shortages in 1941. Dr Vagner and Maxi Barth, two German engineers who were interned in 1940, were released in April, 1941, and they needed assistants for the work they were doing.

The doctor was satisfied with two seventeen year old girls, recruited with 'highers' in mathematics, whom he was able to train in the specialist design of filters and equalisers. But what was needed was to train more like Alan and me, to do the experimental and development work, including the testing of prototypes, and first-off production.

For a spell I worked for Barth on a precision oscillator for the Turkish Government. The company had won a contract, on the strength of supplying these oscillators for calibration of signal sources, but had not been able to develop them.

After six months with Barth, I produced one which met the specification. Only I knew how, and nobody believed that I could do it again. I knew I could. I had a small capacitor hidden outside the temperature control box, which was the only way of compensating for changes when the tuning unit was sealed, but obviously I couldn't admit this to anybody, least of all to Uncle.

Then poor Barth died tragically of a heart attack at thirty-four, and the company discovered to my relief that the Turks only required one calibration oscillator, and never expected any more.

Harry Williams had left to go to a job on maintenance in the BBC and Jimmy Cotton won his appeal against reservation when they were looking for recruits for REME.

When Alan and I left school, over two years previously, just before the War started, the majority were in favour of a war. It would solve employment problems, which concerned getting a job, and then being bored to death for the rest of your life. The enthusiasm for taking part in the present War was now such that even those of degree standard were keen to enter the forces as soon as they had qualified.

The only solution was to employ girls. The first one to arrive was a delightful extrovert blonde girl of twenty-two, who had failed the second year of her medical degree. She was great on biology and the human body. She was appointed to a mathematical design group, and nearly had hysterics when she was given a text book and asked to design 'M' derived filters.

It was not her fault. She had been directed to meet the company's request for suitable staff. Those doing the directing believed anybody having demonstrated some intelligence could do any engineering job. Eventually the poor girl was found a menial task for which she received twice the normal pay. She came to Alan and me at times for help, which we were delighted to give. Unfortunately I couldn't resist pulling her leg over the use of some insulating material. She returned to our office when she found out, and had me on the floor in a fierce embrace, the female equivalent of a half nelson, when Uncle walked in.

He waited looking at the two of us, as we got to our feet, and she slid out the door, and I went to my desk.

'You see what I was saying about Trigsby. Every time I see him near a girl he has her on the floor,' he said to John Picard, who was trying to hide his amusement.

'I don't think he intended to end up on the floor,' John replied, as I sat there embarrassed, trying to think of a suitable explanation if it was requested.

'Whatever he intended, he should not have been doing it on the floor or anywhere else,' Uncle said, shaking his head disapprovingly.

'I think that he has a fatal attraction for the opposite sex,' John suggested, adding to my embarrassment.

'Whatever he has, it frightens me to think what will happen if we employ girls in the laboratory,' Uncle said as he left the office.

The workload was becoming heavier, and something needed to be done, whatever excuse Uncle made for delaying the inevitable. The real problem was that very few girls were interested in taking a job in a laboratory, and the pay did not compare favourably with the office jobs they normally applied for. The increasing demand for technical staff meant that it was easier to lose them, if you could get them, than to recruit them.

Uncle finally agreed that girls would have to be taken on, and to ensure the right types were chosen to resist the charms of Ted Trigsby, he would do the interviewing.

He was astonished that there were so few applications, believing women would be queueing up to work for him. He had no idea how miserably the pay offered, about thirty shillings a week including war bonuses, compared with even the low pay of the factory girls.

Alan and I were unhappy about girls being brought in, unless they were properly trained, and we were not eager to help as we were busy with studying, and Home Guard, as well as our normal work. To survive in this environment the girls would need to be extroverts, with the determination and thick skin of the male equivalent, a fiery attractive blonde like Miss Marple.

We waited apprehensively for Uncle's first choice. Priscilla Wandemere was short and cuddly, shy and introverted, the ideal choice to prove that women could not succeed in a laboratory.

She arrived on the Monday morning, was given a desk at the far end of the main laboratory, and told that a companion would be coming in a few weeks. Tony Rae explained to her about fetching the teas from Mrs Tickle, and how the radio lab, the trans lab, where she sat, and the battery room would have to be kept clean and tidy, the benches requiring regular polishing.

Alan and I found it difficult to talk to her, and as a result spoke very seldom to her, if at all. On the third week Victoria Godsworth arrived; tall, thin with a pale face, and frightened brown eyes like a gazelle. She was even shyer than Priscilla and very much an introvert.

'Uncle asked me to inform you that he does not want to find you on the floor with either of the two girls,' John said, when he returned from his Monday morning chat.

'It's not my fault. They just can't resist me,' I replied as Alan came in.

'I think that we will have to go around in pairs. Those two must have something, or Uncle would never have taken them on,' Alan said, laughing as Victoria swept majestically past the office.

The two girls were terrified of Uncle. One could feel the fear when he came into the Laboratory, which he did most days. It was an unreasoning fear. He had never hurt anyone. He was sarcastic, bombastic, humourless, and, apart from being a pig, quite a pleasant companion, for somebody else. The office staff, including his secretary Miss Shrub, all held him in awe, and rushed about to do his bidding. I had been brought up by Father, and I didn't expect any kindness or consideration from the boss, and I was not disappointed.

Victoria was chosen for the job of iron dust mixing with insulating varnish. It required constant stirring on a hot plate, to prevent the varnish burning, and care to avoid breathing in the unpleasant fumes. It was one of Uncle's pet babies, the only reason why, before the girls arrived, I had never had the honour to assist in this unpleasant task.

Soon after Tony had finished instructing Victoria on the art of not burning the varnish, Uncle came in to see how she was getting on. The poor girl visibly shook as he stood close beside her watching every stir.

'Stir slowly and steadily. You must not let the varnish burn. You understand?' he asked anxiously.

'Yes,' she answered in a barely audible whisper.

'Here, let me show you,' he said, elbowing her aside after watching for several minutes, during which time her shaking hands had brought her near to having some of the mix on the hotplate, and the rest on the floor.

I was working nearby, and sympathised with her, remembering how the first time I had switched on a breadboard for Uncle, the HT leads crossed, and caught fire.

'There you are, that is the way to stir a mix. Did your mother never teach you anything about cooking a cake?' he said, and then shuffled down the lab to where I was working.

'Well, Trigsby, when are you going to have those results ready for Major Hammond?'he asked, as I carefully calibrated the valve voltmeter to make him wait for an answer.

'I'm hoping to finish this afternoon,' I replied. They were ready then, but I had learned to let him wait and check everything several times. He was not pleasant with my mistakes.

He stood waching me for several minutes, and I continued to twiddle nobs, and calibrate the valve voltmeter several times. I was not going to do anything while he stood there.

'Bring them to me as soon as you've finished. I promised Major Hammond that they would be ready yesterday,' he replied, as he turned and walked towards Victoria who was concentrating, trying to stir steadily and smoothly, while shaking with fright in case he spoke to her again.

Priscilla was the one who, if Uncle spoke to her, would dash to the ladies, as soon as he'd gone, and have a good cry. The girls he chose may have had the intelligence for laboratory work, but they were too sensitive for a gentleman like Uncle. Not for nothing was he called the Bastard from Barrow.

22

The directors, FT the father, CH and BJ Coverdale the sons, and Mr Murphy were coming every Monday morning now for a board meetimg with Uncle on the lucrative development contracts, preceeding even more valuable production contracts.

Uncle and Mr Parsons, the work's manager, were the only two in our factory who attended and, like the other four, they wore dark blue suits. Mr Fisher was very important. He wore a smart dark grey suit, and every Monday he came in early to set the scene in Uncle's office, putting out the ash-trays for the cigars, agendas, pencils and paper, and cigarettes in abundance. After the meeting, he filled his large cigarette case before putting the remainder away for the next meeting.

Tony Rae would stand at the window in the office, watching the directors arrive in two Rolls Royces, and a Bentley; he was a great car enthusiast. Many a time he was puzzled why they looked up at him, not knowing we were tapping on the window in the lab, with a specially designed window tapper operated from bench level. Some of us, including my left-wing friends, felt that it was an extravagant use of petrol in war time; all four of them would not have been too uncomfortable in one Rolls Royce.

This was the time when most mechanical and electrical engineers below a certain age received letters inviting them to apply for commissions in the newly formed REME (Royal Electrical and Mechanical Engineers) providing they could be spared without prejudicing their company's war effort. This of course was a golden opportunity for a company to rid itself of unwanted staff, not always to the benefit of the service.

All the technically-minded in the forces were also being requested to consider volunteering for the other ranks.

Neither John Picard, who was not a member, nor Tony

144

Rae, a student member, received letters. Several engineers at the main factory in Dulwich received them, and were induced not to accept by the company offering improved salaries, or by suggestions that they would only be taken back at the level at which they left.

Eric Fisher was repeatedly telling us how his apprenticeship in a dockyard gave him the status of a marine engineer, far superior to an ordinary mechanical engineer; and of course when the Army realised this he would be called to the colours. He wasn't a bad chap, but he could be a bore when he was talking about himself, and having very little work to do, he was forever looking for someone to pass the time with.

'It would be helpful if that little man in Whitehall would hurry up and put us out of our misery,' John Picard suggested, after a particularly long session, when Fisher had learned that Mr Thompson had been given the rank of Major for the installation contract he was supervising in India.

'If he doesn't, perhaps we should,' Alan suggested, and we all laughed.

That afternoon Fisher came back to tell us of another engineer, far less competent than himself, who had been made a Captain. We were amazed we hadn't appreciated that there was such a person.

'I think Alan's right. We'll have to speed things up,' John said, handing Alan a letter he had drafted.

'That will never fool anybody,' Alan said, when he'd stopped laughing.

'It isn't meant to. It's just a joke, hopefully to shut him up for a while.' John replied, pointing for Alan to pass it to me.

'Read it out, Ted, and let's see what it sounds like,' Alan said, handing it to me.

Dear Mr Fisher,

From our investigations, we note your qualifications, and experience as a marine engineer, which would be invaluable to us in the recovery of tanks that break down in the desert.

If you would accept a commission, we could offer the rank of Captain on entry, with prospects of further promotion.

Yours faithfully, J. Hardasher (Colonel).

'That will do, he ought to get the message. How are we going to get it typed? We can't give it to Susan,' Alan said, smiling as he took it from me to have another look.

'Ted, you've several typists in your family, how about one of them?' John said, holding up a buff-coloured envelope he'd just taken out of his drawer.

'Where did you get the address from?' I asked, looking at the one at the top of the page.

'I opened the London telephone directory at the address of the Women's Gas Council. I thought it very appropriate,' he replied, as I took the envelope from him.

'Jean comes home in the evening, I'll ask her. She's just qualified, and loves to type anything,' I said, slipping the note into the envelope.

'You'll need this too,' John said, handing me another piece of paper on which Fisher's address was written.

It all seemed such a laugh. Jean typed it Tuesday evening, I gave it to John to post in London Wednesday night, and he came in Thursday morning with it still in his pocket.

'I've had second thoughts. It's too obvious. He'll screw it up and throw it straight in the fire, and we'll never even know if he got it,' John said, as the door opened and Fisher came in.

He stayed for over an hour, and telling him we were busy had absolutely no effect, he still went on gabbling away about REME, and the same thing happened in the afternoon.

We all wished that John had posted the bloody letter, and I think that he was beginnning to think the same.

Friday was a better day for us. All day Uncle discussed with Eric Fisher the contents of a folder that formed the agenda for the directors' meeting on Monday, and the menu for the lunch, booked at a hotel in Chislehurst.

This was during a term break at the polytechnic. Alan and I were walking along the top corridor from the lab to go home, at about five thirty, when we heard Eric shouting as he came running up the stairs.

'It's come. I told you it would,' he shouted at us, as we stood back to let him pass.

'What was all that about?' I asked, as we continued towards the door.

'Didn't John tell you? He posted the letter last night,' Alan said, as he opened the door for me.

'He shouldn't have posted it on a Thursday. Eric will have the whole weekend to convince himself that it's a joke,' I replied, feeling annoyed with John. I would have expected him to have had more sense.

Alan came in earlier than usual on Monday morning.

Well, how is Eric today?' he asked me, as he sat down at his desk.

'He's not come in this morning!'

'Christ! I hope he hasn't shot himself,' Alan replied, as he sat down at my desk, having just signed the book in Susan Shrub's office.

'He'd miss,' John said, laughing.

'Didn't you ask Susan where he was?' Alan asked me, leaning back on two legs of his chair.

'Of course, that's how I knew he wasn't in. She said that she believes he's gone to Dulwich, but she didn't know for sure. I didn't like to be too inquisitive.'

'What the hell's he doing there?' Alan asked, sitting on the window-ledge with a puzzled look on his face, as he stared up the road.

'Ted, you've got friends in the drawing office. Ring one of them, and ask what they know about it,' John suggested, as we sat looking at each other.

I dialled Elsie's number. She always knew everything.

'Hello, Elsie. Do you know why Eric Fisher hasn't come in this morning?' I asked, conscious of the unusual silence from the others.

'Jim Dooke has advised us not to talk about it,' she replied, cautiously.

'Come on, what do you know? Where is he this morning?' I asked. She didn't sound at all like the rebellious Elsie I'd listened to in the shelter.

'You'd better have a word with Jim.'

'Thank you, I will,' I replied, putting the phone down.

'What did she say?' John asked as I was dialling Jim's number.

'She said that Jim Dooke had told them not to discuss it, so I'm ringing him to find out what it is must not be discussed.'

'Christ! What the Hell's he up to?' John asked, anxiously.

'He couldn't have taken it seriously,' Alan said, shaking his head in disbelief.

'Ted here. Jim, do you know where Eric Fisher is? We
expected him early this morning to prepare for the Monday
meeting.'

'You know he received a letter from REME on Friday?'
Jim said in his usual quiet manner.

'No. Did he? It must have been after I left,' I said, hoping
that I sounded convincing.

'It appears that they were offering him a Commission. He's
gone to head office at Dulwich this morning, to see FT about
it.'

'No! Really?' I said, genuinely surprised and concerned
about the last remark.

'Ted, do you know anything about it?' he asked anxiously.

'No. That's why I rang you, I guessed you would know. We
never hear a thing over here in the trans lab,' I replied,
quickly putting my hand over the receiver as John and
Alan laughed.

'Thank God for that. We reckon that the letter's a hoax. I
thought it was you lot, and I told my staff not to discuss it.
There will be Hell to pay when it's found out. I advise you to
do the same, Ted, the less you know about it the better.'

'Thanks, I don't know anything. I haven't even seen the
letter. Have you?'

'No. Before he went in to see FT, Eric showed it this
morning to Joe Bennet the chief draughtsman at Dulwich,
and he rang me, saying it's the most obvious hoax he's ever
seen.'

'No! What's wrong with it?' I replied, feeling offended, we
thought it was a good letter.

I held the phone away from my ear for Alan and John,
whose heads were close to mine trying to listen.

'There was no phone number for a start. It wasn't in an
HMS envelope, and it says something about a marine
engineer, being invaluable in the desert, looking for broken-
down tanks. Joe said that it was all he could do not to laugh. I
didn't tell him, but I thought it sounded like you lot.'

'Good lord! It does sound suspicious. Do you think we
should point it out to him, if he shows it to us?' I replied,
worried that he would hear John and Alan, who were falling
off their chairs laughing.

'No! The best thing is to go along with it, then you won't be suspected. Once you are, even if they haven't any proof, you'll be in trouble. This one has gone right to the top. He's taken it to FT.'

'I put the phone down, and we all laughed.

'I'm glad our directors have a sense of humour,' John said, grinning with his tongue in his cheek.

'Oh yes, that's obvious by the way they roll up Monday mornings in their hearses dressed for a funeral,' Alan said, nodding his head wisely.

'There's only one person Uncle will blame; you're going to have a job talking your way out of this one,Ted,' John said laughing, and trying to look as if he felt sorry for me.

'Me!'

'It's a pity you haven't a wife and family. They usually take that into consideration,' Alan said, helpful as ever.

'God, it could never be as bad as that. I should plead diminished responsibility, if I were you, Ted,' John said, looking to Alan for support.

'Why me? What about you two?' I said, feeling that they were having too much of the fun.

'You'll get away with it,Ted. Uncle will vouch for you being an idiot. He thinks you're a sex maniac as well,' John said, sitting there smiling as if it were all settled for me to take the blame.

'That's not fair. I fell over teaching Fokki the whisk. He should have knocked,' I replied, determined to put up some defence.

'Whatever you were teaching her, Uncle thinks that you should not have been doing it on the floor,' John said, showing no sympathy for my bad luck.

'You don't want to end up in an asylum, Ted. Couldn't you go to prison, where you could study? There's a good one near Battersea. I could keep in touch and bring you the course work each week,' Alan suggested. They were full of bright ideas for my future.

'That's right. Wormwood Scrubs isn't all that far from Battersea. You could easily call in and see Ted once a month,' John added, warming to the idea.

'Shut up both of you. We ought to be thinking of someone else to blame, not me,' I said, feeling a joke was a joke, but I ought to have some of the fun.

'That's a good idea, Ted. How about Holy Bliss, the one who crosses himself every time the siren goes?' John suggested.

'I'm serious. I didn't know it was going to go like this. What are we going to do?' I asked, trying not to laugh.

'Nothing, we are all innocent, except you, and we'll only give you away if they make it worth it,' John said, still laughing.

'I think I'll go and see Susan,' Alan said at half past ten when we'd finished tea.

He was back five minutes later.

'They will be here at half past eleven. The delay was caused by the directors discussing a letter to REME from the personnel manager claiming our need for Fisher's services were greater than theirs,' Alan said, and we looked at our watches to see how long we had to wait.

'Christ! They must be desperate, no wonder we're losing the war,' John said, and as we laughed we heard the unmistakable sounds of Parson's heavy boots coming up the corridor.

'He's probably going to discuss the meeting with Uncle,' Alan suggested, hopefully.

The footsteps halted outside the door, and we kept our heads down. I didn't even hear the door open.

'How are you lads going to get out of this one?' Parsons asked in a loud voice.

I turned round, the others were pretending they hadn't heard him.

'Pardon,' I said, politely meeting his steady gaze.

'I said, how are you lads going to get out of this mess?' He repeated, slowly and clearly.

'Sorry, I don't understand. What mess?' I replied, looking as innocent as I could, and noticing that Alan was doing the same.

'You know very well what I'm talking about. I must admit I had a bloody good laugh when I heard,' he said, looking at John in quite a friendly manner.

'What on earth are you talking about?' John asked, frowning, and looking the perfect picture of 'je ne comprennais pas'.

'Oh come off it. It must be you chaps. I can't imagine

anybody else being so daft as to involve the chairman of the company in a hoax like this.'

We all shook our heads in turn, trying to outdo each other in looking completely mystified and innocent. Mr Parsons shrugged his shoulders, closed the door and went back down the corridor the way he had come.

At eleven thirty the big cars arrived, like a funeral with three hearses. We watched from the window, being careful not to be seen. Eric was helped out of FT's Rolls Royce by the chauffeur, his dark grey suit looking out of place among the dark blues, but he was obviously feeling very important.

We crouched over our desks concentrating hard to hear the first sounds of their approach.

'Eric's in the lead,' John whispered, as light bouncy steps came first, slowly being drowned by the more elephant-like plods of the other four proceeding nose to tail, the corridor narrowed by the store cupboard preventing a two by two approach.

'That's so that he can open the door for FT, before he crawls into the office with his clean white handkerchief to dust the chair for FT's bottom,' Alan said, peeping through one of the gaps in the wall charts strategically placed to give us a view from a distance wihout being seen.

'Where's Parsons?' John asked, as we heard the door close.

'He's there. He must have come up the back stairs when he saw them arrive,' Alan replied, picking up the phone which had started to ring.

'Leare speaking. Yes, they're all in Uncle's office. No, we haven't spoken to Eric, he hasn't come down to our level yet,' he said, replacing the receiver. 'That was Dooke. He was confirming that they'd arrived,' Alan said, grinning happily.

When we returned after lunch at quarter to two, the meeting was still in progress. It didn't break up until after two. Then our door opened and Parsons came in.

'You can fool them all, but you won't convince me that you're not at the bottom of this one. A marine engineer would be invaluable for collecting broken-down tanks in the desert. That's not the language of the army. Why didn't you tell Eric that they were raising a corps of desert mariners, and bringing a camel round to see if it fits him, before painting it battleship grey,' he said, shaking with laughter.

'You'd better hurry after them, or they'll eat your dinner,' John replied, as we all laughed at the picture Parsons conjured up.

'If you promise not to drop any more ton weights over my head, I won't give you away,' he said, smiling hopefully as he hurried off down the corridor after the others.

It was three o'clock before Eric had the time to come and tell us the news, and give the letter to each of us in turn to read.

'So when will you be going?' John asked him, as Eric passed the letter to me.

'They won't let me go, not with all the big contracts coming along. Uncle leans very heavily on me,' he replied with his usual modesty.

'You can't turn a chance like this down. Further promotion could be beyond Major, to Colonel, or even General,' Alan said, his eyes wide to indicate the wonderful opportunities that Eric could be missing.

'I'm being compensated. Freddie has promised to move me into 'band D' next year, to justify retaining my services. They can't do without me,' he replied, rubbing his hands and dancing from one foot to the other.

'They might insist on you taking your commission. By the sound of the news this morning Monty needs your help to keep Rommel on the run.' I suggested, knowing we couldn't lay it on too thick for Eric at the moment.

The next morning we waited anxiously for John to come back from his usual 'day after' briefing meeting with Uncle.

'Well, what's the news?' Alan asked him as soon as he sat down.

'Eric's going to be a lot worse. FT has authorised his move up in to Band D. Uncle is furious, but he doesn't suspect you, Ted. I told him it was those drawing office wallahs. They have the nerve for anything.'

'That was big of you. Did you tell him to have a word with Parsons?' I said, pleased to think that somebody else was taking the blame.

'Everybody knows it's a joke except Eric, and FT. Eric because he's a stupid big head, and FT because he never bothered to read the letter. He had a long chat with Eric to try to discover why anybody should want to employ him, and told him to take it to Pierce, the personnel manager, who knew how to deal with these matters.'

'Good for him. That's why he employs a personnel manager,' Alan suggested brightly.

'Yes, but all Pierce did was to tell Eric not to worry, he'd drop them a line, gave him the letter back, then did nothing else except laugh his bloody head off. We will now have to listen for ever to Eric telling us how he was offered a Commission in REME.'

'It serves you right for blaming me,' I said as the door opened and Eric came in for the first of many sessions.

23

The experimental and development work was done in our laboratory, and further along the corridor was a smaller lab, the users of which had a large office on the first floor. The fifteen of them were responsible for design of components for production equipment, and they had some extraordinary characters among them.

Johnny Smith and Peter Russell, the two young lab assistants of a similar age to Alan and myself, we knew quite well, but some of the seniors we tried to avoid, and others had no wish to fraternise with us.

One, who found it difficult to converse with Alan and me, was particularly friendly with John Picard, who did his best to discourage him without any success. This was Warnchester, a tall aristocratic figure with a long goatee grey beard; bald on top with an untidy pelmet of grey hair down to his dirty shirt collar. He was, he told John, often and loud enough to ensure that we would also be aware, descended from nobility. This was proven, he thought, by the ghastly coloured herring-bone patterned tweed suits which had been left to him by his Uncle, an earl, who picked them up for a song about the turn of the century and, not ever having worn them himself, for obvious reasons as far as we were concerned, left them all to his nephew.

Warnchester delighted to show us the quality of the material, which made the drainpipe style of no consequence. The earl, having been of similar thickness to Warnchester, these parameters fitted to perfection. Unfortunately, his lordship having been at least four inches shorter in the leg, resulted in the turnups resting about six inches above the ankles.

Warnchester was a bore. He lived in a district which had

many bombs scattered around, and we would have to hear details of every one that fell day, or night. The only release for us was when the siren sounded, which was why the first thing we did when he came into our office was to open all the windows to make sure that he heard it. He would immediately gallop off to the shelter, overtaking anybody who had a start on him, his long legs showing inches below his trousers, looking like beanpoles with shoes on.

To help with our morale, we workers were given badges to wear for continuing to work during air raids. The only one to wear his badge was dear old Warnchester. But he had a phenomenal brain. He never used a slide rule, and would design components by sitting back and doing the mathematics in his head, whether in the shelter or in his office.

C H Coverdale, the younger of the directors, went for a walk along the corridors after a Monday meeting and, seeing Warnchester at work, popped into his boss in the office next door.

'Are you aware that a member of your staff is asleep?' CH asked Mr Otton, who had leapt to his feet when he saw the director standing in the door way.

'No I did not,' Mr Otton replied, looking embarrassed, knowing that one or two of his staff, if they had a bad night due to air raids, would not hesitate at any time during the day to lie on the floor for a sleep, using a raincoat as a pillow, even though he had warned them repeatedly not to do it on a Monday.

'I'll show you,' CH said, leading the way.

'There you are, that's the man, the lanky fellow in the ghastly suit. He hasn't moved since I last saw him,' he said, pointing through the glass top of the door.

'That's Warnchester. He's working. He's our filter designer,' Otton replied, laughing with relief.

'He can't work like that. Tell him to work properly,' CH replied, apparently not impresses by the long figure of Warnchester leaning back on two legs of his chair at full stretch in his light brown suit, the turn-ups half way to his knee, and his eyes firmly closed.

Otton opened the door and led CH into the office. The others had noticed the high level contingent outside the door, but not Warnchester. They stood by his desk for a full minute before he fell forward on to the four legs of the chair, and wrote some numbers on his pad.

'Mr Warnchester,' Otton said, to let him know that they were there.

'Can you come back in ten minutes? If I stop now, I shall have to start all over again,' he replied, his glazed eyes staring in front of him, and closing, as he returned to the two chair leg position.

Otton lead the way out, and they didn't return. CH had had his introduction to Mr Warnchester.

Under the open window of that office, slightly apart from the rest, sat Walter Wiggins. He was responsible for transformer and toroid winding design. A kind honest young fellow in his mid twenties, he could give the minimum information required in the maximum time along with every other item of irrelevance you would never dream of, usually concerned with his passion for amending railway timetables.

On cold days the window nearest to him was always opened by his colleagues because washing was another one of his irrelevances. On warm days all the windows were opened, and a line was marked on the floor beyond which he was requested not to move.

If it could be avoided, nobody visited Wiggy. All requests for information were by memo or telephone. If a visit was imperative you posed your question with a large handkerchief held over the nose, and he was requested to phone the answer.

The resident nurse had discussed the problem repeatedly with all, including Wiggy, who was the least embarrassed, and some believed he had a secret passion for the hard-hearted harridan who was our angel of mercy, as he seemed to look forward to her visits.

I came in to the office to draw some graphs for Uncle, and noticed Johnny Smith and Peter Russell talking in the corner with Alan. I couldn't help overhearing snatches of their whispered conversation.

'Ted, you would like to help the prod lab boys, wouldn't you?' Alan called over to me.

'Depends,' I replied, cautiously, having heard Eric Fisher's name being referred to by Alan.

'Johnny has an idea to stop Wiggy boring them to death

with his railway timetables,' Alan said, holding a piece of paper in his hand.

'You go ahead, Johnny. We'll all be grateful to you,' I replied, getting to my feet. If we were going to be chatting it would be better to be where they were. I didn't want them to come over to me in full view of Uncle if he stood up.

I read the note on the piece of paper Alan handed to me:

Dear Mr Wiggins,
    I am visiting Orpington Station on Monday, and as we understand your factory is only a bus ride away, I would like to take this opportunity of inviting you to come over and discuss our new timetable before we go to print.

Your sincerely,
Norman Pomfrey

'Sounds all right,' I said, laughing at the thought of anybody thinking that they could have a discussion with Wiggy.

'We need a piece of railway notepaper.' Johnny said, taking it from me.

'How are you going to get it?' I asked, genuinely interested as to how they would go about it.

'Alan says you have a friend "George" at Cray station', Johnny said, his brown beady eyes twinkling behind his thick glasses.

'So has he,' I replied, guessing what was coming next.

'It would be better coming from you.' He knows you better than me,' Alan said, as if he was making a serious judgement.

I argued a bit longer. I wasn't too sure I liked the idea. We had been badly mauled when we had tried to bring Eric down a peg, though I couldn't see how things could go wrong this time. In the end I gave in, and three days later handed Johnny an envelope containing three sheets of Southern Railway-headed notepaper. George had been pleased to oblige. He was being called up in a few weeks' anyway.

As far as anybody worked for anybody, Wiggy worked for Warnchester.

'I can't give you time off. My responsibility for you is purely mathematical. You'll have to ask Mr Otton,' he told

Wiggy, as he read the letter we had composed.

'You'll have to make up the time,' Otton said, scrutinising the letter suspiciously.

At eleven o'clock we watched Wiggy striding importantly out of the gate towards the bus stop, laughing at the 'let down' he would feel when Mr Pomfrey failed to materialise.

At two o'clock we watched him striding back past the front offices deep in thought and looking remarkably cheerful for one who had been made to look a proper 'Charlie.'

Johnny came into the office after tea, bursting with news.

'Have you heard what happened?'

'Of course we haven't. We've been waiting for you to come and tell us,' Alan said, moving his legs off the chair so that Johnny could sit down.

'I'll bet he had the red carpet laid out for him. He didn't look as if he'd had his nose bent,' I said, feeling sure that we were in for another Eric Fisher.

'He says he met Mr Pomfrey's assistant, and spent two hours explaining all the changes he required, including stopping the fast train to Bromley and Victoria which goes through Cray Station at five forty.' Johnny said, looking far from happy with the outcome.

'Give your friend George a ring and ask him if he knows what happened,' Alan suggested, picking up the phone and handing it to me.

'OK, get me the number. I'll have a word with him,' I replied. I was as curious as the others to find out how things could have gone wrong.

We sat in silence while Alan asked the operator to connect us to Cray station.

'It's ringing,' Alan said, handing me the phone.

'Hello, George.' Ted here. 'Glad you answered.'

'I suppose you want to know what happened this morning? George said, laughing the other end.

'That's right. Our chap says he saw Mr Pomfrey's assistant.'

'He did.'

'How could he? Mr Pomfrey doesn't exist, how can he have an assistant?' I asked, as Alan and John laughed with me.

'Well, the stationmaster at Orpington thought head office

had made another blunder, so he instructed his most presentable porter to put his coat on, and to pose as Mr Pomfrey's assistant.'

'What the Hell did he want to tell such lies for? Why didn't he tell him he knew nothing about it?'

'Hang on, you haven't heard the half of it yet. When the stationmaster phoned head office, they told him they'd never heard of Mr Pomfrey, but that didn't mean he didn't exist. There had been so many staff changes that they'd have been surprised if they had. They asked the stationmaster to send in a report and they would deal with it.'

'What happens now?'

'I suppose head office will consider Mr Wiggins' proposals and write to him. You'll have to wait and see. Oh, by the way, they were going to stop the five forty here for a trial period anyway.'

'Thank you, George,' I replied, putting the phone down.

We didn't have to wait long. A week later Wiggy got a long letter from head office, he had it copied, and circulated it to every department. The five forty was known as Wiggy's wagon.

24

In 1942 there were terror raids in the daytime, and nuisance raids at night, nothing to compare with 1940, but enough to distract me from my studying, and cause excitement during the long hours we were working with very few breaks.

In July Phyllis was married and left home. In September Margaret did the same. I had several girlfriends, and went dancing some weekends, but all men of my age were away in the forces. They came home on leave every six weeks, and we would go dancing in parties. They were on a week's holiday, looking glamorous in their uniforms. I was working and studying in the one suit for which I'd sacrificed all my coupons, and only had a new tie because I borrowed a coupon from Father when he told me that he didn't need coupons because he couldn't afford to use them.

It was October. Jean and I had gone to 'The Bull' at Birchwood for the evening on our own. She had been very moody since the other two girls left home.

There were seldom more than twenty couples, even on Saturday nights, and we were sitting at the far end of the hall away from the small band.

'I'm going to join the Wrens,' Jean said, as I sat down after handing her a drink.

'I think you should wait a while. Mother is depressed enough with losing Margaret and Phyllis,' I replied, wondering why she whould want to leave home now, after waiting all these years for a bedroom of her own.

'I'm not waiting any time at all. I'm not going to be caught like Aunty Alice and find I'm expected to stay at home and look after my parents for the rest of my life,' Jean said, pulling a face at me, and looking very determined.

'They won't need looking after for years yet. I'm only

suggesting that you wait a few months,' I replied, laughing at her foolish fears.

'If I'm going I'm going now, or I won't go at all. Mother was crying last night, saying how lonely it was without the girls, and how glad she was that she had me for company. I feel sorry for her, but she can't expect me to stay at home. I want to be with young people.'

'What about me? I'll be left with only them for company if you go,' I replied. I hadn't thought of her going away. I was tying her departure to matrimony, for which she had not yet shown any mad desire.

'It's different for you. You're at classes every evening. You don't sit in the lounge night after night with Father reading his paper, smoking that filthy pipe, and coughing his heart up every ten minutes,' she said, looking at the bottom of her empty glass.

'Sometimes I wouldn't mind being called up. It would be more exciting than going to classes, and doing homework all the weekend,' I replied. I didn't mind studying. It had to be done, but I didn't expect her to think that I was enjoying it.

'You said you couldn't go, you were reserved, so you've got to stay at home. It doesn't need two of us to look after Mum and Dad.'

'I can go if I volunteer for air crew.'

'That would be stupid. At least you know you're doing something useful,' she replied, handing me her glass.

'I can tell you that at times I feel a change wouldn't be a bad thing,' I replied. I didn't want to tell her but I was coming round to thinking that it would not be long before I went. There were times when I felt exhausted and miserable, and I wasn't feeling all that cheerful now at the thought of being left alone with Mother and the old man.

We danced after I came back with the drinks, and we were both quite cheerful on the long walk home, never mentioning the subject again.

I arrived home Monday lunchtime to find Mother in tears. I thought that she had been having another row with Father over the housekeeping money.

Father took no money from any of us. He simply stopped from her housekeeping half the money we said we gave to Mother. But of course we gave Mother increases and never told him, and with Margaret and Phyllis leaving, Mother was very badly off.

'Jean's joined the Wrens,' Mother said, and blew her nose miserably on a silly little handkerchief.

'She told me she might. When did that happen?' I asked, wondering if Mother meant that she was going to join.

'She signed on last Friday, she expects to go in about six weeks,' Mother replied, dabbing her eyes.

'I suppose you can't blame her. All our friends are in the forces,' I said, surprised that Jean hadn't told me on Saturday night that she had already signed on.

'She could have waited. There's plenty of time. I told her how miserable it was now that Margaret and Phyllis are married. I don't know how I shall manage now for money,' she said, giving pathetic little sniffs.

'Has she told Dad?'

'No, they don't speak to each other. I told him. He said it was about time that one of you did something besides getting married.'

'That's a cheek. Considering Margaret and I took it in turns to do his local fire-watching, while all he did was lie in bed and shout to the warden that he was awake,' I replied. I was sure that if it hadn't been for us he could have been in serious trouble. He never did a thing if he could avoid it.

'I expect that's why Jean is going. He's hardly spoken to her since she left school over a year ago,' Mother said, giving several little sniffs.

'Come off it, Mother. He's hardly spoken to any of us. He has no interest in anything we do. I doubt if Jean notices him not talking to her. All he ever does is the football pools, reads *The Financial Times* backwards, and keeps lighting his pipe and pushing those filthy cleaners through the stem to try to make it stay alight,' I replied, laughing to try to cheer her up.

'What am I going to do? You'll have to give me more money,' she said, and cheered up when I promised I would, until we had it out with Father.

I never arrived home before half past eleven at night, and I left for work at quarter to eight every morning. An order was established in the mornings so that we didn't clash with each other in the bathroom or toilet, apart from seeing or hearing a door opening or shutting. And as I worked Saturday mornings, I never saw Jean or Father to talk to until Saturday lunchtime.

'I gather you've done it now,' I said, as I sat down at the dinner table.

'Yes, I actually signed up last Friday, but I felt unable to tell you on Saturday,' she said, with one of her gentle smiles.

'It doesn't matter, but why did you choose the Wrens?' I asked. I didn't know anybody in that service.

'I'm going to be in for some years, and I prefer to dress in black and white. I couldn't stand khaki or Airforce blue, they don't suit my natural colouring,' she said, wearily at the effort of having to explain such an obvious reason for her choice of service.

'I thought that you must have given some serious thought before making your choice,' I replied, laughing at her typical approach.

'There was. I hoped I wouldn't have to tell you,' she said laughing.

'I'm pleased to hear that. What was it?' I asked, knowing she was setting me up.

'I love the little round hat,' she replied, giggling with pleasure at the opportunity to tell me.

'War is a serious matter. You children treat it as a huge joke,' Father said, making one of his rare contributions to the mealtime repertoire.

'When are you expecting to go?' I asked Jean. I didn't want to get involved in the horrors of war. We knew how serious it was, and it didn't help to dwell on it.

'In about a month,' she said, reaching for the salt.

'I suppose I shan't receive any formal notice,' Father said, waiting for Jean to finish with the salt.

'What were you expecting? Nine months, the same as when I arrived?' Jean said, laughing and winking at me.

'I don't know how I'm going to manage for money when you go, Jean,' Mother said, keeping her head down to avoid Father's stony stare whenever money was mentioned.

'What do you mean?' I asked, knowing that was what she wanted.

'When Jean goes I shall be back to the housekeeping money I had in 1939, apart from what you give me,' Mother said, carefully preparing some food on her fork, and keeping her head down.

'Surely Dad's given you an increase since then,' Jean said, looking at Dad to reply.

'We've all given you half our cost of living bonuses every year since we started getting them, and you told us Dad was doing the same,' I said, watching Dad concentrating on his dinner.

'Every time I asked for an increase, you told me to get it from the children, didn't you Godfrey? You've never given me an increase since the children started work,' Mother said angrily.

'We'll discuss it when Jean's gone,' he said, obviously embarrassed.

He gave Mother a larger increase than she had expected, but she found out years later that he had been able to afford it for sometime, but had kept her on as little as he possibly could.

25

Alan and I failed our intermediate BSc in July, 1942, which was not surprising. We had missed the first term, and never really caught up. We decided to take correspondence courses as the course work we had done was acceptable for the external examination which we would have to take.

The correspondence course was a saving in travel, but it meant a more monastic existence, shut in my small bedroom from six o'clock, five or even six evenings a week. I became depressed, probably because I missed the company of fellow students, and the excitement and exercise of chasing after trains.

Alan took the exam in December and passed. I had decided to wait until the following July. He said that he would wait for me until September, 1943, but I wasn't feeling too confident about that.

Christmas, 1942 I spent most of my non-study time playing solo with Mum and Dad. Some of my pals were home on leave, but they had more money and time to spend than I had, and when I said goodbye to them, I was determined that I was going to join them, and to Hell with Uncle, Home Guard, studying and everything else.

I had been informed that I was reserved in my job. The only way out was to sign on for air crew. I filled in the form in the daily paper, posted it, and waited to be summoned.

The reply came in the buff-coloured envelope in less than a week, and Mother put it on my side plate for when I came down to breakfast.

'What's that letter about?' she asked, watching me reading it.

'It's inviting me for a medical and an interview for the RAF,' I replied, feeling a twinge of guilt for not having

165

mentioned it to her before.

'You told me that your job was reserved and you couldn't join up even if you wanted to,' she said, her brown eyes looking accusingly at me.

'That's true, but I volunteered for air crew,' I replied, wishing she wouldn't look at me in that pitiful way.

'You could at least have waited until you finished your exams,' she said, starting to sniff.

'The rate I'm passing exams, I'll be too old and feeble to climb into a plane,' I replied, starting to eat my breakfast before it was cold.

'It's Jean's fault. I told her that if she went, you would be fed up and do something silly,' Mother said, before hurrying to the kitchen as we heard Father coming down the stairs.

I cycled to work feeling as if the world had been lifted off my shoulders; in another few weeks I would be finished with this life and starting a new one.

'What's happened to you this morning,' Alan asked when he came into the office and heard me laughing with John and Tony Rae. Recently I had been going straight into the lab and working on a frequency converter I was developing for Uncle.

'He's having a day off on Friday,' John replied, before I could answer.

'I wondered why you looked so cheerful. Getting married or something?' Alan asked, as he took some papers out of his drawer.

'It's not as bad as that, he's volunteered for air crew.' Tony replied, laughing at the look of horror on Alan's face.

'You've done what?' Alan asked, looking at me with his mouth open.

'I've volunteered. I'm not the first one, some others have done it before me.'

'If you think you'll enjoy being an air-gunner. . . .'

'I'm not going to be an air-gunner, I'm going to be a pilot.'
'I should never have let you out of my sight, once you're in you'll be an air-gunner. Why didn't you tell me what you were up to?'

'What the bloody hell has it got to do with you?' I replied. I didn't care what he said, I was going to be a pilot.

I felt strangely happy those next few days. Alan hardly

spoke to me, and I felt sorry for him. I was sure that if he hadn't a widowed mother to look after he would have done the same. I waited until Thursday before telling Uncle.

'I'm going for a medical for air crew on Friday, so I won't be able to come in,' I said, making sure that I didn't ask his permission.

'It would make more sense if you stayed here. It takes six months to train an air-gunner. We've spent three years training you, and we were hoping to get something useful out of you in a few more months,' he said, looking thoroughly disgusted, as if I was taking a day off out of sheer cussedness.

'I'm hoping to be a pilot,' I replied, wishing that I'd never bothered to ask him for the time off.

'You a pilot? They'll be taking a chance having you at the rear with a loaded gun,' he said, standing up as he spoke, and turning his back on me.

I didn't care a damn for Uncle anymore. I was feeling great travelling on the train to London, and when the overweight civilian clerk called 'Next one', I went over to him and cheerfully sat in the chair.

'Date of birth?' he asked, when he'd checked my name and initials.

'20th of December, 1921,' I replied, confidently.

'Oh dear,' he said with a deep sigh, 'twenty-one years of age. You don't look more than eighteen. You kids are all so keen to get yourselves killed. Have you brought your birth certificate with you?'

I handed him my certificate, which he glanced at before initialling the card and handing it back to me.

'Room ninety-four. Next one,' he called, sounding as cheerful as an undertaker.

I spent the whole morning being tested, from my eyes to my feet, and a lot more in between. There were morse aptitude, elementary arithmetic, and some intelligence tests, which must have meant something to someone, but from the many groans only a very few.

In the afternoon we stood in a large room, waiting for I had no idea what. My name was called, and I pushed through the crowd to the voice. It belonged to a very smart sergeant.

'Follow me,' he said, turning sharply on his heel, and marching stiffly along a highly polished corridor to a large door on which he knocked loudly, before pushing it open. After two precise paces into the room, he sprung to attention.

'Mr Trigsby, sir,' he shouted in a loud voice, to three RAF officers sitting only a few feet away at a huge desk under a larger than life-size painting of King George VI.

I assumed that they must be deaf! They gave no more indication of having heard him than his Majesty the King looking down on us from his picture on the wall.

In front of the desk was a small straight-backed wooden chair, which the chairman pointed to as I stood hesitating in the doorway, not feeling too confident that I was going to enjoy the party.

When I had been sitting uncomfortably for some moments, aware of the silence after the sergeant had withdrawn and quietly closed the door, the chairman spoke.

'You are Edward Trigsby,' he said in a voice, that I would not have dared to argue with if he'd told me that I was Jesus Christ.

I nodded, and he continued.

'Why do you want to join the Royal Air Force?'

'I would like to be a pilot,' I replied, looking him straight in the eye.

The expression on his face seemed to indicate that this might not be the right answer.

'Have you no desire to destroy the enemies of our King and Country?' he asked, pen poised to mark a form he had in front of him.

'Yes, and to do that I would like to be a pilot,' I replied glancing at the other two members, one of whom appeared to be suffering some discomfort. He had his handkerchief over his mouth.

'War is not a picnic, Mr Trigsby. You don't choose the part you want to play. You volunteer to take any part you may be ordered to. Without question. You understand?' he asked, his chin pointing aggressively in my direction.

'You asked me why I wanted to join, and my reason is that I want to be a pilot,' I insisted, not liking his manner, and determined that I would not settle for less.

'Squadron Leader Murray,' he said, staring straight in front of him.

I turned and looked at the one who was fidgeting.

'Are you an only child, Mr Trigsy?' he asked in a patronising manner as if I was a kid of fifteen.

'No, I've three sisters,' I replied tersely, feeling annoyed at his attitude.

'Ah, you are an only son,' he said, smiling as if he'd made a wise deduction, and I noticed the chairman nodding his approval at this display of wisdom.

'Of course, but why should that prevent me from being a pilot,' I replied, indignantly.

'Thank you, Mr Trigsby, that will be all,' the chairman said wearily, sitting back and folding his arms.

I left, wondering what I was to do now. How could I go home and tell Uncle they didn't want me? I entered the crowded room again, and sat on a chair, thinking of what a mess I'd made. I must have been mad. Obviously I should have agreed to do anything, and rely on things turning out all right afterwards.

A few minutes later a sergeant with a clipboard spotted me, and came over.

'I've been looking for you,' he said, smiling in a friendly fashion. 'You realise that you've failed your selection board?'

I nodded. There wasn't much I could say.

'Don't be downhearted about it, you'll get another chance. Sign here and you can go straight into the Air Sea Rescue. That's a really exciting life,' he said, handing me the pen and putting his finger on the spot.

I took the pen and was about to sign when I glanced across the room, and saw a young fellow shaking his head furiously at me. I hesitated a moment, then handed the Sergeant back his pen, and walked towards the door, until I reached the young fellow.

'Were you shaking your head at me?' I asked him.

'No mate! I was just telling myself what a bloody fool I am. I've just signed up for pilot, navigator and air-gunner, the lot. There's only one job I'll get and that's bloody air-gunner, and that's what I deserve. I'm a bloody idiot.'

Travelling home I wondered what sort of reception I would receive from my colleagues at work. The only bright spot was that mother would be pleased.

'What happened?' John asked, as I sat down at my desk on Monday morning.

'They turned me down,' I replied, now feeling quite relaxed about the whole business.

'Alan was bloody annoyed with you. He said that you were running away from Uncle in a blind panic,' he replied, smiling cheerfully.

'I was running away from something. It wasn't only Uncle. I'm not that scared of him,' I said, and I could have added that if I had been I wasn't anymore.

'You shouldn't have done it. Uncle was surprised. He said he thought that even you had more sense, and he'd miss you. Mind you, I believe he was looking forward to it,' John said, laughing as Alan came in.

'Hello, I thought you would be over Berlin by now,' Alan said, grimly staring at me as he sat on the desk, dangling his long legs, his hands tucked under his knees.

'Ted's staying. The selection board didn't like the way he interviewed them,' John said, getting to his feet as Uncle tapped on the window for him.

'I was a fool to worry about you, but I didn't think you'd get yourself out of this one,' Alan said, laughing and beating a tattoo with his heels on the front of the desk as John came back and shut the door.

'Uncle only wanted to know how you got on, Ted. When I told him, he sighed and said, 'I didn't think it would be that easy. Perhaps he'll settle down now, and get on with some work.'

We all laughed, but I knew now that I must be patient. The next time I told Uncle I was leaving, there would be no turning back.

26

It was towards the end of February, 1943 and the boys were home on leave again. The first thing they did was to ring me, and ask who was home, and what we were going to do Saturday night. I gave them the usual reply, 'Meet at the station at half past six: on the platform if you don't want to pay for the girls' ticket,'

One of the group not in the forces was Peter, a good-looking nineteen year old training to be a farm manager, whose brother had been killed flying with the RAF just before Christmas.

He passed the factory every Friday afternoon sitting on a pile of manure, and I would make signs from the lab window indicating everything that was organised, and how many were coming, finally ending up with miming a bath.

There weren't many girls at 'The Daylight Inn' whom he didn't know, and this evening I noticed one I had not seen before.

'Who's the little dark-haired girl opposite?' I asked him, at the first opportunity.

'Never seen her before, have you?' he replied, standing up to observe her more critically.

'No, but I wouldn't mind getting to know her. She looks rather nice,' I replied, noticing that the seats were empty on each side of her.

'I'd be careful if I were you. She came in with a Red Beret who's coming through the door now,' Peter said, as he sat down.

I found myself looking at a large khaki figure, marching up the centre of the dance floor, the noise of his boots thudding a second warning to me across the hall. After having a few words with the girl, he turned and marched away again and the band began to play.

'Would you like to dance?' I asked her, a few seconds later having decided that she was worth the risk.

'Thank you,' she replied, after hesitating a few moments.

I managed two circuits, which didn't take long at my dancing speed, but time enough to gain a little information before the big fellow came back with the drinks.

As I steered Annette, towards him, I was sure I recognised him.

'Hello, Steve. I was looking after your partner for you,' I said. I was right. He was a small boy of about fifteen when I last saw him at school three years ago.

'You don't need to bother, I'm looking after her,' he said curtly, handing her a drink and turning his back on me.

I returned to our party, and invited Betty, the girl I had come with, to dance.

'Who's that little girl you were dancing with?' she asked me, as soon as we were under way.

'That's Annette, she's a nurse at Orpington Hospital,' I replied, as if I'd known her for years.

'She's a bit small for a nurse. Are you sure she's not a ward maid?' Betty asked me with a giggle.

I took her through a whisk and then a reverse turn, and she apologised.

'Be careful, Ted,' she said, more seriously as we stopped at our seats.

'What do you mean?' I asked. I was fond of Betty. We had some very good times over the years, and I thought that she would have liked me to take her more seriously.

'I mean that your new girlfriend is with a soldier who had a fight with somebody a lot bigger than you last week. Keep away from her tonight,' she said, laughing, but seeming worried in case I should do something silly.

'Don't worry. I'll see that I get you home safely tonight,' I replied. I was not intending getting into any sort of fracas over a girl.

But a chance came in the Paul Jones, when I found myself somewhere near opposite, and made a dive. I had a promise from her that she would meet me at the station at seven next Saturday, when a violent blow on my shoulder spun me round.

'You'll keep away from my partner if you know what's good for you,' Steve growled, in a most agressive manner.

'Certainly, I only danced with her because we met in the Paul Jones,' I replied, leaving Annette, and retreating rapidly towards our seats where Betty was sitting, shaking her head at me.

The next week dragged at work, and on Friday afternoon, when Peter went by on his load, I gestured to him that only six of us were going to 'The Daylight Inn' on Saturday night, and I didn't bother about the bath.

Saturday evening at the station we were one girl short, and time was running out for catching the usual train.

'It's not like Betty to be late,' Peter said, as we waited for the third girl to arrive.

'It's not Betty, I'm taking Annette tonight,' I replied, feeling anxious.

'Who's Annette?'

'That little dark-haired girl I pointed out to you last week,' I replied, peering at the late-comers hurrying up the hill.

'You're mad! He'll kill you. You said you had a bruise after he tapped you on the shoulder last week.'

'Doesn't look as if she's coming anyway,' I replied, as the clock showed two minutes to seven.

'What are you going to do?'

'I'll wait in case she's late, and come on my own if she doesn't turn up,' I replied, feeling very let down.

'Come on, forget her, She wouldn't be late on her first date if she were coming,' Peter said, moving towards the barrier.

I was disappointed. I had never been stood up before, and although I was annoyed, I found myself looking for her everytime we went to the Daylight Inn.

Some months later, I'd decided to go back on the bus, after lunch, and as I waited at the stop, I heard a bicycle bell behind me. Before I could turn round somebody tapped me on the shoulder.

It was Annette, smiling as she said a cheerful 'Hello'.

'I never expected to see you again,' I replied, trying not to appear pleased at meeting her.

'I'm on nights, I only get every third Saturday off,' she said, leaning on her bicycle as she spoke.

'You didn't turn up when we had a date,' I said, hoping that she had a good excuse.

'That must have been the time I overslept. It's not the first time. I get two days off, and I sometimes sleep right through them,' she said, looking sorry, but I felt that she should apologise.

'Would it be any different if we made another date?' I asked, as the bus arrived, and I ignored it.

'I would like to try,' she replied, looking sincerely at me with her lovely blue eyes.

'How about this Saturday?' I asked eagerly.

'I don't have a Saturday for another three weeks.'

'Three weeks! You'll be bound to forget by then,' I replied, feeling that it was hardly worth meeting her if I couldn't see her.

'Why not a week day?'

'I go to classes all week, the only night I have off is Saturday,' I said feeling that we were wasting our time.

'I might be able to change and have this Saturday off. How could I let you know?'

'That's easy. I'm on the phone,' I replied, feeling for a pencil and a piece of paper.

'When should I ring?' she asked, not looking happy with my suggestion.

'Ring this number any time. Mother will take a message. She'll be at home,' I replied, handing her half an envelope.

'I don't want to ring your Mother. She doesn't know me.'

'I'll warn her that you will be ringing, she won't bite you over the telephone.'

'I'll only ring if I can't come.'

'Good. I must go,' I replied as the next bus stopped just behind us. I didn't want to be too late, Uncle had said that he would see me after lunch.

It was Thursday. Mother was going to the aunts, and the meal was all ready for me. She'd had hers, and would be off in a few minutes to catch her train.

'A girl phoned this morning, and asked for you. I told her you were at work,' Mother said, as she sipped her cup of tea.

'Did she leave a message?' I asked, remembering that I had forgotten to warn her Annette might ring.

'No. When I said you were at work she rang off. She wasn't one of your usual girl friends or I would have recognised her voice,' Mother said, and I could see she was very keen to know who it was.

'It must have been Annette. I met her at a dance a few weeks ago. She said she might ring. I'm surprised she didn't leave a message,' I replied, feeling worried. Annette had said that she would only ring if she couldn't come on Saturday.

'She had an Irish accent. I hope she's not a Catholic,' Mother said, gathering up her things before dashing out of the door.

I had noticed that Annette had an accent, but I had never given a thought to where she came from, but of course Mother would. She was opposed to Catholics, possibly because Father was always threatening to become one.

I went to the station on Saturday evening, hoping that she would turn up, but equally resigned to the possibility that she might not. I kept out of sight when I saw Peter coming with some of the others, and then started to walk down the hill towards the hospital. I didn't want it to be known if I was stood up twice by the same girl.

I was on the point of turning back when Annette came into sight, hurrying up the hill towards me.

'I'm sorry I'm late. I overslept,' she said, panting for breath.

'It doesn't matter. We can catch the next train,' I replied, not having told them that I was going. I thought it might be better if we met them at 'The Daylight Inn'.

We slowed down and easily missed the train, and when we arrived at 'The Daylight Inn', I bought the tickets and went straight into the bar, which was nearly empty.

'I'll hand my coat in,' Annette said as I went to get the drinks, and soon after she'd gone Peter came in with the others.

'Hello, Ted. We didn't know you were here,' he said, coming across as soon as he saw me.

'I came with Annette,' I replied, knowing Peter hadn't met her.

'Where is she?' he asked, looking at the empty chair beside me.

'We came straight into the bar. She's gone to hand her coat in,' I replied, noticing her coming through the door as I spoke.

'Hello Annette. We know each other don't we,' Peter said,

warmly shaking her hand.

'Yes, we have met,' Annette replied, smiling at him as she struggled to pull her hand away.

I didn't ask them when, but I felt furious. Peter seemed to know every girl, and I had hoped Annette was different.

I enjoyed the evening, and was waiting with Peter for the girls to collect their coats.

'How did you come to meet Annette?' he asked, as we were waiting by the door.

'I met her here some time ago,' I replied casually.

'You're welcome to her. She's a miserable little bitch.'

'She seems all right to me,' I replied cautiously, wondering how much he knew about her.

'I met her on the station a few weeks ago. George and I walked her and a friend all the way to the hospital, and she wouldn't even let me kiss her good night.'

'I don't blame her for that,' I replied, laughing to think that at last someone had been able to resist Casanova Pete.

'I hope you like walking because you won't get much out of her, I can tell you,' he said, as the girls appeared and we moved to meet them.

I liked Peter, he was a good friend in many ways, and he certainly did me a good turn that night.

'When shall I see you again? I asked Annette, as we were nearing the hospital.

'Never,' she said, letting go of my hand.

'I can't wait that long,' I replied, not believing for a moment that she could be serious.

'It's too difficult. You can only make weekends, and I only have time off in the week.'

'I could have time off in the week. I'm studying at home, and can make up for it by working Saturday evenings. You say any night except Thursdays, when I'm at Home Guard, and I'll meet you.'

'No, it would be better if we didn't.'

'Why? What harm will it do if we go for a walk in the evening, for an hour?' I replied, catching her hand and stopping her under the large tree near the tunnel.

'All right, Tuesday night at eight o'clock, but I have to be in the home before ten, or I shall be up in front of matron,' she said, squeezing my hand hard to make sure that I understood she was serious.

We walked in silence to the hospital. I had plenty of questions, but I felt that she would tell me the answers in her own time.

For three Tuesdays we met from eight until ten, and on the third evening we were sitting on the Red Cross seat under a tree near the hospital, as we had on the previous occasions, when she told me that she was not on duty, and would see me the following Sunday afternoon.

'Good, you can come home for tea,' I said, pleased to be able to introduce her to Mother.

'I don't want to meet your parents,' she said angrily, as if I'd taken a liberty.

'Why not? We can have tea, and go for a walk afterwards. Mother meets all our friends. They call and see her when they come home on leave from the forces,' I replied, wondering what possible reason she could have for not wishing to meet her.

'You really don't understand, do you?'

'No, I don't. You don't even like meeting Peter and my other friends. What's wrong with them?'

'Nothing's wrong with them, but every time we meet the girls have different dresses or skirts. I have only one dress, and I only have two blouses, because I swop with the girl I share a room with,' she said angrily.

'Everybody's the same with clothes' rationing. You're not expected to have masses of clothes. Anyway, it doesn't worry me. Why should it worry you?'

'Your friends and parents are well-off, you live in fine houses with gardens, and telephones. My parents haven't even got running water or electricity.'

'It doesn't matter. Your parents are miles away, you don't have to tell anybody if you don't want to. I don't care where you come from, I'm only glad you came.'

'That's fine then. You can't meet my parents, so I don't have to meet yours.'

'You know very well that you will have to meet my parents eventually. Why not now?'

'What are you talking about?'

I caught hold of her arms, and pulled her towards me. She didn't resist and I kissed her gently.

'We've hardly known each other a month. Can't I wait a little longer?' she asked, clinging to me.

'No, it's got to be this Sunday. I promise you that Mother will be friendly, and Father won't say a word. He only grunts.'

'I'm terrified, but I'll come if you want me to,' she said, turning her head back for me to kiss her again.

The village hall clock began to strike ten, and she leapt to her feet.

'Quickly, you'll have to help me over the wall. If I'm caught out after ten, I won't get another pass for months,' she said, and we hurried along the well-worn path to where the wall had been climbed so often. I waited until the rustling of the bushes ceased, and turned for the long walk home. It was a lovely evening, and I was pleased that Annette was going to meet Mother.

27

It was four o'clock on the Thursday in September, 1943 after a particularly long board meeting the previous Monday. Uncle knocked on the window; he preferred the knock to the telephone, to warn that he was keeping an eye on us. He usually pointed to John, and one of us would point to anybody but John, and Uncle would patiently shake his head until we got it right.

This time, as I looked up he pointed to me. I desperately pointed to John, and he slowly shook his head, and pointed at me and then at Alan.

'We're wanted, Alan,' I said, as Uncle turned away and went back to his desk.

'He can't want both of us,' Alan replied, making no effort to get up.

'He does. He pointed his fat finger at you and nodded.' I said, waiting at the door for him to come.

'You must have been mistaken. You go and if he does, try knocking on the window,' he said, laughing and refusing to believe me.

'Where's Mr Leare?' Uncle asked as soon as I entered his office.

I walked over to the window, and knocked on it, pointing, I hoped like Uncle, and then slowly nodding my head. A loud guffaw came back at me through the glass. Uncle looked sternly at me.

I sat in the chair he pointed to, wondering if I was doing the right thing. He always had me standing on the mat in his office. Alan came in and sat beside me, and Uncle studied us in silence for several moments, giving me time to have an apprehensive flash back over the past week.

'The first two-off production, six channel racks for the

Army contract will be coming into the laboratory first thing Monday morning. I want you to see them through their inspection and test procedures,' he said, looking over our heads at the wall opposite.

'This Monday?' Alan asked, with an incredulous expression on his face.

'Yes, this Monday. Put the work you're doing aside, and clear the benches to take them. You should finish them in two weeks. The production rate will then be four or five a month to complete in about a year,' he said, pausing to look at some notes on his pad.

I looked at Alan, and he shrugged his shoulders. We'd tested equipment of this type before, but not on this scale. Two of us could never meet a target like this.

'The follow-on production testing will be done by the army under your supervision as part of the training for them as maintenance staff. Mr Picard will provide any technical help you require,' he said, putting his pencil down, and turning his back on us as he stood up, and stared out of the window.

Friday we cleared the lab of all the jobs we were at present working on, and Monday morning we sat in the office waiting for something to happen.

'What time are they due to arrive?' I asked John, as we finished our tea. He should know. He was supposed to be in charge.

'I can't answer that. It's not a technical question,' he replied, appearing to be more amused than concerned about us sitting there doing nothing.

The door opened and Eric Fisher came in.

'Where are the racks we were supposed to be working on first thing this morning?' Alan asked him before he could start gabbling about something else.

'Haven't you got them yet?' he replied, looking surprised at the question.

'We wouldn't be sitting here if we had. Could you find out what's happened, or at least get some circuit diagrams for us to look at,' Alan said, as Fisher began to move towards the door.

'I'll be back,' he said, hurrying out of the office.

'He's been a good lad since they moved him into band 'D', but you have to be firm with him,' Alan said, laughing as he went over to close the door.

'He's probably had the bloody things in his office for a week and didn't know what to do with them,' I replied, knowing Eric only too well.

There was a bang on the door, which Alan leapt to his feet to open, and Eric staggered into the office carrying two large brown paper parcels, which he dropped on to my desk.

'I think these must be the schematics. They came last week, I didn't know who wanted them,' he said, panting from the effort of carrying them.

In those days there were no detailed buzzing instructions, the tester had to follow the circuit diagrams and decide whether it should be connected and give a buzz, or it should be open circuit and remain silent. A buzz, when there shouldn't be one, was important. It meant a short circuit which could burn out a unit when the power was connected.

After the Monday meeting in Uncle's office, John was told that the first two units would be a week late, so we were to resurrect our previous jobs for a few weeks. It wasn't easy for us to find them. We had not expected to want them again for another year. Research and development staff with no experience of production, we had always been told that only R & D was late.

One rack only arrived the next Monday, with many wiring faults, which we had to have a trained girl to correct. We could solder, but it was more suited to the plumber, although the chief engineer once asked when I had worked on a unit, 'Who's the butcher responsible for these joints?'

The second rack arrived two weeks later, and it took us four weeks to clear both of them. By then the first ten soldiers should have arrived, along with five more racks, but nothing like that happened.

The army wanted two more weeks to train the first ten men, to make sure that they would be up to the job, and two more racks arrived, two weeks late.

This suited us, in having something for the soldiers, but it was hardly likely to give them much experience for future maintenance.

The REME boys were hand-picked in a manner of speaking. In order to obtain the men as soon as possible for training without having to wait six weeks for the basic square-bashing to be done by new entrants, the army asked for volunteers from other units. Anybody with the appropriate experience was requested to apply. What happened of course was regardless of any attributes to make them suitable; those fed up where they were applied in the hope of a change, and those superiors fed up with their staff, usually because they were useless, volunteered them.

We had a new group of ten men every six weeks for about a year. The first thing we did was to introduce ourselves, and after a short talk on what they would have to do, we had a chat with each one in turn to find out those who might need the most assistance. We seldom got it right. Those with absolutely no experience or training, and often no schooling after fourteen years, were often as good, and sometimes a lot better, than those who appeared to be well-trained and qualified for the work.

The first morning Eric introduced himself to them after tea break as Uncle's right hand man, and showed each his letter to prove that he could have been their commanding officer. After that we warned them that he was a nut-case, and that they must not comment on the letter, as he could become violent.

Tiger Tomkins was a BSc from Manchester, and one of those volunteered by his unit. He believed that he should be an officer, and his fellow rankers agreed that he had insufficient intelligence to be given very careful consideration.

He sought more guidance than the others, mainly to impress us with his technical knowledge, and would wait on matters of detail which the others would have taken in their stride, or got on with something else until we could give them a ruling.

He was called Tiger, because he was exceedingly volatile, and conscious of his good—looks, and, as his colleagues put it, of his own pissing importance.

We used crocodile clip leads to connect test equipment to the units, and between tests we clipped them on lines strung between the racks. If Tiger was working near some of them, they clipped them on to the bottom of his battledress and, as he didn't notice, most times it didn't matter.

If we were sure that a unit was faulty, we could take it down to the unit test shop, and have it tested to the specification by the pretty girl operator. We soon discovered that certain units were being removed as a matter of course, and we had to insist that no unit should be removed until one of us had checked it.

One time when Tiger went to see one of the girls, she asked him why he wore a tail. He didn't understand until she showed him that he had two crocodile leads dangling from his jacket.

He came into the lab red faced and furious.

'See what some stupid idiot put on my jacket,' he said, holding them out to me.

'Thanks, I need some of those,' Chase, a little soldier in his mid–thirties, said, taking them from him.

'I felt an absolute idiot. How can I receive the respect I should from factory girls when my colleagues behave like morons?' he said, obviously smarting from his loss of dignity.

'Did you get the unit tested? I asked him, not being very concerned with his dignity.

'I left it with her, I was too embarrassed to wait after finding those leads dangling from my jacket.'

'You'd better go back. We have to stay late tonight, to clear your rack,' I said, feeling annoyed at the delay.

'I'll go back right away,' he said, dashing off with the tail of crocodile clips that Chase had clipped on his jacket while we were talking.

He returned in a violent frame of mind, and I was worried. There might be blood shed on our polished lab floor, but it was soon apparent that the big fellows each side of little Chase were there for a purpose, and Tomkins jumped to this conclusion.

Muttering threats, he went to the rack he was working on and connected the new unit in the circuit, as I watched him go to push the plug in the socket, I remembered seeing Chase wrapping fuse wire round the pins. There was a blinding flash and a loud bang as the fuses on his plug box blew. He leapt backwards, cursing above the howls of laughter from his colleagues.

We were supposed to set an end of course test for each batch of soldiers. We discussed this with them, knowing that the treatment of the first batch would set a precedent. The majority favoured our proposal to draw the names out of one hat, and marks all above the pass line from another, and with a very small spread, only Dame Fortune would determine the top and bottom.

'You can't do that. Our army careers may depend on it,' Tomkins said, believing that he would come out top.

'Shut up, Tiger. If you can't see that your career has reached its ceiling, we can,' Chase commented in his high-pitched little voice.

'We have taken a democratic vote and you are a minority of one,' John said, writing the names as he spoke.

'I shall report this to my officer,' Tomkins replied sulkily.

The fates were on our side, Tiger drew the top mark and we never heard another word from him.

The main problems with the groups of ten were the lack of equipment delivered for test. The army insisted that they had to come on the agreed dates, and in the worst case they only had three units which arrived a few days before they left. We gave them talks about possible faults and went through all the circuit diagrams, but it meant that they would have to learn on the job, and fortunately we discovered that most of them were intelligent enough to do this.

Breaks from circuit diagrams were essential for sanity. To pass the time, those who wished would give short talks followed by discussions. We found that the quality of the talks, ranging from horticulture to astrology, from these scruffy characters in khaki were excellent.

In one group was a concert pianist who was keen to expound on music and Communism. He gave a recital one lunch hour in the canteen on an old piano, which was enjoyed by the audience packing the canteen.

Alan was not impressed with his talents when applied to testing the equipment, and warned me to keep an eye on him, and explain again the need to buzz thoroughly to the circuit diagram before switching on.

'Call Alan or myself before you plug in,' I told him, and left him to carry on.

It took about two days to buzz through, and I called on him the next morning. He was standing with his back to the bench lighting a huge pipe, which normally started with a large cloud of smoke and fortunately died after a few minutes.

'How's it going, Charles?' I asked, keeping my distance until the smoke cleared.

'I finished half an hour ago,' he replied, in between a suck.

'You can't have finished yet. It takes at least two days to buzz through,' I said, feeling glad that I'd come in time to stop him doing anything stupid.

'I have, I've just switched on,' he replied, staring out of the window.

I leapt at the power panel and wrenched out the plug. We didn't have expensive switches on power boxes in a laboratory. I had noticed that the smoke wasn't all coming from his pipe. Most of it came from the rack behind him.

It was clear that when I spoke to him he had not understood anything we had been telling him, nor did he care. If he couldn't get a tune out of it he didn't want to know.

They were all interesting characters, and despite nearly a year's break from more technically interesting work, the time they were with us passed quickly, and we were sorry to see them go.

28

'Jean's coming home this weekend. Will you be taking her out on Saturday night?' Mother asked, as she put my dinner in front of me.

'Yes, I expect we'll go to "The Daylight Inn".' I replied, having already heard from several of the others who had arranged to have leave at the same time.

'I'm so glad, I thought that you might be taking that little dark-haired girl who came to tea.'

'You mean Annette?' I replied, aware that Mother had not mentioned her name since she came to tea.

'That's right, I couldn't remember her name,' Mother said, reaching for the salt.

'She has very few Saturdays off, that's why I work most Saturdays now, and see her on Tuesday evenings.'

'I didn't know you were seeing her Tuesdays. I thought you went to the club for a walk and some fresh air,' Mother said, pausing as she was about to pour out some water.

'I used to, but since I met Annette, I've been going for a walk with her for an hour.'

'I would not like you to be serious with her. You know she's a Catholic?' Mother replied, frowning at me.

'Of course I do. It doesn't bother me what she is,' I replied, irritated at her remark.

She said nothing and went out to the kitchen.

'Mixed marriages never work. They only cause unhappiness,' she said, as she came back with a cup of tea for me.

'Mother, I've only known her a few months,' I replied. I certainly wouldn't have dreamed of telling her that we thought of marriage after such a short time, whoever the girl was.

'You will be very foolish not to listen to advice. It's for life

186

when you get married,' she said, looking sad. She knew what she was talking about.

'I'm grateful for advice, but you and Dad are the same religion, and I would not call your marriage a great success,' I replied, laughing as she smiled, and passed me the sugar.

'It was the War that ruined your father. He was all right until he went to the War,' she said, having told me many times before.

'Nonsense, you have told us your mother begged you not to marry him. He was your boss, and you went out of your mind with the glamour of it all.'

'That isn't true. I was in love with him, that was why I married him. He was different when he came home after the War.'

'You married him to save him being called up, and when they changed the rules to only married men with children, you had Margaret, and he's never forgiven her for arriving two days late.'

'Ted! That's not true. You shouldn't say things like that. You don't know anything about it.'

'I know all about it. You've told us often enough. I am going to choose my own wife, and we won't have rows every night.'

'What about your exams? You can't get married until you've passed those,' she said, trying to take the argument away from her and Father.

'There's no law against it, but I've no intention of getting married until after the War, and I might have finished by then,' I replied. I didn't like her objecting to Annette. It would have been nicer if she hadn't, but it would make no difference.

'Ted, don't rush into things. You'll regret it later,' Mother said, looking sadly at me.

'Don't worry. I may never get married now that Annette's met Father,' I said jumping up, suddenly realising that I should have left five minutes ago.

Jean came home at one o'clock just in time for Saturday dinner, and apart from telling her to be ready by six thirty, I didn't say much to her.

'Mother tells me that you've got a new girlfriend,' she said as we were walking to the station that evening.

'I expect she was bursting to tell you. I don't think she approves,' I replied, laughing.

'She certainly doesn't. You know why?'

'I suppose it's because she's a Catholic.'

'Yes, especially as Dad approves of her, and hopes she might be able to do something with you,' she said, looking sideways at me and laughing.

'That's nice. How are things going with you?'

'Don't tell Daddy but they have offered me a commission if I take a technical course on radar.'

'Why not tell Dad? He might forgive you for leaving school. He'd love to have an officer in the family. He can't forget that he was a sergeant in the last war,' I replied, thinking her brains were coming in useful.

'I'm not telling him. I won't pass, I can't understand a word of it,' she said, shaking her head despondently.

'I'll help you. It will only be a course on magnetism and electricity to start with.'

'That's it, and I just don't understand it.'

'You must be able to, I'll go through some with you tomorrow,' I said as we arrived at the station and met the others.

It was a lovely evening dancing with Jean. She was a good dancer, and so full of life. We arrived home about midnight, and Peter and Peggy, his girlfriend, came in for a cup of tea, and a scrape of dripping on toast. There was nothing else to put on it. But it was like old times, telling each other to shush in case we woke Dad and he came down to tell us off without his teeth.

Jean went back Monday morning, and I was sorry to see her go. It would have been a lot worse if I hadn't met Annette. I tried to help Jean with the physics, but she denied understanding any of it.

I was taking my examination soon, and I had to ask Uncle for the time off. We were in the lab, and he seemed quite pleased with some results I had plotted for him, so I thought it was a good opportunity.

'I'm taking the BSc intermediate, and I will need to have three days off next week,' I said, hating asking him for anything.

'The London examinations are in July not November,' he

replied, almost accusing me of falsely asking for time off.

'I'm taking it externally,' I said, resting the soldering iron I'd been using on its stand.

'You'll never pass the external if you failed the internal,' he said, looking scornfully at me with his hands on his hips.

'I'm going to have a try,' I replied, glad that I wasn't looking to him for encouragement.

'You must think you're clever to take it externally,' he said sarcastically, as he turned and walked with his slow tread back to his office.

'Why did you bother to ask him? I didn't. I asked John to tell him I was having time off when I took the exam,' Alan said when I told him of Uncle's encouraging remarks.

'I'm not going to let him think I'm scared of him, that's why,' I replied. I hated him, and I was frightened of him, but I was not going to run away from him.

'I shouldn't ask him for a rise, if I were you,' Alan said, laughing as he sat down.

'I certainly will. If I don't ask, I definitely won't get one,' I replied, not relishing the thought.

It was difficult to get in to see Uncle. One had to hover around, and hope Eric didn't pip you from the door the other side.

I waited around, wasting most of the morning, and then decided that I'd have to try to get in first thing in the afternoon.

I was lucky. Before he had time to sit down I knocked on the door, and went in. He must have seen me but he didn't look up for what seemed like hours to me.

'I've come to ask you for an increase in my salary for the new year,' I blurted out, finding it difficult to speak calmly to him at the best of times.

'Do you think your performance over the past year justifies an increase?' he asked, looking at me with those staring blue eyes of his.

'Yes, I do. I think my money is far too low, and I think that I should have at least a pound a week more,' I said, having decided that I would be unlikely to get ten shillings, and therefore it would be proper to start at a pound.

'A pound! You certainly won't get a pound a week more. I might consider five or six shillings, not a pound,' he said, and

I was pleased that he really seemed shocked at my outrageous suggestion.

'I am working long hours, and have completed a number of difficult jobs, like the precision oscillator for Turkey and the ringing converters. They weren't glamour jobs but somebody had to do them,' I replied, warming to my case. My pound seemed to have rocked him.

'I will consider whether you merit an increase at all, and I can assure you that you will not receive a pound. Nobody gets that sort of rise.'

'I hope that when you've given it careful consideration you will conclude it is not an unreasonable request,' I replied, backing towards the door.

'All right, Trigsby, I'll consider it,' he said, getting to his feet.

'Thank you,' I replied, and hurried out of the room into the fresh air of the corridor.

I hated every second of it, but I was glad I'd told him. Alan was sure that I'd get the minimum for my cheek.

I decided that I would go in every year to seek an increase, and that if I could join something like the Civil Service, where such a humiliating annual experience was unnecessary, I would do so at the earliest opportunity.

It was when we received our pay packet, on the first Friday in the New Year, that we learned if we had been given an increase by the presence of a small slip, and everybody surreptitiously watched everybody else opening his pay packet to see who had a slip of paper, and who had not.

I opened my packet, having covinced myself that I would get nothing from Uncle, and I was pleasantly surprised to find the little piece of paper, informing me that the management was pleased to increase my salary by fifteen shillings a week.

'I've got something,' John said, breaking the silence after the rustling of papers.

'Me too,' Tony said, looking smugly pleased with himself.

'Did you get your pound, Ted?' John asked, as he put his money into his wallet.

'No, he stopped short at fifteen shillings,' I replied, laughing at the looks of disbelief on their faces.

'No! I only got ten,' Alan said, looking astonished.

'He's kidding,' Tony said, laughing and tucking his money away in his wallet.

I passed my note to Alan. I didn't care who knew, my talk with Uncle had paid off.

There was worse for me to worry about than getting a rise that Friday, which probably contributed to the bad headache that I had been nursing all day. The results of the examination I took in November were posted on the notice board outside Imperial College that morning, and postal notice would be received on Monday.

'You don't look at all well,' Mother said as I was packing up the dishes to take out to the kitchen.

'I've a rotten headache, otherwise I'm all right,' I replied, not wanting to tell her that I was worried about the examination results. She would be more upset than me if I failed again, and she'd probably blame Annette.

'Why don't you go to bed? What you need is rest. You've had no holiday since you started work over three years ago, and all that overtime, studying and Home Guard duty, you're exhausted,' she said, getting on to her usual theme.

'I told you, I'm all right,' I replied, thinking that it would be great to go to bed for a week.

I sat in my room trying to read a book, but my eyes didn't seem to want to follow the print. The only way to stop worrying about the result was to find out what it was, and then get on with whatever was necessary. If I'd failed then I'd better get ready for another try. Whatever happened, I must not give up.

'I'm going out,' I told Mother who was in the kitchen, tidying up.

'I do wish you'd have an early night. It would do you far more good,' she said, drying her hands on the towel hanging from the back door.

I felt better as soon as I was out in the cool night air, and hurrying to the station. Once in the train, I began to go over my weaknesses in the subjects I had taken, and how I would make sure that I did not fail again. By the time I was going down to the underground I was in such a mood of grim determination that failure had no fears for me. It only meant that I would show Uncle and the rest that I might be down, but I was definitely not giving up.

I wandered round the outside of the college in the blackout, until I found the notice board, which of course was in darkness and impossible to read.

How could an idiot like me ever expect to pass examinations? I didn't smoke; I had no lighter or matches, and I couldn't see in the dark. Laughing at myself almost hysterically, I walked a long way before I found a dim blue light which indicated a shop open, and bought a box of matches.

I was soon back at the notice board, fumbling to get a match out without spilling them all over the pavement.

The first match broke, and I tried another which went the same way. I presumed that there must be an art in lighting a match which smokers acquired after years of practice.

The next one lit, and as I brought it close to the board, it flickered and went out. Cursing, I took out three matches. They exploded in a blaze of light, and I had to let go as I smelt burning flesh coming from my fingers.

'Can I help you?'

I turned round, and saw two ladies standing behind me smiling. Obviously they had been watching my antics, and found them amusing. One of them was holding the lead of a King Charles spaniel, which was yawning as if it would like to get on with its walk.

'You haven't a torch, have you?' I asked hopefully.

'Of course. Mr Morrison said never to go out in the black out without a torch,' the one holding the lead said, handing one to me as she spoke.

'Thank you,' I replied, also recalling that the Home Secretary never said where one could get batteries even if one had one.

I couldn't find the paper with my number on so I handed the torch back for the kind lady to hold while I used both hands to search. I could swear that pieces of paper do a tour of my pockets, but eventually I found it in the first pocket I had looked in.

The lady shone the torch on it. After memorising the number, I took the torch from her and shone the feeble light onto the noticeboard. There were only about ten numbers under Engineering, and half way down the board my eyes came to rest. My number was up.

29

Now I had made the first positive step towards a degree, my life seemed to have direction, and my whole time was devoted to studying at every opportunity. Annette and I agreed we would marry as soon as the War finished, and were both happy to spend the little time we could have together working at my degree. She was particularly useful in converting my rough work into neat graphs and diagrams for the course work, of which there was a large amount.

The time I could devote to study at work was now reduced to coming in early, and towards the end of overtime spells, when Uncle didn't turn up.

We were allowed three days off from work a year, and as a concession we could take them all at once. It didn't really matter, one got into a rut, and came in automatically. Often we worked for weeks with little time off, finishing about four o'clock on a Sunday. I didn't mind Sunday working. We got overtime, and it was an excuse not to go to Home Guard, which seemed pointless now that it was our turn to invade. We were trained to repel the Nazi storm-troopers with pickaxe handles, not to chase them across The Channel.

The flying bombs provided some exciting times from August, 1944. The equipment being manufactured was urgently wanted by the Allies, for the battles in Europe, and we could not spend all day in the shelters. A tannoy warning system was devised, whereby the head warden went on the roof and gave a commentary on the flying bombs' progress as they flew over. If it stopped and was coming to earth he was to tell us, and everybody was expected to dive under their desks, or whatever cover was available. Some were more fortunate than others. There were the usual rumours, one being that every time Parsons heard a flying bomb, he dived

under his desk with his blonde secretary, the joke being that
there was no desk large enough for them both to get under.

All went well for the first week.

'This is Jim Mason, your Air Raid warden speaking, the
alert has gone and I am watching the flying bombs going
over, well to the East of us.'

'This is your Warden speaking there are three bombs to the
west.'

Then the second week it began again. The poor factory
girls, many with young children being looked after by
mothers, and spending sleepless nights in shelters, were
terrified of these new horrors.

'This is your head Warden speaking, the alert has been
sounded, and there is a flying bomb above the clouds. I can't
see it but there is no danger. It is to the East. Correction, it
appears to be in the West.'

Of course we could hear them if they were any where near,
and this one was coming too near for comfort.

'This is your Warden speaking. This one is going to pass
directly overhead. Do not panic. There is no danger. Its
engine is still going . I repeat, there is no danger. Its engine is
still running.'

Then of course the engine cut out, and he didn't need to
tell us. Everybody dived for cover, except of course Parsons,
a jump ahead of the rest.

There was a large lake fifty yards from the factory into
which it fell and exploded, causing no damage at all. But fifty
girls fainted, and many in the winding shops had quite severe
injuries when they dived against lumps of machinery bolted
under their benches.

After that, if we heard it coming, we listened intently and
some went under the useless cover in slow time, until it was
obviously bound for somebody else. We only had two other
cut outs, which missed, and there were no casualties apart
from those who fainted.

We were not bothered by flying bombs when we went to
classes at Battersea. They seemed to come at odd times but
not between five thirty and eleven o'clock, unless of course
we didn't hear them in the train.

Despite having started part one of the finals six months
behind Alan, I believed that I was making good progress,

especially after meeting Howard Downton. He sat next to me at the classes, and often travelled down with us to Chislehurst, where he lived with his wife and four year old son. He was about thirty−five years old, had an honours degree in civil engineering, and was taking a BSc in electrical engineering to improve his education.

One evening, I was sitting next to him in a pure mathematic lecture given by Parrydean, a Cambridge graduate known to be a genius. He had filled three boards with complex intergrands at a speed which had left me halfway down the first board, but I was aware from his comments that Howard was as usual well ahead of him.

The sweating Parrydean scribbled the last two lines at the bottom of the third board, and in his exhausted state broke the chalk as he tried to draw a line with a flourish to show that he had finished.

When he turned to the class to see if anybody was still with him, Howard was sitting back with his hand raised.

'Yes, Mr Downton. I expected you to be with me,' he said, rubbing his aching wrist and blowing chalk dust off his fingers.

'Can you go back to the first board, about half way down, please?' Howard said politely.

Parrydeen went across to the board and ran his hand down it.

'Here,' he asked turning to look at Howard.

'That's it, if you use integration by parts, you can get the answer in another three lines,' Howard said, smiling modestly.

'I'm sure you're right, Mr Downton. I'll confirm it next week,' Parrydean replied, picking up his bag and laughing with the rest of us as we all fled to catch trains and buses.

That was not a unique occasion. Many times in other subjects such as fluid mechanics and theory of structures, Howard would find simple solutions to complex problems. He seemed to understand everything as if it were simple arithmetic.

'I can't see myself ever finishing. Even when I think I've grasped something, I've forgotten the next week.' I said, on the way home one night, after a particularly intense lecture following a tiring day at work in the lab with Uncle.

'Can I help you?' Howard asked, eagerly.

I hesitated. He was too bright for me. He'd blind me with his brilliant intellect.

'If you would like to come to my place, we could go through old exam papers together. It's much easier with two of you,' he continued, and he seemed sincere in suggesting that I might actually help him.

'I'd like to, the problem is when. If I work later on Sunday, I could come Saturday afternoon,' I said, not feeling enthusiastic.

'That would be fine. Come about two o'clock. We'll work until five, and you can have tea with us,' he said, standing up as the train began to pull into the station, and handing me a card with his address on it.

'How far are you from the station?' I asked quickly as he was opening the door.

'Only five minutes; second turning up the hill on the left,' he called back, before slamming the door.

When I arrived at two o'clock on Saturday afternoon, the front door was opened by Sylvia, a cheerful blonde I judged to be some years younger than Howard.

'You must be Ted Trigsby. I'm Sylvia,' she said, taking my coat and then ushering me into the lounge.

'Where's Howard?' I asked, sinking happily into a very comfortable armchair, and hoping that he had gone for a long walk.

'He'll be down in a minute. I'll bring you a cup of tea,' she replied, hurrying out of the room.

I sat looking round the well-furnished lounge with its thick carpet, and display cabinets of china and silver. I couldn't imagine Annette and I ever enjoying this sort of luxury.

'Help yourself to sugar and biscuits,' she said, putting a tray down on the small table and handing me a cup of tea.

This is great, I thought as I selected a chocolate biscuit. Then Howard came in.

'I told you to show Ted into the dining—room, he hasn't come to sit in an armchair drinking tea and eating my biscuits,' he said, winking at me.

'He doesn't want to start work right away. He needs a rest after the journey,' she said, looking at me for support.

'No he doesn't. Come on Ted, I'll take the biscuits, you

bring your tea,' he said, leading the way, and of course I had to follow.

Howard had the table laid out with paper and pencils, and old examination papers. It looked like a board meeting for two. Once we started we didn't stop, and I found him an excellent tutor. His explanations were so clear that he made every problem seem simple, and I could not see how I was able to fail to solve it myself. But I did repeatedly, and then he made it seem so easy. The time flew by, and Sylvia came in for us to clear up, and lay the table.

We had a very good tea, and I was pleased to become acquainted with Toni, their four year old son, a very forward child. I was glad he wasn't joining us for the test papers. He might have left me behind.

We helped with the washing up, and I took my time. Howard persuaded me to stay the evening to do some more papers, and although I was sure he was teaching me a lot, I felt mentally exhausted.

We started at half past six, a break of an hour and a half, and Howard was still going flat out, when I made my apologies and ran for the ten fifteen train.

I did that for six weeks, and then Annette had a Saturday off and Howard persuaded me to bring her along as company for Sylvia.

It wasn't too bad until after tea, when I felt that I'd had enough, and would have preferred the four of us to spend the rest of the evening in the depth of the armchairs. Howard insisted that after having a break for tea of nearly two hours, the girls had seen enough of us, and we too much of them, and the time should be spent working on some more exciting problems.

'How did you get on with Sylvia?' I asked Annette as we began our walk back to the station.

'I like her, but she is very unhappy,' Annette replied, squeezing my hand hard as usual when she wanted to make a point.

'How can she be unhappy? A lovely house, a charming little four year old son, and a brilliant husband in a good job with sufficient money to keep her in semi-regal luxury,' I replied, genuinely surprised at Sylvia's ingratitude.

'She wants a husband not a textbook. He thinks of nothing

else but studying. When you leave at ten o'clock, she told me he carries on until after midnight.'

'I'm not surprised. He seems as fresh when we finish as when we start,' I replied. I envied Howard his mental stamina, even though he was not in very good shape physically. We left him behind when we ran for a train, and he usually missed it.

'You're getting like him,' Annette said, giving my hand such a squeeze that I cried out with pain.

'Don't do that, you hurt,' I protested, shaking my fingers to get the blood back.

'I meant to. I want to get through to you that you are getting like Howard,' she said, trying to grab my hand, which I was keeping out of her reach.

'I'm not. I haven't the stamina for a start, and we've agreed that while the war is on I might as well study, and you'll help me. There's not much else to do,' I replied, feeling that she was not being fair to me.

'You work night and day. You think of nothing else.'

'I have to, but I see you whenever I can. You're the one who prevents us from going dancing. You can never have a Saturday off.'

'Ted, promise me you won't become like Howard. I couldn't stand the life Sylvia has,' she said, hugging my arm, and nearly having us both on the pavement.

'Of course I won't. I promise you that when we're married I'll always be the first in bed,' I replied, and she got hold of my hand and squeezed it again, until I yelled with pain.

We had the next two weeks off from classes, and I decided that I would surprise Annette by ringing her up on Monday, and arranging to see her every evening.

'Hello, darling, I'm coming round at nine o'clock. We can have an hour together before you go on duty,' I said, eagerly awaiting her amorous response.

'Oh! Ted, I'm sorry, I can't see you tonight,' she replied sadly.

I wasn't too disappointed, another hour's study would be very useful.

'Never mind, I'll see you at nine o'clock tomorrow night,' I replied, cheerfully.

'Sorry, I can't make tomorrow either.'

I was taken aback. I didn't like to ask her why not. We agreed that the most important thing was to trust each other.

'All right, see you same time on Wednesday,' I replied, feeling a little disappointed now.

'I can't make any night this week.'

'Hell! You were the one who warned me about studying all the time, and now I'm trying to ease down you can't see me,' I replied, feeling peeved and curious as to what she was up to.

'I didn't know you would see me in the week, you never do, but it wouldn't have made any difference. There's a mission on.'

'What the Hell's a mission' I asked, having no idea what she was talking about.

'My church has a service every night, and we have to attend to obtain a very special blessing,' she replied, laughing at the other end of the phone, as if picturing the bewilderment on my face.

'All right, you win, I'll meet you at the station Saturday night at the usual time,' I said, accepting graciously that my plan to take things easier was completely wrecked, but at least she had Saturday off and we could go with the others to 'The Daylight Inn' for the dance.

'I told you, I'm going to church.'

'Not Saturday night as well!' I shouted, down the phone.

'If you want to see me you can come too,' she replied, laughing and I sensed expecting me to say no. So of course I said 'yes'.

'Good, see you at seven o'clock outside the hospital and don't be late or you'll have to stand. I must dash, darling, I'll be late for supper,' she said, cheerful as a pigeon keeping one awake in the morning.

By Thursday night I thought I needed an hour off. I rang Peter, and we went to the sports' club for a game of snooker. It was a pleasant break, and I felt it did me good, until Peter said casually as we parted,

'See you at the usual time at the station on Saturday?'

'No, I'm afraid we can't make it,' I replied, remembering that I had told him last week that Annette had the Saturday evening off and, fool that I was, I assumed that we'd be going to 'The Daylight Inn'.

'Poor Annette, I suppose her day off has been cancelled,'

he said with great sympathy.

'No, not at all, she's taking me to church,' I replied, knowing that he would like that.

'On a Saturday!' he said, his eyes and mouth wide open.

'It's the end of the mission. All those who go for a whole week get a right good blessing,' I replied, pleased to air my knowledge of these ecclesiastical matters.

'What the Hell are you going for? They surely don't have special blessings for heathens like you?' he asked, laughing and slapping me on the back.

'I'm going to hold Annette's hand while she gets blessed,' I replied, and we both laughed.

I didn't feel quite so confident when I arrived outside the hospital, and saw hundreds of people hurrying towards the church on the hill opposite. I felt conspicuously unholy, and jumped a foot when somebody came up behind me, took my arm and began hurrying me across the road. Then I realised with relief that it was Annette.

'It was good of you to offer to come,' she said, panting as we arrived at the entrance, and we paused as she dipped her fingers in the holy water and flicked it over me.

I looked anxiously round the church. It seemed very full, but Annette marched us up to the front where there were plenty of seats.

'I thought you might like to watch what goes on,' she whispered, when she got off her knees and sat beside me.

'What time does it start?' I asked her after we had been waiting twenty minutes by my watch, and I noticed much shuffling, indicating that I was not the only one impatiently waiting for something to happen.

'It was supposed to be half past seven. Something must have gone wrong,' she whispered, checking her watch again.

'What could possibly go wrong?' I asked. I had hoped that we might yet get out early enough to go to 'The Daylight Inn'.

'Shush. Say a prayer.'

'Me? What do I want to say a prayer for?'

'Pray for something to happen.'

'You try. You're better at it than I am.'

She giggled and slid to her knees. I sat trying to remember standard integrals.

Holy music started up and we listened until my watch said

eight o'clock. Then a strange silence descended on us all, followed by an awesome sighing. I turned and, looking over the bowed heads, saw a priest in resplendent yellow robes swishing along at a holy pace, reverently bowing at intervals to the altar like a high-stepping nag. I watched him climb the steps, and then gracefully rotate to look down on his flock assembled before him.

I stared fascinated as he gathered his holy thoughts to make a momentous announcement.

'Father O'Reilly,' Annette whispered to me.

'Oh, yes,' I replied, hoping that the information might one day prove useful.

'The most Reverend Monsignor Rion regrets that he is unable to be with us tonight.' He paused to allow us to recover from our disappointment. 'His car has broken down at Bromley North. The most Reverend Father O'Hare will give you a most holy blessing, and he will be with us in fifteen minutes. God willing,' the Holy Father announced, and then went to the altar, and sank to his knees.

'What's he praying for?' I whispered.

'That Father O'Hare will turn up,' she replied, digging me with her elbow.

His prayers were answered. In fifteen minutes the music stopped, a bell clanged at the back of the church, and it became very quiet. The congregation slid to their knees, except one. I leaned forward, watching the priest with a splendid hat and gown proceed slowly past me swinging the bowl of incense, and every now and then one of his followers clanged the bells. Those round me seemed to kneel lower as if it were a warning to keep one's head down.

The service went on for a long time with hymns, and readings of Latin prose. Annette passed me her Bible with a translation, but the English made no more sense to me than the Latin.

Suddenly there was a change of tempo, and I knew the blessings were about to begin as the priest stood tall, and moved away from the altar.

'There are many of you who have shown great holiness and have fulfilled the mission, attending this holy place for every night of the week, and to you shall be given the most holy of blessings.' He dipped a raffia—type crumb brush into the holy water and shook it in the direction of the kneeling congregation.

He then talked of those who had managed fewer attendances, and each received a lesser blessing, and he obviously ceased to give blessings at an attendance level of two.

'What about me?' I whispered to Annette. I thought I deserved something for missing the dance at 'The Daylight Inn'.

'Shush!' she replied, smiling in contentment with her maximum blessing.

'The good among you have been blessed, and yours shall be the kingdom of Heaven, you are believers who have accepted the word of the Lord and done his bidding. But . . .' He paused and drew himself to his full height and with his high hat he looked a formidable messenger standing looking down on us, eyes burning with passionate holiness. 'There are amongst us those who are evil; those who do not believe in the word of the Lord. Disbelievers! They will be destined to perish in the fires of Hell for ever!! A . . . men'

The congregation reverently echoed A...men, and he dipped his brush deep into the holy water, and shook it furiously in all directions, and the bells dinged out many times. Above it all I heard Annette whisper in my ear.

'That's you.'

30

Living with the flying bomb was bearable because the invasion was going well, and we were promised the launching sites would soon be overrun. A junior minister announced in September that the Battle of London was won, except for a few last shots. Those last shots continued for another seven months, and there were things to come which many of us found even worse.

These were of course the gas mains which our leaders wished us to believe were exploding all over the place. In fact most of us had friends in the RAF who had been bombing rocket sites for months, and whispering horrifying descriptions of the havoc that would be caused if they didn't. So when we heard a clap of thunder followed by the noise of an express train, and a second explosion some distance away we referred to them as flying gas mains. Then one day Mr Churchill announced in the Commons that they were rockets, as if they were not serious enough to have been worth a mention before.

At work in the factory many of us felt jumpy. Slamming of doors was unpopular, without many of us wanting to admit why.

At home Mother still relied on me to console her. I had let her down on many occasions, like identifying high flying planes as ours, and a few minutes later having to admit that the bombs that were whistling down were theirs: but there was nobody else for her to turn to.

We had had several of those loud claps like thunder followed by the roar, and Mother found them very frightening, and became even more nervous, and jumpy. This was despite the night's sleep which was now reasonably free from tension in the Morrison shelter in the dining-room in which she slept at night, and off which we ate in the day time.

'How much longer do you think those beastly things will be coming over?' she asked me one morning in March, 1945 as she stood up after tidying the bedclothes in the shelter on top of which I was eating my breakfast.

'It can't be for much longer. The sites must be nearly overrun by now,' I replied, as Father came in for breakfast.

Mother brought in the porridge, leaving Margaret, who was now living with us with her three year old son Paul, to finish getting the breakfast while she went upstairs to dry out the bathroom, Father being one of those who spurned a face flannel, preferring to throw the water from the washbasin with his hands roughy in the direction of his face and neck.

A few minutes later, after a quick look at the paper, Father began to dish out the porridge. I heard a strange noise and a cry from Mother upstairs, and watched Paul pick up a piece of wood in the shape of a cross, and put it on the plate that Father was about to take for his porridge, after handing me mine.

'Don't do that, you naughty boy,' Father said, impatiently, picking it up and looking at it, without any idea what it was. Usually Paul put his teddy-bear on the table.

'That's part of our window,' I said, looking at the hole in the wall where it had been a few moments ago.

'You have it,' Father said, handing it to me, having no idea what I was talking about, the window being behind him.

I was still puzzling how long the window had been out when the dining-room door opened and Mother came in. I jumped up and took her to the chair by the fire. Her face was white. She was shaking violently, and trying to speak through her chattering teeth.

'Ted, something has happened. The bathroom window cracked and a wind blew all round me,' she said, sobbing with fright.

'What's happened?' Margaret asked, having just come in with the toast and seen the window was missing.

'I didn't hear a thing. Mother heard something in the bathroom, but I think she's only shocked,' I replied, bending over her. She was still clinging to my arm, and shaking violently.

'It couldn't have been much. I didn't hear anything,'

Father said, continuing with his breakfast by tucking into the toast.

I disengaged Mother's fingers, and Margaret tried to comfort her, while I went upstairs to find out what other damage had been done.

There was very little to see. The bathroom window was cracked, and there was some dust on the floor. The only window missing was in the dining-room, the glass had been sucked out, and the wooden frame had blown in afterwards. The other way round would have been very much worse.

Father went off to catch his usual train to London, leaving me to find some plywood in the shed to fill the hole where the dining-room window had been.

Before I left for work, Margaret came in with the mail. Poor girl, her husband was in France and she watched for the post every day.

'The postman says a rocket fell behind the cinema. It took most of the blast, and certainly saved us, but the little girl in the cakeshop opposite was killed by flying glass, and many others were injured,' she said, as she handed Mother a letter from Jean.

'Ted, do you think there will be many more?' Mother asked, still looking shaken but with a little colour in her cheeks.

'No, of course not. The distance they're coming, you'll never get two falling in the same place. We'll never get another one as close as that,' I said, confidently, and was pleased to see her smile with relief. She still had faith in me.

It was nearly half past nine when I hurried off to catch the bus that would get me in by ten o'clock, which was very late for me.

'That rocket must have been close to you this morning. We thought you'd caught it this time,' Alan said, when I entered the office.

'It was, it fell just behind the cinema.'

'Did you have much damage?' he asked, handing me a cup of tea.

'Very little. I didn't hear a thing, but poor Mother's nerves are frayed a bit more,' I replied, hoping that she wouldn't suffer any worse effects.

We chatted as we drank our tea, and I felt that we were all

on edge. The rockets were not numerous, like the flying bombs, only three or four at the most fell within earshot in a day, but you never knew when they were coming. They just arrived out of the blue.

About eleven o'clock an air bang made us jump and we knew that it was within a few miles radius, but we had no idea where. I was sure that it would be nowhere near Mother. We waited in the office with the doors open so that we could hear the announcement on the tannoy. One couldn't hear it in the laboratory. After a few minutes it crackled into life.

'This is your Air Raid Warden speaking. A rocket has fallen at the corner of Hill Rise and Orchard Avenue. Anybody living in that vicinity is advised to go home as damage is extensive. Repeat, it fell at the corner of Hill Rise and Orchard Avenue.'

I was stunned. That was less than half the distance from the cinema.

'You'd better get home, I'll switch everything off.' Alan said, coming over and pushing me towards the door.

The drill was that squads descended on the repairable houses, and made them weather-proof, and as I came up Hill Rise I was pleased to see men on our roof.

I hurried up the path. The front door was leaning against the wall with the hinges and lock torn off. I noticed, despite most of the tiles having been lifted off the roof, that all the windows were open and none appeared to be broken. I went through the hall, opened the dining-room door and went in.

Mother was sitting in her armchair drinking tea with Margaret and Mrs Bush. I glanced round the room but not a window was broken. The only damage was from the morning. My hasty repair had gone.

'Are you all right?' I asked. They all looked so cheerful that I wondered if they knew what had happened.

'Yes, thank you,' Margaret replied smiling as she sipped her tea with Paul sitting on her lap.

'I told Mrs Bush that you said we'd never have another one anywhere near, and she said that it was a nice morning and just in case we should open all the windows,' Mother said smiling and looking very relaxed.

'I was very worried when I heard it on the tannoy. It must have been even nearer than the one this morning,' I said, amazed at Mother looking so different now.

'I'm not worried any more. Mrs Bush says you never get three in a row. They send them in pairs,' Mother said, as Mrs Bush handed me a cup of tea, and gave me a large wink.

31

The end of the War was obviously approaching, but it was difficult to see how it would make any difference to the problems that confronted us.

I wanted to leave home and get married. That required money to buy or rent a house, and there was a shortage of houses. I wanted a change of job, and there would be thousands looking for jobs when the forces were demobilised.

We were all war weary, and longing for it to end. But many had been glad to join the forces to get a break from the boredom of travelling to work by crowded trains each day. If we'd stayed at home, it had been five years of all work and no play. Would it all be better when everybody came home, and we had holidays again, and freedom to change our jobs?

'We're going to get a whole week's holiday,' Tony Rae announced one morning.

'What about the back holidays they owe us? I suppose we'll get three months when the War is finally over,' John said hopefully.

'You'll be lucky! The staff, represented by Wendy for the Association of Scientific Workers, wanted the Saturday off before, and the management said they can't afford it. So we won't be able to go away Friday night. It will have to be Saturday night, or even Monday if you plan to go to the West Country,' Tony said, sipping his tea.

'That is really mean! Can't we do anything about it?' I asked, feeling angry.

' The drawing office is having a protest meeting in the canteen, if you want to go,' Tony said, looking at me as if he was making the point that I could go if I wanted to.

'Are you going?' I asked, knowing he wasn't one to stick his neck out.

'I can't, we have an evening meal at six o'clock,' he said, in that superior manner of his.

'Tell your wife to keep it hot,' Alan, suggested, winking at me.

'I'm afraid, Ted, now that the war is nearly over, you are going to find out some of the hard facts of life,' John said, looking seriously at me.

'Come on now, be fair. The company has to adjust itself to peace time, the same as we do,' Mr Thompson said sternly.

'Surely it won't cause a major crisis if we have the Saturday morning off before a week's holiday?' I asked, wondering why John didn't reply.

'That is the wrong attitude to take. You must learn to accept the judgement of the directors of the company,' he replied, pointing his pencil at me.

'Well I think the least they can do after the hours we've worked is give us a proper full week's holiday,' I said, and nobody else said anymore until Mr Thompson left the office.

'What are you going to do?' John asked me as soon as Mr Thompson closed the door.

'I'm going to the meeting. I've never been to a gathering of workers before,' I said, seeing no reason why I shouldn't.

'Mr Thompson was trying to tell you that you shouldn't go. Have you forgotten that he gave us our first chance?' Alan asked, confirming my belief that he would not be doing any protesting. He'd changed over the years, never questioning those above him.

'I haven't forgotten, but it doesn't mean that I am forbidden to protest at injustices, if I want to,' I replied.

I had not been pleased with the way all my Socialist friends except Wendy were sacked for all manner of trivial reasons as the end of the War approached. Bill Gurre in particular had been sacked for criticising the quality of the canteen food. I had laughed at their stupid arguments, but now I was beginning to have second thoughts.

There were about forty of us at the meeting in the canteen, including Mr Bennet the chief draughtsman, who had been encouraging his staff to come along and listen to the talk by a member of the Association of Scientific Workers.

Wendy had made all the arrangements and chaired the meeting. It was a very quiet gathering.

The A.Sc.W. man told us that scientists were poorly paid and needed to be organised to demand the pay and conditions appropriate to their contribution to the wealth of the companies they worked for.

The meeting lasted an hour. It was good humoured and many spoke. When it came to the item concerning the Saturday morning off before our week's holiday, Joe Bennet said he understood our feelings and would bring them to the attention of FT, the chairman of the board of directors on Saturday morning, when he visited head office.

It was my first introduction to a meeting expressing the views of the workers, and I was sure that Mr Bennet could not fail to convince the directors of the justice of our case, bearing in mind all the points we had made.

A week later Wendy put the reply from FT on the notice board in the main hall.

> Dear Mr Wendean,
>
> As I am sure you will be aware, with the termination of hostilities the company will require even greater efforts on the part of all staff, including the directors, to improve our productivity and enable us to compete successfully in peace time commercial markets.
>
> I am displeased therefore to learn that there are some employees who do not appreciate the part they are expected to play, and question our decision to require attendance at work on the Saturday morning preceding a full week's holiday with pay generously granted to all members of staff.
>
> I only wish more had the attitude of Mr Bennet, my chief draughtsman, who has unstintingly given of his time, and never once faltered in his loyalty and devotion to myself and the company.
>
> Signed.........

It was several weeks before Bennet was seen in the factory. Undoubtedly, as a modest fellow, he found such adulation from the chairman of directors embarrassing.

'Trigsby, I gather that you went to the meeting,' Mr Thompson said when he heard us discussing the letter.

'Yes, and I'm glad I did, I have learnt quite a bit about

being shopped by our senior management,' I replied, pleased that he did not seem too annoyed.

'You will not progress in any company unless you listen to the sort of advice I gave you,' he replied, scribbling on a pad in front of him.

'I did listen, but surely it can't be wrong to protest about an injustice that you feel strongly about,' I replied, knowing that he would not agree with me, or like me to defend my action.

'You have some good qualities, which I have seen developing as you have grown up in the company. But you must understand that you are never in any position to argue with the chairman of the company. Unless you can accept that, you are wasting your time here, and I advise you to look for a job in national or local government service,' he said, in such a manner that I was able to see the wisdom of his advice, and many years later I was grateful to him for helping me to shape my future career.

32

Jean was demobbed before the War ended, and the oil
company she had worked for as a temporary before she
volunteered agreed to take her on the permanent staff when
she had passed a medical.

I was looking for another job, but decided to wait and
compete for a post as an engineer under the Civil Service
Reconstruction scheme before trying for another post in
industry.

Phyllis's husband had been taken back in his previous job,
and she was living in a fine house a few miles away.

There was an air of frustration at home now. Margaret's
husband was still waiting to be demobbed, and she was living
with us with her four year old son. Every weekend they went
out hunting for a house to buy, but it wasn't easy to find one.
So many had been destroyed in the last six years. I also
wanted to leave, and get married, but the chances of finding
somewhere to live on what I could afford were more difficult
than finding another job. Jean had no steady boyfriend, and
was still worried about becoming an old maid now that she
had turned twenty-one. But Mother somehow found enough
food for us to invite friends to tea on a Saturday or a Sunday.

I arrived home from work on Saturday morning, looking
forward to playing tennis that afternoon. Jean and I and two
others were cycling the eight miles, leaving in time to be
there by half past two, and returning at seven o'clock in time
to change, and go to a dance with a party of about a dozen.

I came through the kitchen as usual, and the house seemed
empty. In the dining-room the meal was all laid, and I
expected to find Jean changed for tennis, and Margaret
playing with Paul as they waited for me to come home to
dinner. I hesitated before going upstairs to change, and

Margaret came into the dining-room carrying Paul.

'Hello, I wondered where everybody was,' I said, as she came past me, and I noticed that she looked as if she had been crying.

'Ted, something terrible has happened,' she said, sitting down in an armchair.

'What's happened? Is it Mother?' I asked, knowing that she had been weepy and nervous lately.

'No, but she's had a terrible shock. The phone rang this morning, Jean answered it and the man the other end asked to speak to Mrs Trigsby. Mother spoke to him, and when she'd finished she came in here and sat down and cried her eyes out. We couldn't get anything out of her at first and then she managed to tell us. It was the doctor from the oil company where Jean had her medical. She has a spot on her lung, and they have arranged for her to go into a sanatorium on Monday,' Margaret said, dabbing her nose with a handkerchief.

'If they take her in right away, they can save her. Where is she?' I asked, as Mother came through the dining−room to the kitchen.

'She's in her room. She says she doesn't want any dinner.'

I hurried up the stairs. Jean was lying on her bed and looked up as I came in, her eyes red with tears.

'Come on, Jean, you'll be all right. They saved Ron with that new treatment that they have been using for months now. You'll be all right. I know you will,' I said, hoping that she would respond to my optimism.

'It's Aunty Jane's curse, I knew it would happen,' she said, burying her face in the pillow and sobbing.

'Don't be silly, it hasn't happened to me and you will get better. I know you will,' I replied, taking her hand and pulling her upright.

'How do you know you haven't got it? You haven't been X-rayed,' she said, looking tearfully at me for an answer.

'Of course I haven't, I couldn't play tennis, and hockey if I had TB.'

'Don't be silly. I was doing that a week ago, I must have had it then. I didn't get it last night,' she said, dabbing her eyes.

'Come and have some dinner. You must eat if you are

going to get better,' I said, pulling her gently off the bed.

'Don't tell the others I've got TB. You can get a four when you get there, tell them I don't feel well,' she said as we went down the stairs to dinner.

It wasn't the same without Jean. Of course I told Annette when we met to go to the dance, and she was very helpful, telling me that she was sure they had caught it in time to save her.

I tried not to think about it, but I wondered if Aunty Jane was wiser than I thought she was. I didn't sleep a wink all night, and as I wasn't seeing Annette until nine o'clock Monday evening, I decided to go and see Dr Grant immediately after tea. He had been Jean's doctor before they all changed to the lady across the road.

'Hello, I haven't seen you for a long time. What can I do for you?' he asked, as I sat down in front of his large desk.

'I've been quite well, but Jean has gone to hospital with TB. I'm worried in case I may have it,' I replied, feeling very nervous and foolish at being afraid.

'I'm sorry to hear that. She's the youngest isn't she?' he said sympathetically.

'Yes, she's just twenty-one,' I replied, feeling pathetically miserable.

'How old are you now?' he asked, writing something on his pad.

'I'm twenty-three,' I replied, pleased to be over Aunty's predicted life span for me.

'Are you still studying?' he asked, scribbling as he spoke.

'Yes, I have a long way to go yet.'

'Are you working the same sort of hours you told me about last time I saw you?'

'No, I don't have any Home Guard now. It makes it much easier.'

'What holidays did you have last year?'

'Three days, but we're getting a week this year.'

'Are you looking forward to going into a sanatorium?'

'Pardon!' I thought I must have misunderstood him.

'Are you looking forward to going into a sanatorium, because that's where you are going to end up. No fresh air, no proper holidays, and working day and night.'

'I have the same holidays as the others where I work.'

'I can't help the others, but you're my patient. Your sister is a war casualty, caused by long hours and excessive mental strain, and you are going to end up the same unless I can do something about it. Do you want me to help you?'

'Well yes, of course,' I replied meekly.

'That's encouraging,' he said, writing furiously as he spoke, and I sat there wondering how many pills I was going to have to take.

'Here you are. Come back and see me after the month is up,' he said, handing me a certificate.

I stared at it in disbelief. I don't know what I expected, but he seemed to have a one track mind.

'I can't have a month off work. I have a job to do,' I said. He didn't seem to realise that some people had to work for a living.

'You can't be any use to anybody in your mental state. You're a nervous wreck,' he said, looking at me, and shaking his head.

'I'm not. I'm no different from any of my colleagues at work. I only came to see you because I was worried I had TB,' I replied. I was feeling annoyed with him. I expected him to listen to my lungs with his stethoscope, not write me a chit for a month's holiday.

'Listen, young man. I've seen a lot like you grow to be drivelling idiots. Nobody notices except me because society expects them to behave like that as they grow older. I'm trying to save you, even though you're halfway there already.'

'Couldn't you make it two weeks instead of a month?' I asked. He seemed so sincere that I felt I should go some way to humour him, and Uncle would go beserk if I sent in a certificate for a month.

He smiled sadly, shaking his head and holding out his hand for me to return the certificate.

'Now, for the next two weeks, I want you to have all the fresh air and exercise you can. Play tennis, cycle, go swimming, and if you return to sanity in that time, you will accept the other two weeks when you come to see me,' he said, handing me the certificate and showing me the door.

I wandered up the road in a daze, I was not ill. I couldn't stay at home for two weeks. What about the job Uncle was chasing me for every day?

I felt more cheerful after walking the two miles to the hospital, laughing to myself about the doctor telling me to play tennis. Who did he think I would play with? He didn't seem to realise that people went to work, and only played tennis at weekends.

'He's right,' Annette said, when I told her as we sat on the Red Cross seat.

'He's daft, I'm not ill. I suppose I shouldn't have gone to see him.'

'You are. If you were not mentally ill you wouldn't be so frightened of admitting the truth,' she said, holding my hand and looking as if she thought I might take offence at her remark.

'I don't need to send it in. I could go to work and forget about it,' I said, as the thought suddenly struck me. I didn't have to take the doctor's advice.

'Please send it in, and have a week and see how you feel,' she said, and the next morning I rang the personnel manager and told him that a certificate was in the post, and to convey my regrets to Uncle.

Mother was pleased that I was at home, and she spent an hour telling me about Jean, who was going to be operated on in a week's time, and the surgeon had told her the success rate was going up all the time.

'I'll answer it,' she said, when the front door bell rang.

'It's Bobby Copling,' she said, leading him into the room as I stood up to see who was coming.

'Hello, fancy meeting you,' I said, laughing with pleasure as we shook hands. The last time we had met was three years ago, playing tennis. It was the leave before he was taken prisoner.

'I hoped I'd find you at home,' he said cheerfully. He hadn't changed much, except that he was a lot thinner.

'You're lucky, I could have been at work,' I replied, pleased I wasn't.

'Dr Grant told me to call on you. He said you needed exercise and fresh air, to recover from mental strain, same as I did.'

We did all the things the doctor had suggested, and the weather was glorious for tennis and swimming. Bobby received extra rations for being an ex-prisoner of war, which he insisted on sharing with me.

After those two weeks I was ready to go back to work and face a dozen Uncles.

'Well, are you going to take another two weeks?' the doctor asked me, when we had chatted about how I was feeling.

'Yes, I think I will, but may I have the final certificate now so that I know I am returning in another two weeks?' I said, after hesitating for a few moments.

'You won't get TB or become a drivelling idiot if you learn from this break that work is no good to those who let it kill them,' he said, laughing, and seeming genuinely thrilled at the change in me in a fortnight.

I returned to work after that month, sun−tanned and bursting with energy. The work so desperately urgent a month ago had never been touched. After teabreak, Uncle came into the lab, shuffled up to where I was working, and stood looking at me.

'You're back,' he said, standing a few paces away with his hands on his hips.

'Yes,' I replied, feeling completely relaxed.

'When do you think you will start getting results?' he asked, staring at me coldly.

'In a couple of weeks,' I replied, as I calibrated the valve voltmeter.

'You said a month before you stayed away,' he said gruffly.

'That's true but I feel fit enough to work twice as fast now,' I said hopefully, expecting that he might be pleased.

'Don't overdo it, I would hate you to kill yourself,' he said sarcastically as he turned away.

'Thank you. I don't think I will ever do that,' I replied, remembering the doctor's advice.

33

After a year in a sanatorium Jean came home. She had to go back to the hospital every month, but was allowed to get up after dinner, and sit in the garden to read, providing that she stayed in the shade. She was making good progress and would one day be fit for work again.

'Aunty Jane was wrong,' I said when we were talking about her experiences in the sanatorium.

'She would have been right if the technique had been developed a few years later,' she said, looking very thoughtful.

'Did she write to you?' I asked, laughing, having seen some of Aunty's letters to Mother.

'Yes, about eighteen pages. With all those instructions, she must have thought that I was there for ten years. But we laughed about it for months, so it did some good.' she said, closing her book and putting it on the table by her bed.

'I wonder when she's coming to see you,' I said, amused at her look of horror at the thought.

'It had better be after your wedding, or Annette will change her mind,' she replied, sliding off the bed to come downstairs for dinner.

'I shouldn't think it would be before then; it's only two weeks. We invited her, but she declined. I don't think she's recovered from seeing Mother marrying Father.'

Jean's friends came to tea on Sundays and we had the usual gathering of ten on the Sunday before our wedding. Annette couldn't come. She was on duty all day.

Father hardly spoke, but it would have been difficult for him to join in our banter. He excused himself as usual and retired to his armchair in the lounge. We were sitting noisily chatting, drinking tea, and finishing up the bits, when the front door bell rang.

218

'Whoever it is, is too late for tea this time,' I said, as I left to see who it was calling at such an unusual time.

I opened the door, and was brushed aside as Aunty Jane came through dragging Clare, her fifteen year old adopted daughter, by the hand.

'Hello,' I said, smiling with pleasure. This was going to be something I knew our friends would never forget.

'I can't stop, Ted, I must catch the next train back. Clare has to be at school by half past eight. Where's Florrie?' she said, all in one breath, and only pausing in the hall for directions.

I pushed past her and, opening the dining-room door, stood blocking the entrance as I looked at Mother, her eyes indicating that she was anxious to know who had rang.

'Aunty Jane and Clare have come to tea. They apologise for being late,' I announced loudly, to silence the chatter.

'No! Don't be a fool, Ted. Who was it?' Mother said, half rising from her chair.

Jean laughed. I knew she would appreciate the joke, and then I ushered them in. There was silence. Except for Aunty Jane.

'I can't stop, Flo. I came to see Jean. How is she? Where is she?' she asked, peering round the table through her dark glasses, shielded by the flat brim of her dark brown hat.

'Jean, put you hand up,' I said, as Mother came to take Aunty's coat and hat.

'I haven't time to take my hat off,' she said, smacking Mother's hand away.

Mother began clearing two spaces between Jean and her friend June by moving two of the boys to where Father had sat, and I set in the spaces the china and knives that I had just taken from the sideboard.

Aunty protested she did not want to sit down, but Mother and I persisted, until she was sitting next to June with Clare between her and Jean.

'How are you? Did you get my letter? When did you come home? How long were you in the san?' she asked, firing the questions at June who was almost falling off her chair with laughing.

'I'm not Jean, she's there,' June managed to say at last, pointing to Jean who was giggling.

Aunty turned on Jean sitting on the other side of her, and repeated the questions adding a few more.

'What's that?' Aunty asked, opening the sandwich that Mother had just brought from the kitchen, and put on Clare's plate.

'It's only lettuce, and tomato, it can't possibly do her any harm,' Mother replied, as Aunty peered critically at the contents.

'I think that's all right. Don't eat too much,' she said to Clare, and then to the rest of us, 'She doesn't need any tea. She had dinner.'

'Let her eat what she likes,' I said, horrified at the docile manner of poor Clare.

Mother caught my eye, and shook her head violently for me to be quiet.

'What was I saying? What was I saying?' Aunty asked as if I had distracted her by interrupting.

I looked round the table. They were all laughing helplessly.

'You're getting married in a week's time. I can't afford much, I'll give you a cheque. Four pounds be all right?' she asked, opening her large black purse, and fumbling to find her chequebook and a pen.

'Thank you very much. We are very grateful,' I replied, watching her writing out the cheque.

'I'm not giving it to you, Ted. It's for the bride. Here you are,' she said, handing it to June, as she stood up.

'Come on, child. You can't sit here eating all night. We've got to catch the train,' she said, standing over Clare.

'You can't go yet, Clare hasn't even had a drink,' Mother said, getting to her feet.

'Give her some milk, that will do. She can't be thirsty,' Aunty said, taking the milk jug and pouring a tiny drop into her empty cup and holding it out for Clare to take.

Mother came round the table to show them out. I collected the cheque from June, and for five minutes nobody could stop laughing. But I could have cried for poor Clare. It really wasn't funny.

That evening I met Annette and told her about the visit of Aunty Jane.

'Now you understand why I was glad when you had a month's holiday. It was to stop you becoming like Aunty

Jane,' she said, as we walked towards the Red Cross seat.

'Rubbish! It's me who should be worried. Mother told me that all nurses ended up like her,' I replied, pulling my hand away quickly.

'She would say that, but I won't be a nurse all my life,' she said, cuddling up to me as we sat down on the seat.

'Aunty Jane said that you were mad already.'

'She didn't!'

'She did. She said that we must both be mad to be getting married in less than a month with nowhere to live, and me looking for another job.'

'I don't believe that, do you?' she said laughing.

'No, of course not. She's mad. Everything will be all right once we are married,' I said, and we both believed it.